CW00872035

Death Devours

Mortis Series: Book Four

J.C. DIEM

Chapter One

It was after midnight, which meant that it was late enough for most of the humans in the seedy hotel to be asleep. Not being human myself, it was still pretty early for me. Only when dawn came knocking would it be bedtime for my kind.

Luc still looked slightly rattled by the call that we had received only a few minutes ago. I couldn't help but share his unease. Kokoro, a prophetess for the Japanese vampire nation, had been on the other end of the line. Unfortunately, she hadn't called to bring us good news, but to advise us of imminent danger.

Just last night, I'd put an end to the First. He was an ancient vampire that was master to a horde of grey skinned creatures that I liked to call imps. He and his offspring had been the greatest threat that vampirekind, or humankind had ever faced.

I hadn't fought the monsters alone. My recent and reluctant ally, Colonel Sanderson, had commanded an army of American and Russian soldiers during the battle. In a combined effort, we had slain every last creature that had been lurking in the First's underground lair.

I hadn't actually expected to be victorious. I'd kind of figured I'd be converted into an imp myself the instant I came face to face with the First. Unlike every other vampire who had set foot inside the vast cavern, my shadow hadn't taken control of my body. In this case, being different from everyone else had worked in my favour. My holy marks had prevailed, my nemesis was now dust and his offspring had been reduced to chunks of meat.

You'd think my problems would now be over, but apparently a new threat was already rising. It was very tempting to fall into bed, pull the covers up over my head and pretend that everything was fine. I was emotionally, if not physically exhausted and I just wanted to rest. Unfortunately, this was the kind of news that couldn't be ignored. Like it or not, I had certain responsibilities that I couldn't shirk no matter how badly I wanted to.

"After you," Luc said, breaking me out of my reverie and gesturing towards the door. The rest of our team needed to be advised that further trouble was on its way.

Luc gallantly allowed me to precede him from the room. Our hotel was in the heart of Russia, a country I'd never expected to travel to in my lifetime. Technically, I'd been correct about that. I'd only travelled overseas after my life had ended and my unlife had begun.

We made our way downstairs and Gregor answered the door at my soft knock. Dark blond hair framed his ruggedly attractive and somewhat surprised face. As always, he was wearing a natty tweed suit. His attire seemed out-dated for a man who appeared to be somewhere in his early forties. Dapper and suave, the aged vampire successfully managed to pull off the vibe of a professor.

Stepping aside, he gestured for us to enter. "Natalie, Lucentio, how nice of you to re-join us." His surprise at seeing us again so soon was masked by a strained smile. I had the distinct impression that he was secretly relieved we had returned.

Glancing past him, I saw why. I hadn't returned from my fight with the First alone. Nicholas, a courtier from the French vampire Court, had defected after I'd killed the First. He'd sought me out and had begged to come along with me. Knowing how sadistic the Comtesse was, I couldn't leave him behind to suffer her not-so-tender mercies. She was one of the nine Councillors who ruled the Court. With so many of our kind dead now, I wasn't even sure how many of them still remained.

My friends weren't reacting well to the newest addition to our ranks. Standing in the tiny area that passed for a kitchen, Igor and Geordie mirrored each other. Their arms were crossed and they wore matching frowns. Nicholas sat innocently on the threadbare couch in the living room. He was either unaware of the impact he was having on the group, or he was ignoring their discomfort.

The object of my scrutiny stood as I entered and smiled at me widely. White teeth flashed in his all too handsome face. Sculpted muscles peeked out from beneath his black jacket.

His shirt had been too filthy to bother with after his captivity in the First's cavern of doom. He'd chosen to just wear the grimy jacket without anything beneath it. No one had offered him a change of clothes yet. He would probably be too muscular to fit into them anyway. Luc was the only one who came close to Nicholas in shoulder width.

Our newest member had been one of the guards who hacked my body to pieces at the Comtesse's order some months ago. Somehow, he'd been elevated from being a lowly guard to one of the glittering courtiers. The sudden transformation didn't make much sense to me, but I wasn't exactly an expert in vampire law. I would get around to questioning him about all this, but I had more pressing business to attend to first.

"My Queen," Nicholas said with a bow before I could launch into the reason why Luc and I had returned.

"What did I tell you about calling me that?" My tone was slightly annoyed and very embarrassed. It was bad enough being called something so ridiculous in front of the humans, but if was far worse when it was done in front of my friends.

A tiny frown marred the perfection of his face. "You asked me to call you Natalie," he recalled in a small voice.

"Did he just call you 'my Queen'?" Geordie said incredulously. He was torn between amusement and alarm.

"Was it not prophesized that she would one day rule us?" Nicholas responded.

Geordie looked at me, looked at the former guard then back at me again. "You think Natalie," he pointed at me, "should rule us? You think the "gnat", our Ladybug has what it takes to tell us all what to do?" His lips trembled, then he doubled over with laughter as amusement won out. I couldn't blame him for his hilarity, not when I found the idea of me being a ruler to be almost as funny as he did. Still, he didn't have to laugh quite so hard.

Gregor was well versed in our rules and decided to clear up the issue once and for all. "It was prophesized that Mortis would destroy the damned and that only a remnant of our kind would survive." He gave Geordie a stern look and his giggles tapered off. "It has never been prophesized that she would rule the remaining vampires."

"Thank...goodness for that," I said, coming close to stuttering on a word I could no longer say out loud. "I don't want to rule anyone." *Based on Geordie's reaction, no one would take me seriously anyway.*

Luc's next statement effectively dampened all amusement. "Natalie has had some disturbing news from our Japanese kin."

Reminded of the reason we'd hurried downstairs, I gave them a quick explanation. "Kokoro, their seer, called to warn us of her latest vision." It had come to her while Luc and I had been getting reacquainted in the bedroom. I decided it would be best to skip over that part of the story. Geordie was already jealous enough of my relationship with Luc. I didn't want to send him into a sulking fit.

"What did she see?" Gregor asked. Sensing the news wouldn't be favourable, he was already beginning to frown.

"More doom and gloom, of course," I replied. "It seems that killing the First has unleashed a new problem."

"What problem?" Despite being two hundred years old, Geordie looked like a fifteen year old kid. His dirty blond hair always appeared to need a wash even after he'd just scrubbed it. He was still young enough in vampire years to have a faint ring of blue around his pupils. From what I understood about our kind, his pupils would grow to consume his irises in another hundred years or so.

"I'd better fill you in on some back history," I told them. Kokoro had passed this story on to me when I'd visited her in her temple. Now it was time to pass it on to my friends. "When the First was created, he made ten followers. I think they were like his disciples. He had complete control over them and they hated it. They plotted against him, planning on killing him somehow and making an army of vampire slaves."

Killing your maker wasn't only frowned upon, it also guaranteed your own death. Unless you were me, that was. I'd survived murdering my maker just fine. I had no idea how the disciples had planned to kill their leader. It didn't really matter, since they had clearly failed.

Igor shook his shaggy head at the disciple's desperate plan. "It is a very tricky undertaking to kill your maker." Roughly fifty in mortal years, his unkempt black hair rarely had contact with a brush. Craggy and unhandsome, Igor was Russian and spoke with an almost unintelligibly thick accent. I'd known him for months now and still had trouble interpreting his speech.

I grimaced in agreement. "The First was either super paranoid, or he somehow found out about their plot. He banished his disciples and ordered them to bury themselves. They've been stashed somewhere beneath the ground for over forty thousand years."

We all shared a moment of silent horror at the thought of facing such a fate. I'd been buried once myself. I'd been on the verge of going crazy after only a few short days. Admittedly, I had a short attention span and became bored fairly easily.

"Now that their maker is dead, his order will no longer apply," Igor deduced. "These 'disciples' are presumably free to rise again." Unlike Gregor's and Luc's penchant for wearing expensive clothing, Igor habitually wore rough woollen clothing and a plain white shirt.

"There's no way they could still be alive now," Geordie scoffed. "Even if they are, why would it be a problem for us?" As Igor's apprentice, he mimicked his mentor in his clothing choices. I hoped we would have the chance to go shopping sometime. It would be fun to introduce the teen to a more modern wardrobe. He had the potential to be cute beneath his perpetual grime and unkempt hair.

"It's going to be our problem because they haven't fed their blood or flesh hungers in a ridiculously long time," I responded to his bewildered question. "They'll go on a feeding and humping frenzy." Geordie pressed his lips together, presumably to keep in a giggle at my terminology.

"I understand your concern yet I am also unsure why this would affect us," Gregor said.

None of them seemed particularly worried so far, but that was about to change. It was time to hit them with the rest of the bad news. "Kokoro's visions told her that the disciple's blood is purer than ours. She thinks this is because they were made directly by the First. She says that their blood will be a lot stronger than a modern vampire's. Any new vamps they make will be stronger, faster and generally nastier than any of us. I'm pretty sure they only need to feed humans their blood once to turn them into vampires."

According to the cave paintings the First had made in his cavern of doom, he'd only tasted the alien's blood once to become the first of our kind. Nowadays, it took three nights of feeding our diseased blood to a human to turn them.

It was finally dawning on everyone just how bad this could be. "Each new vampire will create dozens of our kind in a few short days," Luc mused. "The humans will soon be faced with an epidemic." Not only was he tall, dark haired, hot bodied and handsome, he was also intelligent. I wouldn't pretend that his brains were the sexiest thing about Luc, but they were a definite bonus.

"Perhaps once the authorities become aware of the threat they can help us to contain it," Gregor suggested.

"We can only hope," I replied. "But Kokoro believes the humans won't be able to fight the new vamps very effectively. It looks like it'll be mostly up to us to take them down."

Nicholas ventured a question, drawing an instant scowl from Geordie. "Why do we have to kill our own kind at all? Do they not have just as much right to live as we do?"

Igor fielded this one before I could voice what would most likely be a sarcastic reply. "How will any of us survive if all humans on the planet are turned into vampires?"

Finally grasping how dangerous it would be to let the rogue vamps create billions of our kind, Nicholas was abashed. "Then we should formulate a plan on how we are going to defeat our newly awakened kin."

Geordie's emotions were easy to read. He didn't like Nicholas and resented him being in our group. The new guy had been with us for less than an hour and he was already trying to call the shots.

"Emperor Ishida has a proposal for us," Luc interjected into the tense silence before the surly teen could voice his displeasure. "He suggested that we should work together and has asked for us all to meet to discuss our options."

Rubbing his hands together briskly, Gregor took a seat at the tiny two seater table. "Did Ishida mention where he wants us to hold this meeting?"

I took the vacant chair before anyone else could beat me to it. "He's leaving it up to us to think of a location that will be safe for all of us."

Luc moved to stand behind me. He was close enough that I would have felt his body heat if he'd had any. Geordie threw a mistrustful glance at Nicholas and took up a spot at my side. Nicholas was undecided as to where he should stand, then gracefully walked over to stand at my other side. Igor leaned against the wall behind Gregor, unintentionally making himself look like his bodyguard.

Surrounded on three sides, I felt like I had a collection of shadows following me around again. I'd had eight of them for a short time, but was back to only having one now. The shadows had been far less intrusive than the guys were being. Geordie brushed up against my side, Luc rested a hand on my shoulder and Nicholas leaned against my arm.

I was happy enough to have Luc touching me, but I could have done without the physical contact with the other two. Geordie probably just needed reassurance that I cared about him. He obviously felt threatened by Nicholas. If I had the chance to speak to the kid privately, I'd ask him why he disliked the muscle bound vamp so much.

The newest member of our group was still a mystery. I didn't know what he wanted, or what his motives were yet. He'd begged to join us because he had run away from the

Court. If the Comtesse ever saw him again she'd brand him as a traitor and would have him killed.

Deep in the depths of my subconscious, I wasn't sure that that would be a bad thing. I had an uneasy feeling about the handsome vampire even though he'd given me no reason to mistrust him. Not yet anyway.

Chapter Two

"Do you have any idea where the First's ten followers are?" Gregor asked me, drawing my attention back to our discussion.

"I'm pretty sure at least one of them is in Africa," I replied reluctantly. I was always uncomfortable with revealing how weird I was. I preferred not to bring my strangeness to my friend's attention. Unfortunately, I didn't have the luxury of hiding my peculiarities from them this time.

Igor lifted a heavy eyebrow. "What makes you think they are in Africa?"

Shrugging uncomfortably, I kept my answer short. "I've had a couple of weird dreams and I think they were about one of these guys."

Gregor leaned forward to rest his arms on the table and stared at me intently. "Can you describe these dreams to us?"

I really didn't want to recite my dreams out loud and took comfort from Luc's cold hand resting on my shoulder. Despite just how different I was to the rest of my kin, he never held it against me. "I was in a clearing in a jungle," I began. "A deer that I'm pretty sure I've seen on African documentaries stepped into the clearing and sensed something that frightened it. I felt it, too. It was like a super strong hunger coming up from beneath the ground. The deer bolted away then fell down dead." It didn't sound so bad when I said it out loud, but it had been far creepier in my dream.

"What did it die from?" Geordie asked, eyes wider than usual.

"Terror," I replied and he hunched his shoulders.

Gregor was nodding, as if he understood why it had freaked me out so badly. "Was the second dream similar to the first?"

"Yeah, but this time it was birds. They flew over the clearing, then went crazy. They ended up colliding and falling to the ground. One of them died on impact, but the other one just had a couple of broken wings." I remembered its frantic scrambling as it tried to escape from the overwhelming hunger that had again risen from beneath the ground. "I walked over to them and was caught up by the buried creature's hunger. I snatched both birds up and drained them dry."

I wrinkled my nose at the memory of being taken over by another's need to feed. I'd always managed to maintain command of my blood hunger and I hadn't liked the momentary lack of control at all. For a few brief moments, I'd finally known what normal newborn vampires felt like when they rose for the first time. I pitied the humans that would fall prey to our ancient starved kin and any servants that they made.

Geordie scrunched his face up as well, but I believed it was at the thought of drinking animal blood more than anything. It had tasted the same as human blood to me in the dream. I'd been too hungry to care about what I was putting in my mouth at the time.

Igor shifted uneasily. "Are you saying that its hunger took control of you and forced you to feed?"

I shrugged then nodded reluctantly. "I'm pretty sure that wouldn't happen in real life, though." I actually had no idea if this was true or not, but I doubted it. The disciples, if that was who I'd been dreaming about, were only the second generation of our kind. Since they hadn't made us, they wouldn't have any control over us. The First was the only one who'd had that capability and he was about as dead as you could get. The holy marks on my palms had seen to that.

Gregor fisted a hand and rested his chin on it, musing silently for a few moments. "It is auspicious that Emperor Ishida has agreed to join forces with us against this new enemy. We have you to thank for making it possible, Natalie."

The European and Japanese vampire nations had been at war for tens of thousands of years. They didn't agree with each other's cultures. Both thought they should have ultimate control over our kind.

I'd spent four months on the Japanese vamp's island learning how to fight in their style. During that time, I'd softened their attitude towards the Europeans to some extent. I found this to be pretty ironic considering I'd been born and raised in Australia. My distant ancestors were

English, but that was about as close to being European as I could claim.

"Does anyone have any idea where we could meet that could be classed as neutral territory?" I asked the small group.

"Kazakhstan would be my suggestion," Igor put forward.

Gregor agreed. "It is fairly neutral ground."

Luc increased the pressure on my shoulder to draw my attention. "You should call Kokoro and advise her of our decision." His mobile phone came into view over my shoulder. For someone so old, he was comfortable enough using modern technology.

Dialling the last number on record, it was swiftly answered by the Japanese seer. "We will be pleased to meet with you and your friends in Kazakhstan," Kokoro said before I could even open my mouth. "We will meet you there three nights from now."

"Ok. Good." It was disconcerting to have someone rummaging around in your brain from thousands of kilometres away. "Just pick a spot and I'll find you when we get there." We said our goodbyes and hung up. Luc tucked his phone back inside his jacket. As usual, he wore all black. I had to admit, the darkness of his clothing made a striking contrast to the paleness of his skin.

Being in central Russia at the moment, we weren't all that far from Kazakhstan. We could probably drive there in the allotted time, if we hurried. Flying would be far quicker, but also far less secure. We were restricted by only being able to move at night however we chose to travel to our destination.

Nicholas shifted away, breaking our contact to look down at me. "How will you be able to find the Japanese scum, my...Natalie?" he asked me curiously. He managed not to call me his queen, but only just.

Rubbing temples that should have been throbbing with annoyance, I bit back a nasty response. The courtiers had long been conditioned to hate their Japanese rivals. I couldn't expect them all to get along immediately just because I thought their feud was petty and ridiculous. "I can sense other vampires," I said instead of the acidic comment about racism that I wanted to voice. It probably wasn't a good indication of Nicholas' compatibility to our group if he was already managing to bring out the worst in me.

"How is this possible?" The ex-courtier's astonishment was unfeigned.

"Natalie gained this ability after you helped hack her to pieces," Geordie said curtly. His voice was a couple of pitches higher than usual and his gaze was accusing. "It happened after you and your friends stuffed her into eleven tiny little boxes and left her to starve to death." Overcome with sorrow for the predicament that I'd suffered, he stifled a sob then turned his back and crossed his arms.

"Natalie has many talents the rest of us do not possess," Luc said coolly to Nicholas.

Shifting so that he was pressed up against my arm again, Nicholas spoke softly. "I would very much like to hear about your many talents, my...Natalie."

His tone was suggestive and almost baiting. I suddenly couldn't stand to have him near me, so stood and wrapped my arm around Geordie's shoulder. The teen turned and hugged me, shooting a triumphant glare at our newest team member.

Igor rolled his eyes at the theatrics and I badly wanted to emulate him. We didn't have time to bicker amongst ourselves. I'd only just put down one threat to our survival and now we had another one to face.

Once it became known that a pack of newly risen vampires was on the loose, we would all be in danger. It was unlikely that humans would differentiate between us and any of the new fledglings that would shortly be unleashed on them. We would all become their enemies and we'd be put to the death if we were recognized.

"We should get a move on if we want to get to Kazakhstan in time," I suggested. "Gregor, Igor and Geordie can fill you in on all of my talents during the trip, Nicholas." I kept my tone dry to indicate I didn't appreciate his behaviour.

Lowering his head submissively, Nicholas sent me a heated glance. *Great, now I have three men lusting after me.* Once upon a time, I would have been ecstatic at the idea of having so many guys wanting to jump my bones. Heck, even one man wanting to get into my pants would have been nice.

Unfortunately, one of these 'men' was a teenager and the other was still almost a complete stranger. Luc was the only one out of the trio that I wanted to get naked with. Come to think of it, he was the only vampire I'd met so far that I'd been attracted to. While I was drawn to Nicholas' body, I wasn't particularly enamoured of his personality. He was far more impressed with himself than I would ever be.

Standing briskly, Gregor launched us all into action. "We will meet you in the parking area shortly," he said then gave Geordie a light shove towards what must have been his bedroom.

Taking the stairs back up to our own room, Luc and I silently gathered our belongings. My backpack contained one intact black leather suit, my twin swords and various other articles of clothing when I was done.

The red suit I'd worn to kill the First had been in roughly the same condition as he'd been after the fight; destroyed beyond recognition or any possibility of ever being repaired. I was used to my clothing being torn, stabbed and sliced apart, but I usually squeezed more than one wear out of them. I'd been sad to see the suit ruined, but it had served its purpose as both protection and a distraction.

Luc and I beat the others to the underground parking area, but only by a couple of minutes. Geordie was sulking, shooting glares at Nicholas as they emerged from the stairwell. The overly muscled vamp sent smug, condescending smiles at the kid. His ego seemed to have swollen with his lofty new position as a courtier.

I decided it was high time to question Nicholas about his sudden change of status. My curiosity wouldn't let me wait for dawn when we would have to stop to find shelter for the day. "How did you manage to get upgraded from being a guard to a courtier?" I asked him bluntly. I rarely wasted time in getting to the point. Patience was a virtue that I had only a passing acquaintance with.

Nicholas almost stumbled a step in surprise. *Wow, you can see the wheels cranking in his head,* my subconscious roused itself to say. It seemed that my inner voice thought

Nicholas was searching for a suitable lie. I was glad its sarcasm was directed at someone else for a change. Being on the receiving end of its criticisms could be bruising to the ego at times.

"When the courtiers began to mysteriously disappear some months ago, the Comtesse decided to increase their numbers. She rewarded some of the more faithful guards by allowing us to become her courtiers."

I'd learned to read Luc's controlled expressions to some extent. He was doubtful, but hid his scepticism well. He'd been a prisoner of the Comtesse during this time and had mostly been kept in her bedroom. He'd noticed the diminishing numbers, but apparently hadn't been advised of the elevation of the guards to positions within the Court. "Did no one care that the courtiers were disappearing?" he asked. Nicholas just shrugged. "What did the other Councillors think of this decision?"

Nicholas looked uncomfortable as he answered, which gave my subconscious' scepticism some weight. "They thought the courtiers had defected and agreed that increasing our numbers was the wisest thing to do."

Gregor looked openly disbelieving at that. Although he was a lord, he had distanced himself from the Court hundreds of years ago. He understood their politics far better than I ever would.

Despite my lack of knowledge about Court intrigue, even I could tell that this was a hard story to swallow. As far as we'd known, the courtiers hadn't been defecting anywhere. They'd in fact been sacrificed to the First by the Comtesse. She'd sent them to the cavern of doom to be turned into imps.

When the First had sent out his mental call to draw the rest of the possessed vamps to him, the Comtesse had scooped up everyone from the Court. She'd made her way to Russia along with hundreds, or even thousands of our kin.

With the First's death, the possessed vampire's shadows had become normal again. They would have undoubtedly been confused at suddenly finding themselves inside a cave surrounded by gun wielding soldiers and an army of grey skinned monsters.

Elevating the low vamps on the food chain into new positions within the Court hierarchy had been a clever distraction, if Nicholas' story was true. The praying mantis had managed to keep her part in the fate her people had very nearly suffered a secret. She was a devious old hag and I'd hate to have to match wits with her. I had a feeling that I would lose rather badly.

Chapter Three

Igor took the lead in his large black car and Luc and I followed a short distance behind him. Nicholas and Geordie sat in the back of the midnight coloured sedan. They took turns glancing back at us with monotonous regularity. Our headlights were too bright for them to make out my face clearly, but it didn't stop them from checking to make sure I was still there.

Luc dropped his speed enough to draw back from our friends a little more. "Do you trust your hulking new admirer?" he asked softly. Our hearing tended to be exceptional and he wanted to make sure our conversation remained private. As if sensing we were talking about him, Nicholas turned to peer backwards once more. His silhouette was far larger than Geordie's and it was easy to recognize him.

"Nope," I responded immediately, smirking at my beloved's apt description of Nicholas. "I can't shake the feeling that he's lying to us."

Nodding, Luc's expression remained serene. "I share your unease. It is doubtful that the Council would agree to elevate lowly guards to a position within the Court for such a paltry reason as he described."

I wasn't so sure that bolstering their ranks after their numbers had begun to dwindle was a paltry reason to promote the guards into higher positions. I hated to agree with the praying mantis about anything, but I did in this instance. My curiosity about the new addition to our ranks was now raging. "What do you know about Nicholas?"

Luc sent me a quick look, but something in my expression reassured him that I wasn't interested in the newbie on a personal level. "I know very little about him. Courtiers have minimal interaction with the lesser servants. He was a guard long before I was made and that is the extent of my knowledge. He has never drawn any particular attention to himself and I do not know of his origins."

Luc had been turned by the Comtesse seven hundred years ago. That meant Nicholas also had to be pretty old. Not knowing about the former guard's origins meant Luc had no idea who had turned Nicholas into one of us.

"Maybe Igor will know more about him." Igor was at least several thousand years old, even older than Gregor. If anyone would know more about Nicholas, it would probably be him.

"Lord Aventius might also have some information about Nicholas," Luc said thoughtfully. "We need to speak to him anyway. We should warn him that the Comtesse is most likely on her way back to the mansion. Perhaps you could mention our new friend and see what Aventius knows about him." He fished his phone out of his pocket and handed it to me.

Sorting through the list, I found the number for the Court. It rang half a dozen times before it was answered. "What?" a young man barked with an audible sneer.

"Who am I speaking to?" I asked.

"Jacob," the young male vampire answered in an even surlier tone. I remembered him well although I'd only met him once and our contact had been brief. He'd tried to get his master to kill me, which had understandably left a lasting impression on me. That had only been a few short nights ago, but I felt like an entire lifetime had passed since then.

"Put Aventius on the phone."

"Why should I?"

I could picture Joshua standing there pouting sullenly. Joshua was still very new and hadn't gotten a handle on his hungers yet. Being constantly hungry was enough to make anyone cranky.

"Because you're speaking to Mortis," I told him bluntly. "I'll hunt you down and rip your tongue out of your head if you don't put him on in the next sixty seconds."

I hated having to resort to pulling the Mortis card. I'd learned that my status as being death to our kind was the quickest way to deal with my fellow vamps. Nearly everyone feared me. My friends were the only ones who didn't cringe every time they heard my title being mentioned.

Silence reigned for a few seconds, then the phone thumped down and rapid footsteps hurried away. More footsteps sounded within the specified time. The Councillor who had fled from the Court several months ago answered. If he'd been human, he would have been gasping for air after rushing to the phone so quickly. "This is Aventius," the elderly vampire said with quiet dignity.

"The Comtesse is on her way back to the mansion," I warned him without preamble. "You'd better get everyone out of there." The praying mantis would have them all killed the instant she saw them. Aventius would have a target on his back because he'd defected to my side. His way of showing his support for me had been to sacrifice humans in my name. I hadn't appreciated the gesture nearly as much as he and his small band had assumed I would.

"You did not kill her?" He was almost as disappointed as I was that she was still unalive and well.

My answer was almost curt with self-annoyance. "Unfortunately, no. She and her lackeys escaped after I killed the First." I ignored the small sound of wonder he made at that revelation. "We have bigger problems than her." As hard as that was to believe, it was indeed true. "I need you to muster up every vampire you can find and head to Africa asap."

"Africa?" he replied after a baffled silence. "Why on earth do you need us there?"

"After the First turned to dust, ten followers he banished forty thousand years ago were freed from their forced burial. They're about to rise and create a new race of rabid vamps. They'll quickly grow in numbers and will begin spreading like a virus."

"I see." This time, the ex-Councillor's short silence was thoughtful. "I will gather as many of our kin as I can find. We will join you in Africa as soon as we can."

I liked the fact that he didn't waste time bombarding me with questions, or arguing with me. I'd been ready to dismiss Aventius as being beyond redemption due to his origins. Maybe he wasn't as bad as I'd presumed. I hadn't heard particularly flattering things about the Council, so my expectations of their leaders were low.

"News reports of vampire attacks will probably help us narrow down exactly where they are quickly enough," I advised him. "By the way, do you know a Court guard called Nicholas?" It wasn't exactly a smooth attempt to work the muscle bound one into the conversation. Luc sent an amused smile my way before returning his gaze to the road.

Thrown by the switch in topics, Aventius fumbled for a reply. "Er, Nicholas did you say? Can you describe him?"

"He has dark brown hair, a pretty face and way too many muscles."

"I'm sorry, but he doesn't sound familiar," was his not unexpected reply. "I'm afraid I take little notice of the guards."

Well, that was a bust. "Never mind. We'll see you in Africa in a few days." I handed Luc back his phone, glad we'd have at least some help trying to contain the rabid vamps that were about to be created.

As dawn drew closer, we discovered our chances of finding somewhere to sleep were limited. The towns we passed through were too tiny to support hotels or inns. Civilization disappeared altogether, taking the highway with it, as Igor veered onto a smaller road. Luc seemed unconcerned with our change of direction. If he trusted the taciturn Russian, then so would I.

We bumped over an increasingly decrepit road. Our jeep handled the rough terrain better than the large black car we were following. We passed several driveways that led to distant houses and farms. The earth was beginning to warm with the advent of dawn when Igor finally chose a driveway and nosed his vehicle onto it.

Luc's grip tightened on the wheel at how close we were cutting it to certain incineration. He flicked a glance at his watch and narrowed the distance between our vehicles as, if silently urging Igor to hurry.

Cresting a short rise, we spotted a large farmhouse and exchanged relieved glances. The dwelling was rundown, but the roof and walls were intact. Smoke curled from the single chimney, indicating that someone was home. Whoever they were, they were about to be confronted with six desperate vampires.

With only moments to spare before the sun arrived to chargrill us to death, we scrambled from our cars and approached the house. It was in dire need of a new paintjob and the stairs were splintered with age and wear. Gregor, the most presentable and charming member of our group, knocked on the door.

Huddled at my side, Geordie threw a frantic look over his shoulder. I copied him and squinted against the faint touch of light that was beginning to bloom. "If we do not make it, *chérie*, I want you to know how much I adore you," the teenager said solemnly. For a brief moment, I was touched. Then he had to ruin it with his next comment. "And how very badly I want to see you naked." Luc's lips twitched in amusement. Nicholas gave the kid an affronted stare, as if he was insulted on my behalf.

Gregor abandoned his usual civilized demeanour when no sounds of approach came from within. He shouldered the door open, breaking the flimsy lock.

We piled inside what turned out to be a kitchen. Luc closed the door a millisecond before my friends could be turned into moist stains on the porch. As the sun finally burst into life in its usual suffocating blanket of heat, Geordie lost consciousness. I caught him as he became limp and draped his arm over my shoulder.

A thick curtain on the door blocked the pale light effectively, but the curtains on the windows were far flimsier. Twin beams of sunlight speckled the worn linoleum to either side of us. To step into the light would cause instant immolation.

Taking a look around the kitchen, I saw that it was in desperate need of repair. Once dark brown and now faded to tan, the wallpaper was peeling. Water damage showed in several places.

The linoleum was grey, stained and scuffed. It was difficult to tell what colour it had been when it had been new. Most of the appliances looked at least forty years old. The general atmosphere, coupled with the musty smell of mothballs, indicated that an elderly person lived in the house.

As we huddled together, we heard the almost dainty snores issuing from a human somewhere in the building. "What do we do now?" Nicholas asked softly. With Geordie currently unconscious and hanging limply at my side, there was no one to scowl at the overly muscled vamp for simply daring to open his mouth.

"One of us needs to approach the owner of this house and request that we be allowed to spend the day here,"

Gregor said. There was no way to tell how safe the rest of the house was from the sun until it was searched.

Gee, I wonder who is going to have that privilege? "Since I'm the only one who won't die immediately if the sun touches me, I guess it'll have to be me," I said wryly.

Nicholas gave me an incredulous stare. "Are you saying the sun cannot kill you?"

"I thought you guys were going to fill Nicholas in on my strange and whacky powers," I said to Gregor and Igor, neatly avoiding the question.

Igor shrugged, then gestured at his unmoving apprentice. "Hand him to me." I gladly foisted Geordie off onto the Russian, then moved away from the door. The others clustered closer together in an effort to stay out of the still weak, yet deadly rays flanking them on both sides.

Staying within the band of shadow, I crossed the room and pushed open the door. The living room furniture was overstuffed, but looked comfortable. Rows of framed photos lined the mantle above the fire, which had almost burned out.

It was much gloomier in here and was far safer than the kitchen. I motioned for the others to join me. After some careful shifting, Luc held Geordie by the feet and Igor had his hands wrapped securely around the teen's torso. Shuffling forward, the group managed to make it into the living room without incident. With the door closed, they would be safe from the sun for the moment.

Following the snores, I moved past three dim bedrooms containing double beds and pushed open the door to a fourth room. An old woman lay on her back beneath a mound of blankets. Her toothless mouth was slack, allowing her snores to escape unhindered.

Pure white hair lay on the pillow, almost blending in with it. For a second or two, she strongly reminded me of the Romanian prophet. Ancient and wrinkled, she looked almost as much like a mummy as he had. The only difference was that she smelled like mothballs rather than cinnamon.

I didn't want to wake her, but my friends needed to rest. Clearing my throat loudly made her twitch and mumble something unintelligible. Clearing it louder worked and she woke with a start. Sitting up, she groped for a walking stick beside her bed. "Is someone there?" she asked in a voice that quavered slightly. The room was dim, but she was looking right at me. Her gaze was centred over my shoulder and I realized she was blind.

"Hi," I said in English, hoping she could understand me. "I'm sorry to intrude, but my friends and I…" My explanation trailed off when she shifted the stick to her shoulder. *That's not a stick, that's a shotgun.*

"So, you and your friends thought you could break in and rob me blind," the old lady said in mangled English. She'd homed in on my voice and both her gaze and gun were pointed unerringly at me.

"Well, technically, you're already blind," I pointed out. "Anyway, we're not here to rob you, we just need somewhere to spend the day."

Glaring in my general direction suspiciously, she shifted her grip on the weapon, but made no move to put it down. "Why were you travelling at night instead of during the day?"

Thinking frantically, I gave her the only explanation I could think of. "There's a lot less traffic at night and we can make really good time." Her suspicion didn't waver at all and only deepened. "We can pay you," I said with a hint of desperation. Being blind, it would be impossible for one of the guys to bamboozle her into submission and I didn't want to kill or incapacitate her.

Brightening immediately, she swung the weapon down and placed it against the wall again. "Why didn't you say so?" Holding out her arthritic hand in my direction, she was all toothless smiles. "I am Irina."

"I'm Nat," I replied as I shook her hand carefully.

An expression of commiseration settled on her wrinkled face and she patted my hand consolingly. "You poor thing. Some parents have no shame. Imagine naming your child after an insect!"

Gregor's muffled laugh floated down the hall to me loud and clear even if the old lady didn't hear it. I was just glad Geordie wasn't awake to hear her. He'd never have been able to contain his shrill giggles.

I gave Irina a few moments alone to dress, followed her to the living room. After introducing my friends, and Nicholas, to our hostess, I was glad for her blindness. Explaining Geordie's condition would have been difficult. *You could have told her he's narcoleptic,* my subconscious said sourly. That had been Luc's explanation to curious airport staff when I'd fallen dead asleep while travelling by air once. Being lugged around while dead to the world was embarrassing, even if I didn't actually remember it.

Sharing a very quiet and private conversation with the others, I volunteered to stay awake. Someone had to make sure Irina didn't accidentally kill anyone by opening the curtains in the bedrooms. It was doubtful she would, since housekeeping didn't seem to be one of her top concerns.

A fine layer of dust lay on the furniture and carpet. Airing out the bedrooms was probably fairly low on her to-do list.

Hoisting Geordie over his shoulder, Igor disappeared down the corridor and took the first room on the left. Gregor and Nicholas followed, branching off into the other two spare bedrooms. Nicholas hesitated in the hallway, sending me another heated glance in an unspoken invitation to join him. Luc's response was to pull me in close and kiss me. It was long, thorough and had my flesh hunger rising by the time he pulled away. The ex-courtier entered his chosen bedroom and slammed the door shut. Wearing a smile of self-satisfaction, Luc sauntered down the hall to join Gregor.

Pottering around in the kitchen, Irina was oblivious to the petty, silent squabble. She emerged minutes later and I hurried over to help her with the tray that she carried gingerly. She'd made a pot of tea and insisted on pouring me a cup despite my protests that I wasn't thirsty. Pretending to sip the hot liquid, I heaved an internal sigh. I had a feeling it was going to be a very long day.

Chapter Four

I'd never been so grateful for sundown when the last rays of light finally departed and my friends rose for the night. When they were all ready to leave, I thanked Irina for her hospitality. Gregor pressed some money into her wrinkled hands and we were on our way again.

"I would like to travel with you tonight, my Queen," Nicholas said formally as we approached our vehicles. Geordie cut him a glare and his lips thinned in annoyance. "I believe I would find your company to be far more pleasant than some." He might as well have turned and pointed a finger at the only teen in our midst.

While I could sympathize, knowing just how irritating Geordie could be, I didn't want to be burdened with the newbie. I was cranky after spending the entire day without any sleep and attempting to converse with Irina. She was in her nineties and her idea of entertainment was to listen to ancient music that held absolutely no appeal to me. She didn't even have a TV or books. The few magazines I'd scrounged up had been thirty years old.

Geordie had a simple solution. "If I annoy you so much, then I will ride with Luc and Nat," he said testily. His double usage of our nicknames sounded weird in his French accent.

Luc nodded before I could shoot the teen down. Crestfallen at his request being denied, Nicholas climbed into the back of Igor's car sullenly. Following the dark sedan at a greater distance than usual, Luc revealed the reason why he'd agreed to let the kid ride with us. "What have you learned about Nicholas so far, Geordie?"

Resting his arms on the backs of our seats, Geordie had squirmed as far forward as he could get. He wore a light scowl, but at least he had transferred his hostility from Luc to Nicholas for the time being. "I have learned that he is an egotistical fool who thinks he is the most handsome vampire to have ever walked the earth."

While I sniggered, Luc waited patiently for Geordie to calm down. "Have Gregor or Igor attempted to question him?"

Nodding, Geordie swiped his hair out of his eyes. "They have asked him many questions about the Comtesse and her fellow Councillors. He says he is not aware of their plans. He says that his only goal was to escape from them so that he could be at Natalie's side." Scorn at the idea made his scowl more fierce than usual.

"What did he plan to do once he was at her side?" Luc queried softly. I noticed that his shoulders had risen slightly, as if he were tensing.

Geordie's answer was as dark as his scowl. "I think we both know the answer to that question."

They think Nicholas wants to do the horizontal mambo with me. Unfortunately, I thought so, too. "That's not going to happen," I said. "Yes, he's pretty to look at, but he gives me the creeps."

Cocking his head to the side, Geordie sent me a coy look. "Are you saying that you do not find Nicholas to be attractive?"

That was a hard one to answer. My flesh hunger had come close to forcing me to jump the ex-courtier's bones. I'd managed to resist it, mostly because he'd been asleep at the time. I'd never been drawn to unmoving corpses.

"He's attractive, but I'm not attracted to him." Neither man seemed to understand. "Haven't you ever seen a woman that you thought was beautiful, but you didn't particularly want to have sex with her?"

Luc met Geordie's eyes in the rear view mirror and they shared a decidedly sexist chuckle. "No," they replied in unison.

Giving up, I changed the subject. "Are you deliberately trying to drive Nicholas nuts, Geordie?" The kid was often unintentionally annoying. I could only imagine how irritating he'd be if he really put his mind to it.

Geordie's reply was unabashedly honest. "Yes. I am hoping to drive him away, but it does not seem to be working."

"Maybe he's telling the truth and he really does think the praying mantis will kill him if he returns to the Court," I mused.

Geordie sniggered at the nickname I'd given the Comtesse. At just under five feet tall, she had a small waist, voluptuous hips, white-blonde hair and was beautiful in an exotic way. I'd named her after a creepy insect due to her wide-set, soulless eyes. The praying mantis was minus a hand now, thanks to me. She had kept Luc as her sex slave after she'd ordered him to chop off my head. My retaliation had been to relieve her of one of her body parts. I hoped one day to relieve her of a lot more than that.

Luc allowed Geordie to answer for both of them. "He is up to something, *chérie*. But do not fear, I shall keep a close eye on him."

Wow, I feel a lot safer now. I kept the semi-sarcastic thought to myself, not wanting to hurt his feelings. "Thanks, Geordie," I said, carefully hiding my grin. "I get the feeling you didn't like Nicholas much even before he joined our group." It wasn't a question, but I lifted an eyebrow in enquiry.

Squirming on the seat with reluctance, Geordie finally fessed up why he disliked the muscle bound courtier. "He used to make fun of me when I was newly made." His lower lip pooched out in a pout.

"Why?" I didn't want to pry at old wounds, but my curiosity made me ask.

"Do you know about my origins?" he asked me and slanted a glance at Luc.

I nodded in sympathy. "I badgered Luc into telling me a bit about you and Igor." Luc drove with serene calmness, listening in, but contributing nothing.

"Then you know that I was turned by a young girl." The teen hung his head at the painful memory.

"I know she was killed for breaking the rules," I said so he wouldn't have to.

Nodding, Geordie raised his head again and stared at the car ahead of us. "Nicholas used to torment me about it. He made fun of me because I was turned by someone so low in the Court hierarchy." He scowled at the hulking outline of Nicholas in the sedan ahead. "He said I had no right to exist and that I should have been killed, as if I was a runt not worthy of survival."

Reaching back, I put my hand on his narrow shoulder in wordless support. My esteem for the ex-courtier had just managed to drop even lower.

"Why didn't you mention this to Igor?" Luc said with a tone that seemed calm, but held undercurrents of anger. "He would have put a stop to the taunts."

"I did not want anyone to know the horrible things he was saying to me," the teen said with heart wrenching dignity. "Besides, what could have been done about it? Taunting unwanted fledglings is not against Court rules." He sounded very cynical for someone who looked so young.

"Let me know if he says anything like that to you again," I told Geordie. "I'm not going to put up with any bullying." He gave me a grateful look, then subsided back against his seat. Geordie remained quiet for far longer than I'd thought possible. His wounds might be old, but they were far from faded.

We didn't want to make it too obvious that we didn't trust Nicholas, so the next night Geordie swapped cars with him. I was far from comfortable with the newbie sitting in such close proximity. I might not be able to die, but I just didn't trust him where I couldn't see him. My solution was to turn and engage him in conversation. Since most Europeans thought I was uncouth anyway, maybe it was time to use that trait to my advantage.

"I've been wondering about something, Nicholas." He lifted a sculpted dark brown eyebrow in invitation to ask the question that was on my mind. "Who made you?" Ok, that was blunt even for me.

"My master was a rogue servant of little importance, my…Natalie." He smiled apologetically, but the phrase was beginning to grate on my nerves. The irritated look Luc flicked him in the rear view mirror told me I wasn't alone in my annoyance.

"Tell me about it," I offered. We knew practically nothing about him and I wanted to dig for as much information as I could. If he really thought I was his liege, then he should have been all too happy to answer me. "Why did he make you and what happened to him?"

Casting his eyes downward, the ex-courtier gathered his thoughts. "I was made because my master's master enjoyed men and my master did not." It took me a couple of seconds to wrap my brain around that. "Jacque, my master, was more inclined towards women," Nicholas continued. "He thought that if he could present his master with someone attractive enough, he would be spared from his master's advances."

My lips were wrinkled back from my teeth at the idea of being made simply to satisfy my master's sexual desires. I was pretty sure that had been what my maker, Silvius, had intended for me. Thankfully, I'd speared a cross into his heart before he could do anything worse than kill me and turn me into the undead. "I gather Jacque's plan didn't work out so well?"

Shaking his head, Nicholas' shoulders slumped. "Jacque was killed for his imprudence and I very nearly suffered the same fate. One of the Ladies saved me from being destroyed and offered me a position as a guard for the Court."

"How long ago was this?" I was always fascinated by when and why my kin were made. We all seemed to have one thing in common; none of us had asked to be turned into monsters. The decision had been made for us. We'd all had to learn to adapt to our new circumstances, no matter how horrendous they were.

"I was turned shortly after the Court was formed…Natalie." He grinned at me for remembering to call me by my name that time. If my one true love hadn't been sitting right beside me, I might have been tempted by Nicholas' pretty face. Since my shrivelled heart already belonged to someone else, the courtier's beauty had little effect on my libido.

If Nicholas was telling us the truth, then that meant he was about two thousand years old. I'd have to speak to Igor and see if he could corroborate this story.

"You were a lowly guard for two thousand years then the Comtesse suddenly turns you into a courtier." I was silent for a few seconds, trying to think of a diplomatic way to say what was on my mind. "Why would you turn traitor against her after I killed the First? You could have stayed with the Court and become one of the high and mighty. By joining us, you've pretty much guaranteed that you'll be just a lowly commoner again."

Nicholas struggled to come to terms with this revelation. "Will you not be forming a Court of your own?" he asked uncertainly.

"Hell no," I scoffed. "Why do you think I keep telling you not to call me your Queen?" He still seemed not to get it. "There will be no Court surrounding me because I am not a ruler. Lord Luc and Lord Gregor are just plain old Luc and Gregor now."

"My name is Lucentio," Luc corrected me archly. "Only you, and apparently now Geordie, use that horrid nickname." I could tell he didn't really mind me calling him Luc. Even if he did, I was confident that he'd get used to it, eventually.

Crushed, Nicholas slumped back against the seat. "So, I am to be a mere lackey again," he said bitterly.

"There won't be any lackeys, either," I told him. "We've been a bit busy to work it all out yet, but I don't see any reason why we can't form some kind of democracy. If we stick to the rules you've all been abiding by for thousands of years, we should be fine."

Our rules were pretty simple. The most important one was that we weren't supposed to bring attention to ourselves, or to reveal our true nature to humans. We weren't allowed to kill humans when we fed, but had to befuddle their wits instead. We could only have one servant at a time and could only make a minion in the event that our maker died. The final rule was that we weren't allowed to kill our own kind unless we were defending our own lives.

I'd recently broken rule number one in the worst kind of way. I'd been careless when feeding from a Russian soldier and had been captured in the act on video. Since almost every human on the planet probably knew about our existence by now, I guessed that the first rule no longer applied. It wasn't just me who had been spotted. All five of our original team members had been caught fighting the imps on film. Our secret was well and truly out and it couldn't be put back in.

Musing about the idea, Nicholas smiled tentatively. "Then I will be a free man? I will no longer have to bow and scrape to anyone?"

"That's the plan," I replied. *How often do your plans work out as you intended them to?* My subconscious was at it again, pointing out things I didn't want to hear. The answer to that, of course, was rarely.

Chapter Five

Several hours later, we crossed over the border into Kazakhstan. I sent out my senses to locate our Japanese kin. Detecting a large group of our kind somewhere to the southeast, I passed the news on to Luc. He fished his phone out and I called the others. "Hi, Gregor," I said when he answered. "Can you tell Igor to let us pass him? I've got a bead on Ishida and his people."

"Can you estimate how far away they are?" he asked.

"It'll take us a few hours to reach them, but hopefully we'll find them before dawn." I couldn't judge distances with exact accuracy, but had some idea of how long it would take to reach them.

"I'll pass the message on." Even as Gregor spoke, Igor slowed, having overheard my end of the conversation. Luc overtook the black car with a nod of thanks. Geordie waved at me forlornly as we glided past. I solemnly returned the gesture

Nicholas had lapsed into a moody silence in the back seat. His arms were crossed, holding his jacket shut over his naked torso. He wasn't happy that we were allying ourselves with the Japanese and was making his opinion about our choice very clear.

I hadn't wanted him to tag along after we'd left the cavern of doom and had only reluctantly allowed him to join me. He'd insisted on following me around like a puppy and now he was forced to live with our choices. I wished he'd do so graciously instead of sulking about it like a child.

Concentrating on the group that I assumed was our allies, I directed Luc towards them as best as I could. It wasn't an exact science and we had to backtrack several times after heading in the wrong direction. At last, we reached an isolated property with time to spare before the sun was scheduled to rise.

Luc turned into a dirt driveway and I squinted at the house in the distance. From afar, it looked like a rundown piece of crap. Up close, it was even worse. The roof was gone and most of the walls had collapsed. From the remaining charred wood, I deduced that a fire had swept through the dwelling. Stepping foot inside would almost guarantee an injury if we'd still been human.

The barn was in slightly better condition than the house. Three of the walls were still standing and only half of the roof had fallen in. This was due to age and the weather rather than from a fire.

Luc spied the tail end of a large vehicle parked behind the barn and pointed it out. Before I could examine the vehicle further, dozens of warriors boiled into view.

Dressed in familiar black leather suits and masks that covered the lower half of their faces, they were armed with samurai swords, axes, throwing knives, crossbows and various other weapons. Luc wisely parked some distance away and turned the headlights off. Igor coasted to a stop a few feet behind us and switched his lights off as well.

Disembarking from our cars, we gathered in a circle. "You'd better let me meet them alone," I said into the silence. Luc was reluctant to allow me to endanger myself and Nicholas went as far as shaking his head. "Put your hand up if you're indestructible." Naturally, my hand was the only one raised. It wasn't that I didn't trust Ishida and his people. I just didn't want an incident to occur that might strain our international relations before they'd even begun.

Raising my other hand to show I was unarmed, I strode across the grass. I'd left my swords in the car as a show of good faith. I'd dressed in jeans and a jumper, but should have donned one of my suits. I would have been instantly recognizable wearing it.

"Natalie, is that you?" a young male voice asked. Being twelve in mortal years, Ishida was short enough to be hidden behind a wall of guards. His young voice was instantly recognizable. His guards shifted enough to give me a glimpse of his face.

"It's me, Emperor Ishida. Have you played any good zombie games lately?"

Pushing his way through his warriors, Ishida's normally stoic face broke into a grin. "I have missed your company, Mortis. No one on our island knows how to play computer games."

"Neither did I until you taught me," I pointed out. We clasped forearms rather than hugging outright. As the leader of the Japanese vampire nation, Ishida had an image to uphold. Speaking of image, he wore a modified black leather suit with the same metal plating that my red suit had contained. It protected his chest and back from swords, spears, arrows and many other weapons. The addition of a thick metal band around his neck would stop anyone from easily beheading him. It had been padded to add bulk to his wiry frame, but it wouldn't be polite for me to point that out.

Kokoro emerged from the protective ring of warriors. She stood out not just because of her pale kimono, but also because of her eyes. Unlike every other vampire ever made, her eyes were pure white instead of black. She'd been either gifted, or cursed with visions when she'd been turned and had lost her sight at the same time. She could read minds as well. It was a talent that I personally found to be rather intrusive at times. She glided through the crowd and I stepped forward to meet her. We brushed a kiss on each other's cheek in greeting. "I am glad you and your friends have arrived safely, Natalie."

"This is quite a…place you've picked for our meeting." That was as diplomatic as I could force myself to be about the broken down house and grounds.

Ishida waved away my scepticism. "I have no intention of sheltering in these ruins," he assured me. "We have suitable transportation and sleeping quarters."

My curiosity was piqued, but I had duties to attend to before I could investigate this claim. "Is it ok for my friends to join us?" I asked the emperor.

Ishida cocked an eyebrow at Kokoro. I presumed her short pause was due to scanning my friend's minds for any signs of treachery. "I see you have added someone new to your ranks," she said.

I grimaced at the reminder. Since she couldn't possibly have actually seen him, she'd either picked up on Nicholas' thoughts, or on the thoughts of those around him. "Nicholas defected from the Court and has chosen to join our cause." I had to say that because, despite the distance between our two groups, the muscle bound vamp could no doubt hear every word I was saying.

Ishida cast a curious look at my friends. "Gather your people, Mortis. We must parley before dawn."

I hid my smile at his old fashioned terminology. He was far older than anyone on my team, or so I assumed. We had to respect him just for surviving for so long. At my wave, my team ambled over. Surrounded by around fifty masked male and female Japanese soldiers, our group was badly outnumbered, but I wasn't expecting trouble. The whole purpose of our meeting was to deal with a threat that could prove to be detrimental to us all.

First, I introduced Emperor Ishida and Kokoro, then named everyone on my side. Kokoro gave everyone a polite smile. Ishida inclined his head briefly, giving Geordie a longer look than the others. The two teenagers were only three years apart in mortal years, but were ten thousand years apart in vampire age. Like most teens, they were automatically curious about each other.

Ishida bowed to our group formally. "Please follow me." He gave Kokoro his arm to lead her back around behind the barn. She walked gracefully, holding her kimono a couple of inches off the ground with her free hand.

Gregor immediately followed them, eager to become acquainted with our new allies. Igor stumped along behind him. He was far less eager, but knew our cooperation with the Japanese vamps was necessary. Geordie was more subdued than normal and remained at my side. Luc kept his emotions hidden, offering me his arm as Ishida had with his seer. I took it with a smile and pretended for just a few moments that I wasn't just a lowly commoner.

Nicholas brought up the rear. He'd donned a shirt that Luc had loaned him and it strained to cover his shoulders. His heavy scowl tempted me to tell him to wait in the car. I decided it would be a better idea to keep an eye on him rather than allowing him to wander around on his own.

Rounding the barn, I ogled the sleek black motorhome that Ishida and his people had acquired from somewhere. I wasn't sure if they'd paid for it, or if they'd bamboozled a human into giving it to them. It didn't seem polite to ask. A large truck was parked a few feet ahead of the motorhome. It would be a tight squeeze, but the Emperor's guards would be able to hide inside it during daylight hours.

At a slight nod from their young ruler, the Emperor's guards took up their posts around the vehicle. Ishida entered first, followed by Kokoro. Gregor graciously allowed me to enter next. Pushing Geordie aside, he was right on my heels. The teen gave him an indignant glare that shifted to Luc when he also rudely pushed past him. Igor shoved Geordie ahead of him and Nicholas brought up the rear again. I had a feeling it was a position he was quickly going to have to get used to. We might not have a Court, but it appeared we had our own form of hierarchy.

As a show of trust, Ishida didn't allow any of his guards inside the motorhome. Kokoro knew I had no intention of hurting any of their people. It was thanks to Ishida and his warriors that I'd gained the fighting skills that had allowed me to take down the First and his unnatural offspring. I'd always be grateful to him for making that possible.

Taking a seat at the roomy circular dining table, Ishida indicated for us to join him. The table was topped with pale pink marble and the curved bench seat was covered in cream leather. Geordie stared around the luxurious motorhome in wide eyed wonder. Although he'd lived in the Court mansion for two hundred years, his quarters had been a tiny cell in the extensive catacombs that had been dug out beneath the grounds. The expensively appointed furniture and state-of-the-art kitchen were more opulent than he was used to. For the child king, it was probably a short step up from being bearable. His mountain fortress on a secluded Japanese island was far more spectacular than the motorhome.

I took the seat to Ishida's left and Kokoro sat on his right. Luc frowned at Geordie when he tried to slide in next to me. Giving Luc a sheepish smile, the kid took the next seat over. When we were finally settled, Gregor kicked things off. Flicking his hair back from his face in a habitual gesture, he got straight to the point. "There have been no reports of vampire uprisings so far, but it is only a matter of time now."

Kokoro nodded in agreement. "The First's ten 'disciples' fed very well when they rose three nights ago. They will shortly have dozens of fledgling servants."

Damn it, Kokoro has been rummaging around inside my head again! My thought was decidedly cranky. She must have been prying because she was using the name I'd given the interred ancient vampires. The seer's expression was grave and I was glad I didn't share her visions. The sight of ten starved vamps feeding on helpless humans wouldn't have been pretty. The picture of them feeding their flesh hunger would have been even worse.

"Even now, their victims are waking to join their ranks," she continued. "Tonight, the newly risen servants will in turn begin to feed. This will begin a cycle that will endanger the existence of both humans and us."

"Do you know where they are?" I asked the prophetess.

"Your dreams were correct, Mortis. They are in Africa." I wasn't comforted that my own version of a vision was accurate. This meant I had some kind of connection with our new adversaries.

Igor put forward a suggestion. "If you know they are in Africa, then we shouldn't waste time waiting for official news to spread before heading there. If the disciples have any intelligence at all, they will target remote villages. They will attempt to remain undetected for as long as possible."

Gregor nodded thoughtfully. "If they are careful, it might take days before their attacks become known to the authorities." Everyone was speaking English so translation wasn't necessary. Since I was the only one who could understand every language on, and presumably off, the planet, this saved me from repeating everything that was said.

Ishida glanced at his seer for her opinion on how we should proceed. He might be the ruler of his small nation, but he knew Kokoro's worth. She nodded to back up

Igor's idea. "I suggest we make haste and fly there immediately," she said. "The longer we wait, the more of our kind will need to be dispatched."

For a stunned moment, I thought she meant she and her people could actually fly. Then I realized she was talking about using a plane. Her lips quirked slightly in amusement as she caught my thought. Thankfully, she kept my embarrassing mistake to herself.

"I don't suppose there is an airfield with a plane large enough to carry us all anywhere nearby," Geordie said with a profound lack of hope.

"Actually," Ishida replied, "we will find what we need only one hour from this location."

I had a sneaking suspicion about how they'd travelled from Japan to Kazakhstan. "You didn't steal a plane, did you?"

Inclining his head haughtily, Ishida confirmed my hunch. "Kokoro foresaw our need and arranged for our transportation. The plane is waiting to take us wherever we need to go."

Gregor smiled at the teen. "Excellently done, Emperor Ishida." He was clearly the most diplomatic person in our group. I was glad we had someone with his skills on our side.

If dawn hadn't been lurking just over the horizon, I would have suggested that we head for the airfield straight away. Like Kokoro said, the longer it took us to locate the rogue vamps, the more of them we'd eventually have to put down. I didn't relish the idea of another lengthy fight against thousands of monsters. *Then you're doomed to disappointment,* my subconscious warned me. I gave it a mental grimace.

"We should find somewhere safe to spend the day," Luc said.

"Good idea," I agreed. That would probably mean digging a tunnel because I hadn't seen anywhere suitable where we would be able to avoid the sun.

Kokoro had a solution for our predicament. "Our soldiers located a cellar beneath the farmhouse. It should be safe, if you care to use it."

"Thank you," Gregor said with a bow. "I am sure it will suffice."

"You may use the second spare bedroom of my trailer if you wish, Natalie," Ishida offered gallantly.

"It would be our pleasure," Luc said smoothly. I admired his ability to let the teen know that I wouldn't be sleeping alone without treading on anyone's toes. Ishida inclined his head in agreement. Geordie and Nicholas scowled their displeasure and opened their mouths to voice a protest. Before they could, Igor reached out and dealt them both a blow to the backs of their heads.

Before the pair could retaliate and embarrass themselves, or me, further, I put an end to their antics. "Luc and I will be happy to use the spare room. Geordie and Nicholas, grow up and behave yourselves. We all have to at least try to pretend to get along until this is all over. What you do after that is your problem."

Abashed, they followed Gregor and Igor from the motorhome. "Sorry about that," I apologized to Ishida and Kokoro.

Ishida waved the apology away. "I have heard that the Europeans are less than respectful to their rulers. Their behaviour comes as no great surprise."

I opened my mouth to tell him I wasn't anyone's ruler, but Kokoro subtly shook her head. "Does this mobile palace have a bathroom? I'd like to wash up if I can," I said instead.

"I will show you where it is," the seer replied and stood. She navigated her way to the bathroom that was in the middle of the motorhome almost as if she were sighted.

Turning on the tap, I hoped it would muffle the question I was about to ask. "Why do you want me to pretend to be in charge of our group?" I kept my voice so low that it was practically soundless.

"Why do you feel as if you will be pretending?" she shot back just as quietly.

"Because I'm just…me. I'm not exactly ruler material." Anyone who knew me even slightly could figure that out.

Her white eyes seemed to look right through me. "Who are you, Natalie?"

I saw where she was going and wished I could still heave a heavy sigh. That sort of thing took practice when you could no longer breathe and it didn't come easily to me. "I'm Mortis," was my unhappy reply.

"For that reason alone, you are now the leader of your people." With that less than comforting statement, Kokoro glided away and left me alone to get cleaned up.

The bathroom was also in shades of pink, with a marble floor and basin and a tiny shower. A shower would have been welcome, but I contented myself with washing quickly, but thoroughly instead.

Luc was already in the miniscule bedroom I found near the back of the vehicle. He lay on the bed with his hands crossed behind his head. Black hair framed his face and accentuated his cheekbones. His talented lips tilted up at the corners under my scrutiny and I lifted my eyes to his.

"Don't even think about it," I warned him softly at his interested expression. I knew that look well. It usually ended up with me naked and moaning loudly. There was zero possibility of us engaging in sex with the emperor of the Japanese vampires only a few metres away. Ishida didn't need to die for the day as the youngest of our kind did when the sun rose. Out of all of us, Geordie was the only one who was still too new to stay awake at will.

Shrugging, Luc climbed beneath the covers of the king-size single bed still fully clothed except for his shoes. He didn't trust our allies enough to let his guard down yet. I did, but I also climbed into bed without undressing. Frankly, I didn't trust Luc not to strip me off and have his wicked way with me. Once his hands and mouth touched me, I found it very difficult to resist him.

My most favourite companion behaved himself and merely folded me into his arms. When the sun rose, he slumped against me, suddenly heavy with death. I stayed awake for a while longer, listening to Ishida pace in his bedroom.

Kokoro had taken the other tiny bedroom. She was either asleep, or was doing a good impression of it from the lack of noise coming through the flimsy wall. Some of the warriors were still awake and were on guard. They exchanged worried conversation in the back of the truck, but spoke too quietly for me to be able to make out what they were saying.

Finally, I closed my eyes and sank into darkness, hoping I wouldn't have any weird dreams or visions. Naturally, my hopes were dashed.

Chapter Six

Opening my eyes, I peered at the dirt walls of my prison in utter hopelessness. I'd been banished to this existence by my hated master so long ago that I'd almost lost all concept of time.

The First had known of the treachery that my nine brothers and I had planned for him. His cruel punishment had been to exile us beneath the earth and to forbid us from ever rising again. We were doomed to starve for all eternity, or until the God who had abandoned us so long ago finally relented and sent our master to his well-deserved death.

Over time, my physical strength had begun to fail. To compensate for my body's inactivity, my mental strength had increased. It had taken centuries, but I'd learned to touch the minds of my brothers buried nearby. I even learned how to sense creatures in the area around my prison. Knowing my brethren were near and that I was not alone in my despair was a small comfort in an otherwise unbearable existence.

Eventually, after what was probably thousands of years, even my mental strength had begun to fade. I'd subsided into a coma-like state for untold centuries until a few nights ago, when I'd sensed a strange presence.

At first, I thought it was our master, possibly returning to gloat, but he had left this land long ago. Whoever it was, they were unknown to me. Then I'd sensed something that had drawn my attention away from the stranger; food.

Bound by my master's orders, I could not leave my prison. Forcing my hunger upwards, I could only hope that the food would be drawn to it. My gambit failed and my hunger remained unsated. The being standing above my grave faded when the animal fled, almost as if they had just been a figment of my imagination.

Some time later, the being had returned again and this time I sensed them more strongly. After my long slumber, I was inexplicably beginning to rouse. When more food appeared, my thirst for blood became overwhelming. I sensed the stranger standing above me, feeding on what should have been my prey. I sensed the being so strongly that I could almost taste the blood that flooded down their throat.

Rousing from my musings, I became aware that something had changed. Reaching out, I sought the minds of my brothers nearby. Unlike me, they had given up hope of escape many thousands of years ago. Being the second vampire to be created, my will to survive was stronger than theirs. I had never entirely given up hope that we would one night be freed from our forced imprisonment.

Turning my head slightly, I tried to tell what had changed. I went still as I realized what it was. The compulsion to remain in my underground tomb was gone. This could only mean one thing; our master had at last succumbed to death and my brothers and I were now free to rise.

Resting on my back with my hands laced together on my chest, I had not moved in so long that my limbs would not obey me at first. Forcing my hands into action, they creaked as desiccated tissue reluctantly submitted to my will. My vision was cloudy from far too many years of starvation, but I saw how wasted I'd become. My once dark brown skin was now grey. My flesh had wasted away to nothing and my bones were prominent.

My sticklike fingers flexed, then touched the ceiling of the prison that I'd hollowed out of the ground so very long ago. I stroked the soil to test whether my mind was simply playing tricks on me or not. Grains of dirt broke free and fell onto my face. Still disbelieving that my long confinement was over, I dug my hands deep into the earth. Only when I tunnelled upwards to the surface high above and felt air on my withered flesh did I finally begin to accept the truth that my exile was over.

Climbing out of the ground, I tottered and almost trod on the stinking corpses of two birds. One had died from a broken neck, but the other had only suffered from broken wings. Strangely, I found no teeth marks in their tiny bodies from when the stranger had fed upon them.

Further away was the carcass of a large deer. I looked at the animal longingly. It would have made a fine meal and could have partially satisfied my hunger. Unfortunately, it had been dead for far too long. Its blood would be foul and undrinkable by now.

While uppermost in my mind, feeding would have to wait for just a little while longer. As the Second, it was my duty to rouse my brothers from their eons of banishment. Sending out my senses, I touched their slumbering minds. The Third was reluctant to wake and resisted my efforts. Finally, his eyes cracked open and he heeded my call. His astonishment was equal to mine when he began to dig his way upwards.

Soon, all nine of my brethren were free. We had been imprisoned closely together and it did not take long for us all to gather. All were as withered, shrunken and ashy skinned as I was. It would take vast amounts of blood to restore our bodies to their previous strength.

"Food?" the Seventh croaked and cocked his head to the side. It had been a habit of his since we'd been children in our cave. Even after becoming a monster, he hadn't outgrown the gesture.

"This way," I said and led my friends in a shuffling walk towards where I sensed prey. Many animals made the jungle their home, but they would be too difficult for us to catch. Humans would always be far easier food for us to capture.

It took us many hours to reach the tiny community. Where they'd once lived in large groups in caves, humans were now separated into family units. Their dwellings were small and were made of mud and grass. Their language had evolved and I could barely understand what the few that were still awake were saying. Touching their minds made understanding their speech easier.

Moving slowly and quietly, my brothers and I surrounded what our food thought of as a 'village'. The three men sitting around a fire exchanging conversation were silenced before they even knew they were in danger. I captured one of the humans with my gaze. His will seeped away and the vacant stare that I had not seen in far too long replaced his fright.

My fangs tore through my stiff lips, but the pain was forgotten when they pierced the villager's neck. Thick, salty blood poured into my mouth and I drained the man dry. I then opened a vein in my wrist with my teeth and dribbled a few drops of the black substance between the man's lips.

My brothers and I were weak in both strength and numbers. These humans would rise in three nights and would become our servants. I had no way of knowing how many humans occupied the world now, but I suspected it would be a great many. Increasing our small band would help to ensure our survival.

Strength flowed into my desiccated veins and my flesh was partially renewed. It would take many meals before I would be completely restored. There were enough villagers to begin the process for all nine of my brothers and myself. We would have to take pains to ensure the sun didn't kill our new servants when it rose. We'd have to hide them somewhere safe.

Stealthily, the Third and I entered a hut together. My brother had yet to feed, so I gestured for him to take the male. Two small children lay sleeping on a mat in the corner. Apart from the blood their tiny bodies would offer, they would be of no use to us. I fed from them, then destroyed any chance that they would rise again by tearing their hearts from their chests.

We had experimented briefly with turning children into our kind when we had first become creatures that drank blood to survive. Most of the undead children had been destroyed when their minds broke beneath the hungers that assailed them. We'd learned that a certain level of sexual maturity was required to become one of us.

Finished with the male, the Third turned to the woman. She woke as he pushed her drained husband away, but he ensnared her before she could voice a scream that would alert her neighbours. While my brother was preoccupied, I fed the drained man my blood and made him mine.

I pulled the Third away from the female before he could drain her completely. Most of the women in this village would serve two purposes tonight. They would feed both our blood and flesh hungers. Nudging my brother aside, I tore her loincloth away and pushed her down onto her back.

I enjoyed our prey's fear when I unleashed my flesh hunger on them. This one was too deeply ensnared to be afraid, but my body didn't care. It was demanding that I feed it and I was happy to comply. My blood smeared her lips when I was finished with her. She and her husband would become my fledglings. They and many others would soon rise to do my bidding.

Waking with a shudder, I sat up. It was impossible to wipe the sight of the poor woman being mauled by the Second from my mind. The image was lodged in there tightly and would be in my memory for a long time. I'd been glad I hadn't shared Kokoro's visions, but something obviously thought I should witness the atrocities for myself.

"Bad dream?" Luc asked from right beside me and I started so hard I nearly fell off the bed. For once, he didn't look like he wanted to jump me. Night had fallen a few minutes ago and it seemed that all of the vamps were up and moving around.

"Horrible dream," I muttered, wishing not for the first time that I hadn't been cursed with being Mortis. Latin for 'death', it was a name that I'd lived up to so far.

"Do you want to talk about it?" my one true love asked.

I studied his face to see if he really meant it. None of my other boyfriends had ever expressed an interest in hearing about my dreams. Then again, I'd never dated anyone long enough for things to evolve to that stage.

Luc and I spent a lot of time together, when I wasn't off saving the world or either of us was being imprisoned, but I wasn't sure if we could be defined as dating. His sincerity seemed to be real, so I took him up on the offer. "I just saw what happened the night the Second realized he had been freed from his master's influence."

Sitting up, Luc frowned. He knew as well as I did that my dreams had a disturbing tendency of coming true. "The Second? Is that what he calls himself?"

I nodded and scooted back so we were sitting side by side. "They refer to each other from the Second to the Eleventh. Whatever their real names were, they've been forgotten a long time ago."

"What did you see in this dream?" Luc took my hand and I wrapped my fingers around his. We might not be able to give each other warmth, but we could at least offer the comfort of touch.

"He can sense not only our kind, but humans as well," I said. I thought I was the only vampire who possessed that particular talent. Maybe we all had the innate ability to do so, but it took dire need to bring it out of us. "He managed to call his nine brothers out of their comas, then led them to a village."

Concerned, Luc squeezed my hand. "Did you see them feed, Natalie?"

Nodding, I swallowed down a lump of either fear or sorrow for the humans. "They fed from everyone, then used the women to feed their flesh hunger. The Second is forcing the humans to taste his blood so they'll rise as vampires. Since the children were useless, they drained them before tearing their hearts out." I kept my tone as emotionless as possible, but my anguish still leaked out.

"We should join the others," Luc said quietly. I didn't realize that they had already gathered in the motorhome again until we stepped into the living area. Geordie's eyes were round, indicating he'd heard every word I'd said. Gregor and Igor looked grim. Ishida and Kokoro shared a glance that she could sense, if not see.

Nicholas, either oblivious or uncaring about what my dream portended, swept his eyes from my feet up to my face. He lingered on my chest for a moment too long. "Good evening, my…Natalie." He offered me a smile that might have melted my socks off if I'd been wearing any, or if I'd had even the slightest interest in him.

Geordie opened his mouth to utter an acerbic remark, but Igor shot him a warning glare. The teen closed his mouth and muttered whatever he'd wanted to say beneath his breath.

Ishida saw no reason not to voice his opinion. "You should reprimand your servants when they show disrespect to you, Mortis," he said idly. "If any of my people were to behave in such a manner, I'd have them flayed and thrown into the pit."

I'd spent some quality time in his pit and knew that it meant death to our kind. For me it had meant a few hours of intolerable pain after being half boiled by the sun from my waist down to my toes. It had taken me hours to regenerate, but Nicholas wouldn't be so lucky. "I'll keep that in mind," I said with unfamiliar diplomacy.

"We heard the dream you described to Lucentio," Gregor commented. I admired the way he smoothly turned the conversation to a safer topic. "Do you have any idea whereabouts in Africa they might be located?"

"Somewhere that has a jungle, deer and birds," I replied unhelpfully.

Geordie giggled and Ishida almost cracked a smile. The child king had grown used to my weird sense of humour during the time I'd spent on his island.

"I believe we will very shortly discover where the disciples and their newly made servants are located," Kokoro said. "For now, we should head for the airport. Our pilot is waiting to take us to our destination."

Ishida stood and that was our cue to file outside. Nicholas insisted on riding with Luc and me again. Geordie pouted and retaliated by also joining us. The pair sulked silently in the back. Luc discreetly rolled his eyes as he waited for the motorhome to rumble to life.

Now I know what it feels like to have kids. When I'd still been alive, I'd felt as if I'd missed out since I hadn't settled down and raised a family. *If this is what it's like, then I didn't miss out on all that much,* I decided.

Our car was third in line of the small convoy as it departed from the farmstead. Ishida's truck full of soldiers went first and the motorhome rode between it and our jeep. Igor brought up the rear. Some of the guards had been transferred to the motorhome, presumably to give the others in the truck more room to stand. It would have been very tight quarters with all fifty of them squeezed in together.

That reminded me of something. "How was the cellar?" I asked the morose pair in the back.

"It was adequate, Natalie," Nicholas said and flashed me a grin. His eyes remained curiously flat and emotionless. *How could I not have noticed that before?* My subconscious had an answer ready. *Because you're usually staring at his chest and abs and rarely bother to look at his eyes,* it pointed out snidely, but accurately.

Geordie shot him a look of disgust, then leaned forward to mostly hide the muscle bound vamp from my sight. "It was draughty, damp, full of bugs and cold, *my Queen.*" I glanced into the rear view mirror in time to see Nicholas narrow his eyes at the barb.

"That's a shame," Luc said insincerely. "Natalie and I spent a wonderful night in the Emperor's spare bedroom."

"Exactly how 'wonderful' was your night?" Geordie asked suspiciously.

"Not that wonderful," I said dryly.

Nicholas smirked and Geordie smiled brightly. "If you ever have need of someone else to spend the night with, *chérie,* I humbly offer my services."

Luc had a comeback ready. "That will not be necessary, Geordie. Natalie and I have agreed not to share our flesh hunger with anyone else."

Nicholas lifted a brow in surprise. "You mean you are willingly limiting yourselves to only one bed partner?"

"Natalie is more than enough woman for me," Luc said with a hint of a smile. "I have no need of anyone else in my bed."

Geordie sent me a stricken look. "Is this true, *chérie*? Have you committed yourself to Lucentio?"

I didn't think my sex life was anyone's business, but mine and Luc's, but I could see the advantages of answering the question. "We love each other," I said simply, hoping the admission would keep Nicholas off my back. Surely, even creatures like us had to respect love.

"Our kind does not 'love'," the over muscled vamp said with a lip curl, immediately dashing my hopes that he'd take the hint. "We eat, sleep and fuck. There is nothing else for us."

I'd heard that exact same sentiment before, when I'd been a guest in the London sewer vamp's lair. Gregor had shown me with his cultured manor and library full of books that this didn't have to be the case. Luc had shown me with his memories after I'd accidentally bitten him that it was indeed possible for us to love.

"I feel very sorry for you if that's what you truly believe, Nicholas," I said coolly.

"I also love you, Nat," Geordie said in a small voice.

"I love you right back, Geordie." I kept my tone light so he didn't read too much into it.

Uncharacteristically serious, the teen studied my face. "But you do not love me in the same way that you love Lucentio."

"No," I broke to him gently. "I love you like a…" I almost said pet, but that would have hurt his feelings even more. "Little brother," I said instead.

Leaning forward over the seat so our faces were only inches apart, he looked through me rather than at me. "I was a brother, once. I had two sisters that were older than me. When I was small they used to dress me in their clothes and pretend I was a girl." His smile was sad and held more than a hint of embarrassment.

"I promise I won't ever make you wear a dress, Geordie," I said sincerely.

"*I* don't promise you anything," Nicholas muttered. "I think you'd make an excellent girl."

Turning to glare at him, I lifted a hand to stop the kid from spiralling into a tirade. "If you are going to continue to be a pain in the arse, we'll stop and let you out, Nicholas." I maintained eye contact with him and he seemed to understand that I was being serious.

"That will not be necessary, my Liege." His reply was stiff and formal.

"If you truly believe that Natalie is your ruler," Luc said, "then I suggest you begin to treat her as such. You would not want to get on her bad side."

Nicholas had seen me fighting the imposter pretending to be me the night he had helped to dismember my body. I'd popped her head like an overripe pimple, so he knew just how dangerous I was. Luc's warning seemed to slide off the newbie without sinking in.

Subsiding back into a sulk, Nicholas turned his face to the window. His reflection was ghostly, but I could still make out his annoyance. *Maybe we* should *get rid of him,* my subconscious muttered. It was being more talkative than usual. *We'd be better off without him,* it advised.

It was rare for me to be in agreement with my subconscious. The fact that I agreed completely this time probably meant that I should take heed of its advice.

Chapter Seven

Reaching the outskirts of a medium sized city, we drove past a motorhome dealership. I noticed a vacant slot where a large vehicle had recently been. Coincidentally, it was roughly the size of the sleek black vehicle travelling in front of us.

No one ran out onto the road bellowing in anger, so maybe Ishida had paid for the motorhome after all. Then again, the dealership had closed for the night. Maybe there was just no one around to see us as we glided past.

Not far past the town, we turned onto a dirt track that took us to our destination. A small collection of buildings made up the airport. A single airplane sat on the tarmac. One look at the pilot waiting beside the plane as we pulled to a stop was enough to tell me that he was well and truly hypnotized.

His vacant eyes latched onto Kokoro as she exited the motorhome on Ishida's arm. Despite her blindness, she had still managed to ensnare the guy. I wasn't sure if I thought that was cool, or creepy. Maybe a bit of both. I was definitely impressed that he'd remained beneath her spell for so long.

White and shiny, the plane looked expensive. Inside, it was plush, but not extravagantly so. There was plenty of room for all of us. There were even a few spare seats for our luggage. Ishida chose a seat near the front and motioned for me to sit beside him. It would have been insulting to refuse the offer, so I complied with his silent request. Luc sat across from me, discouraging anyone from taking the window seat by placing our bags beside him.

Kokoro sat in the seat in front of Ishida. It was a surprise when she allowed Geordie to sit beside her. *She's used to spoiled kids after ten millennia of dealing with the Emperor.* I hoped she didn't pick up on my thought. I had some small hope that Geordie would behave himself while in her presence. If he propositioned her for sex, I'd slap him up the back of the head so hard he'd end up facing the wrong way.

I understood why my young friend had chosen to sit beside Kokoro when he launched a dozen questions at her. He wanted to know what life was like on their island. As the seer did her best to answer the kid's questions, the teen at my side sent me a worried glance. Ishida's warriors had taken all of the other seats around us, so Gregor, Igor and Nicholas had moved to the back of the plane.

"What's on your mind, Emperor?" I kept my voice low enough that only the first few rows of his men and women would be able to hear us.

"Kokoro's visions have been very…disturbing," he spoke even more quietly than I had.

"What has she seen?"

He pondered for a few seconds before leaning in to answer me in his native language. "She sees death coming."

That particular prophecy wasn't new, but my blood wanted to drain out of my face anyway. Unfortunately, it had lost the ability to do so months ago. "Do you mean we're all going to die?" I'd thought putting an end to the First would also put an end to the annihilation of our species.

Ishida gave me a disturbed shrug. It was a habit he'd picked up from spending too much time in my company. "She does not know for certain. All Kokoro will tell me is that she sees death and then darkness."

Chilled, I wondered how the First's ten disciples could be an even bigger threat than their master had been. We weren't facing beings that had been transformed into living, breathing, breeding monsters this time. They were just vampires, even if they were more virulent than normal.

During the long flight, I shared further quiet conversation with the child king. We discussed many things, ranging from our doom, to the suits and weapons he'd given me, to the zombie games he loved so much.

Our conversation was interrupted by the pilot towards the end of our ten hour journey. "Emperor Ishida, I was told to inform you of any strange news coming out of Africa." His voice came through discreet speakers at several points around us.

The pilot flicked a switch and a news report started playing. "A small village in western Africa has been attacked by what is believed to be a rogue pack of vampires." Only a few short days ago, our kind had been a myth. Now, thanks to me, everyone knew we existed.

"Every adult in the village has been taken and every child has been slain," the reporter continued solemnly. "There were rumours that vampires helped stop the uprising of the grey monsters in Russia only a few short days ago. Many are wondering if the vampires are now seeking to take the 'unknown entity's' place with a plan to force humans into bondage and slavery."

"And so it begins," Kokoro said softly and with grave finality.

I could almost hear the nails being driven into our figurative coffins. The freshly risen disciples wouldn't yet be aware that our kind was no longer a secret. They would quickly be hunted by soldiers and that would only add to the problem. Some of the soldiers were bound to be taken. They would then be turned and would become the very things that they'd been sent to hunt.

Now that he had a firmer idea of where we needed to go, the pilot altered his course slightly. Our shutters were down to stop the sunlight from filtering inside and incinerating us when dawn arrived. When it did, heat engulfed the plane then was quickly gone. None of those who had chosen to remain awake showed any signs of discomfort. Maybe the heat was only in my head.

Being extremely elderly, Ishida kept me company when we landed on a secluded airstrip somewhere to the western edge of central Africa. We'd heard several more updates over the radio. It was enough to know the village that had been attacked was somewhere in the jungle. We couldn't get any closer by plane and would have to arrange for ground transportation.

When the pilot emerged from the cockpit, Kokoro drew him aside. She instructed him to find suitable transportation for all of us. He was to search for a large truck or any type of enclosed vehicle. He had plenty of time to search since we had all day to kill before we would be able to leave the safety of the plane.

Opening the main door would be bad for our health, so the pilot disappeared back behind the curtain that hid the door to the cockpit. At a grating sound coming from up front, I assumed he had some kind of escape hatch and was using it to exit from the plane.

Something had been bugging me, so I took the opportunity to draw Ishida and Kokoro aside. Luc joined us with only a slight frown from the child king. To Ishida, Luc was just a lackey and was of very little importance.

Sliding my arm through Luc's, I let the emperor know just how important my most favourite companion was to me. "Emperor Ishida, why did you come on this journey yourself?" I asked. "Why not just send your warriors to help us fight the disciples and their minions?"

Kokoro shifted slightly, as if she wanted to field my question, but deferred to her ruler. She and I were the only ones who knew that she had turned Ishida. As Ishida's true maker, she had the capacity to rule their nation through him, if she wished. I had the feeling she only rarely used her secret status and only to nudge the kid in the right direction. His origins were kept a secret from his people, which added to his overall mystery.

"Kokoro foresaw that it would mean my death if I did not join you in this battle," Ishida said. He hid it well, but a shadow of fear crossed his young face. After living for so long, death would be a frightening prospect. "She also advised me not to bring more than fifty of our warriors."

"Can you tell me why, Kokoro?" I'd wondered why they had brought only a quarter of their force with them. After I'd culled their damned, there had only been two hundred Japanese warriors left.

She hung her head for a few moments before responding. The seer struggled to explain something she didn't fully understand herself. "To bring more would have resulted in disaster. Staying behind would also have ended badly. Our only hope for our people was for the Emperor and his chosen few to aid you in battle."

Wow, she couldn't be more vague if she tried. Kokoro winced and I knew she'd caught the thought.

"I have asked Kokoro to be more specific," Ishida said with a hint of dryness. "She either cannot, or will not say more."

From the stubborn tilt to her head, I figured it would be a waste of time to question the seer further. "Let's just focus on one disaster at a time," I suggested. We'd have plenty of time to worry about the coming 'death and darkness' once the disciples were dead. Or so I hoped.

With hours still left before the sun would scurry into hiding, I checked on the rest of our team. Half of the Japanese soldiers were sleeping. I knew most of them by sight and nodded to those I recognized. Toward the back of the plane, a much more familiar face stopped me. The instructor who had taught me how to wield a sword sat in an aisle seat, watching over the emperor from afar. I bowed and he nodded slightly in reply. His face held even less expression than most of his people, but I was pretty sure I saw a hint of pride at how I'd turned out from his tutelage.

Sitting in the back couple of rows were the rest of my friends and Nicholas. The ex-courtier's pretty face was slack with death and his head lolled against the window. Geordie had joined the others before the sun had risen. He sat across the aisle from Nicholas and was almost dainty in comparison. His face was pinched as if he was trying to frown even in his unconsciousness. Igor was also asleep. His arms were crossed and he held a knife in one hand.

Gregor had elected to stay awake. He stared pensively down the aisle, but acknowledged me with a brief smile. I took the seat beside Igor, being careful not to jab myself on his knife. I had only a few changes of clothing left and they would no doubt be ruined quickly enough.

"I take it Kokoro has foreseen something that concerns us all," Gregor said.

There was no use lying, or trying to smooth the coming disaster over, whatever it may be. "Well, she hasn't exactly seen rainbows and pots of gold waiting for us ahead," I replied quietly.

"Being friends with you will never be boring, Natalie," Gregor observed.

"You think this is my fault somehow?" I hadn't heard any accusation in his tone, but I could have missed it.

"No," Gregor replied without hesitation, which eased my worry a little. "I believe we have always been doomed and that our fate is simply finally catching up to us."

I do not like the sounds of that. "What do you mean?" My worry was back with a vengeance.

He motioned me closer and we leaned across the aisle towards each other, striving to keep our voices almost soundless. "The only reason we exist is due to an alien landing on our planet," he reminded me, as if I could ever forget that fact. "It was an anomaly that shouldn't have happened. If not for our long dead Father, we would never have been created."

His point was chilling. "You think fate or destiny or whatever, is trying to correct a mistake it made millions of years ago when the alien landed here?" Summed up like that, it was a scary thought.

Gregor inclined his head. "It is just a possibility that has occurred to me recently."

Now I understood why Kokoro was so concerned. If Gregor was right, and he was rarely wrong, we could indeed be facing our doom. I only wished I had some idea of how to fight it.

There's no use trying to fight it, my subconscious advised me. *Haven't you learned by now that you can't escape your destiny?* Not for the first time, I wished it would keep its opinion to itself.

Chapter Eight

By nightfall, our pilot had located two small trucks and a van. The trucks had once been used to ship milk, judging by the sour smell. Ishida's lip curled in disdain at the sight of them. He might be a revered ruler, but he would be crammed into the back of one of the trucks along with the rest of his people when the sun rose again.

Helping Kokoro into the passenger seat of one of the vehicles, he climbed in after her. A female warrior took the wheel. The pilot remained behind, presumably to guard the plane.

Igor appropriated the van and our team piled inside. I called shotgun, much to Geordie's disgruntlement, and sat beside the grizzled Russian. Frequent news updates had confirmed that two more villages had been hit while we'd been on our way to Africa. We knew roughly where we needed to go and Igor took the lead down a narrow, bumpy dirt track. Branches screeched unpleasantly against the sides of the van, putting my fangs on edge.

There was just enough room in the back for Nicholas, Gregor, Geordie and Luc, as well as our baggage. Unfortunately for them, there weren't any seats. Geordie sat next to Luc, sending the occasional glare at Nicholas sitting across from him. The muscle bound vamp crossed his arms and looked down his nose at the teen.

Gregor, crammed in beside the ex-courtier, ventured a suggestion. "Natalie, are you able to sense the disciples and their fledglings?"

I'd had the same thought and shook my head. "I could try, but I don't think it would be a good idea. The Second might sense me searching for him and I don't want to tip him off that we're on our way."

Igor agreed with me. "We should try to remain unnoticed for as long as possible and strike when their guard is down."

Luc wore a slight frown. "It will be difficult for us to find their exact location if you can't sense where they are."

I'd thought that problem through as well. "We'll just have to map where they've hit and try to guess the most likely place that they'll strike next."

"With the attacks being broadcasted to the general public, I assume the local army has become involved by now," Gregor said more to himself than to us. "They should have the information that we require."

While I wasn't looking forward to dealing with foreign armed forces, it would probably be for the best. The last two armies I'd dealt with had ended up co-operating with me to take down the First's offspring. They'd tried to kill me only once before we'd come to an agreement.

Igor drove along seldom used dirt tracks for several hours, then turned onto one that was far more frequently used. Fresh tyre tracks led in the direction we wanted to go. From the size and shape of the tracks, it was easy to guess that the soldiers had beaten us to the first village that had been attacked.

The tracks turned sharply to the left and lights blazed in a clearing several hundred feet ahead. Igor wisely continued along the path that suddenly became narrow and seldom used again. He parked well out of sight of any soldiers that might be on patrol. The pair of trucks trailing us stopped just behind our van.

Ishida's leather clad soldiers jumped from the backs of the trucks. They'd all drawn their weapons and masks covered their faces. I'd armed myself as well, but hadn't drawn my swords yet. The sheaths crisscrossed my back. I had only to reach over my shoulders to draw the blades.

I'd patched up the straps of the sheaths as best as I could after they'd been sliced apart during my fight with the First. I was just glad the handcrafted sheaths and samurai swords hadn't been damaged during the battle.

"What is your plan?" the child king asked me. I was a bit surprised that he was willing to let me take charge, considering my overall lack of vampire age and experience.

"We should sneak in and scout out the area," I replied. "We need to discover which villages have been attacked and where they are."

"I take it we do not want the soldiers to see us?" Ishida surmised.

Nodding, I examined his people. In their midnight black suits and masks, they would be all but invisible amongst the trees. "They'll probably shoot us once they figure out what we are. We'll have to try to convince them that we are their allies."

"Someone should stay behind to protect our vehicles," Gregor wisely suggested.

I had just the person in mind for that job. "Nicholas, I want you to guard our van while we recon the area."

He instantly scowled, but smoothed his face out when Ishida glanced at him imperiously. "As you wish, my...Natalie." The courtier bowed, but his expression was bordering on insolent. Igor's hand twitched, as if he was forcing himself not to smack the muscled one up the back of the head again.

Geordie's lips thinned into a straight line and he quivered with unvoiced indignation. Luc patted the teen on the shoulder to calm him down. *What is Nicholas' problem?* I scowled lightly as I asked myself the question. He'd started out worshipping me and now he was being as difficult as possible.

"I will remain behind as well," Kokoro said. "Creeping stealthily through a jungle isn't easy in my condition." I doubted that being blind was really that much of a disability for her. She was just using it as an excuse, but I was grateful she volunteered to remain behind. It took the sting out of my dismissal of Nicholas.

Ishida pointed out ten of his men and women to stay with her and the rest of us entered the jungle.

Once upon a time and not all that long ago, my journey through the undergrowth would have been far from stealthy. My usual style of travel had been to blunder through the trees, tripping over roots and falling headfirst into bushes. After my intense training with my Japanese instructor, I'd learned to become far less of a klutz. I could now slip through the dense vegetation with barely a sound.

Luc was at my side and the others followed a short distance behind us. Ishida and his people melted away with the intention of circling around the village. My jeans and sweater were dark enough to help me blend into the shadows as we neared the tiny township.

We stopped at the edge of the clearing and studied the soldiers that had gathered in a large group. Most were dark skinned, but some were Caucasian. I saw the American flag on some of the camouflage uniforms and surmised that Colonel Sanderson had to be somewhere in the area.

Thank God for that! I won't have to waste time convincing a new army to help us. It would be far easier to convince the men that I was on their side if some of them had already seen me take down the First and his horde of imps.

As if my thought had conjured him, a tall, thin blond man strode into view. Standing in the middle of the village, Sanderson put his hands on his hips and glowered at the ashes of a campfire. Blood had pooled on the dirt, but it was only a small amount. After starving for so long, blood was too precious for the disciples to waste by spilling it.

A pair of soldiers emerged from one of the twenty or so huts, carrying a tiny bundle in a black body bag. The sight of the deceased child made the colonel scowl. "I knew we should have killed the vampire vermin as soon as we discovered what they were," he muttered to himself. New lines had been etched on his forehead over the past few days. He looked bitter now, as if he blamed himself for this latest attack.

"Did he just call us vermin?" Geordie murmured. He insinuated himself in between Luc and me and slipped a hand around my waist. I believed it was more for comfort rather than a sexual overture. His attitude towards me had changed since Luc had divulged that we were an exclusive item. I only wished Nicholas would take the hint as well and stop being such an idiot.

"Yeah, he did," I replied unhappily. From the first moment I'd realized that our species was no longer a secret, I'd been worried that humans would try to eradicate us. Sanderson's muttered sentiment increased my concern substantially.

Ishida materialized from the shadows, making me start. "We cannot let this insult go unpunished," he said frostily. His young face showed a hint of outrage that a mere human dared to look upon us so unfavourably.

"Look at it from their point of view," I said reasonably. "We feed from them and then either kill them, or force them to forget that we've stolen their blood. How are they supposed to react now that they know we really do exist? Especially after seeing that." I waved a hand at the small bodies that had been gathered together in a grim, yet tidy row. Ishida turned thoughtful as he viewed the deceased.

Bright lights had been set up around the village, chasing most of the shadows away. It would be impossible to sneak in and speak to the colonel without being spotted by his troops. Once seen, I could only imagine what their reactions would be. I suspected it wouldn't be friendly.

Gregor had been studying my face and knew me well enough to voice a question. "What are you planning, Natalie?"

"I've dealt with Colonel Sanderson before," I reminded him. "Despite what he just said, he can be reasonable." After a few more moments to think about the wisdom of my plan, I reached a decision. "I'm going in."

Taking off my sheaths, I handed them to Luc. He took the proffered weapons with a frown. I knew my friends would worry about me, but they would be in far more danger than me. "Be careful, Natalie," he warned me then leaned down to kiss my forehead.

"You plan to walk into that village alone?" Ishida said in astonishment. "Are you not worried that they will shoot you?"

"Oh, they'll shoot me," I replied dryly. "That's pretty much a given. Hopefully, the Colonel will be willing to hear me out after they run out of bullets." Geordie giggled, then cringed away from Igor when he raised his hand threateningly. "I suggest the rest of you vacate the area in case any stray bullets come your way," I told them. I waited for them to melt away before bracing myself and stepping out into the light.

It didn't take long for me to be spotted. If I'd been in Russia, it would have only taken a few seconds to be recognized before being gunned down. Since I was in Africa, they probably hadn't seen quite as much footage of me munching on a Russian soldier on TV. It took these men a bit longer to understand that I wasn't human.

Noticing me almost immediately, a dark skinned soldier pointed his gun at me. "Put your hands up!" he barked in his native language. Drawn by his shout, more men came running as I dutifully lifted my hands into the air.

Sanderson turned to see what the ruckus was. Recognizing me instantly, his jaw went slack with surprise. He opened his mouth, but he didn't get a chance to speak. The soldier pointing his gun at me beat him to it. He'd been examining my far too pale skin and unnatural beauty and his eyes widened when he cottoned on to what I was.

Instant terror overwhelmed him. "Vampire!" he screamed shrilly. "Kill it!" He opened fire and his comrades jumped on board in an utter panic.

My body jerked and shuddered as I was propelled backwards by the barrage. I managed to stay on my feet, which frightened the men even more and proved that I was definitely not human.

During a short pause as they reloaded, Sanderson roared an order. "Hold your fire!"

His terror extreme, the first soldier to shoot ignored the Colonel and aimed at my head this time. His mouth was stretched wide in a grin of fright. I decided I didn't want to waste time regrowing my head and darted forward. My speed was far too quick for a human to track, let alone to counter. Snatching the weapon from the soldier's hand, I bent it in half then handed it back to him. He stared at the ruined gun uncomprehendingly.

Another soldier raised his gun to shoot me and Sanderson put his pistol to the back of the African's head. "Son, if you pull that trigger, I will paint the ground with your brains."

American soldiers had come at the run when the first bullet had been loosed. Surrounding their leader, they protected him, and inadvertently me, from the African troops.

A short, stocky, dark skinned soldier with a collection of colourful medals on his chest strode forward. "You are siding with this...monster?" he demanded in passable English. His nostrils flared with rage that his men were being threatened by soldiers who were supposed to be their allies.

Sanderson took the machine gun from the terrified African soldier's shaking hands, then put his pistol away. "General Merwe, this is Natalie." I was given the once over by eyes that were almost as dark as my own. "She is the vampire who helped my men to take down the army of unknown entities in Russia."

Contempt and fear warred on the general's face. "Why are you here?" he asked me bluntly. From the way his hand strayed towards the gun on his right hip, he was itching to put a few bullets into me.

"I was advised by a seer that ten ancient vampires have broken free from captivity. They rose a few nights ago and have begun to create a horde of our kind." Dread swept through everyone who heard me. I hardly needed to spell out what this meant for the soldiers, but I did anyway. "That will be bad for all of us. My friends and I want them dead as much as you do." Eyes widened as they realized that I hadn't come alone.

"You mean there are more of you here right now?" another terrified soldier asked. His voice cracked on the last word and he peered fearfully at the dark jungle beyond the circle of lights.

"Yes. They're nearby, waiting to hunt down our kin."

"We should talk privately," Sanderson decided and lifted an eyebrow at the general to see if he was willing to join us.

Nodding reluctantly, the leader of the African troops pointed towards a small green command tent at the edge of the village. It wasn't much of a headquarters, but it was better than nothing and would give us some privacy to discuss our mutual dilemma.

A tiny metal table with four foldup seats hunkered in the centre of the tent. A bedroll sat to one side, neatly packed away and waiting for use. Several rolled up pieces of laminated paper beside the bedroll were most likely maps of the area. Hopefully, I'd be able to examine them, but first I had to establish some trust. The general took a seat and indicated for us to do the same.

"You mentioned ten ancient vampires," Sanderson said. "Should I assume they have something to do with the stick figures we saw in the Russian cavern?"

"You assume correctly. The First made ten disciples when he was created. They had a falling out and he banished them. He ordered them to bury themselves and he assumed they'd eventually die from starvation, but that didn't happen. When I killed him, they were freed from their compulsion to remain buried."

Wearing an expression of almost dazed disbelief, Sanderson struggled with the concept. "You weren't aware that this would happen when you killed their leader?"

I shook my head in denial. "Nope. I had no idea they even existed. That's the fun part about the visions that our prophets are sent. They can only see so far into the future. Once one problem is solved, another seems to pop up to take its place." I didn't mention that I was also on the receiving end of these brief and shadowy glimpses of the future.

"How long have these ten vampires been exiled?" queried the general. He was having an even harder time believing my story than Sanderson was.

"About forty thousand years or so," I said as matter-of-factly as possible.

Sanderson's eyes bulged at my answer. "Is that why they've gone on a rampage? Because they haven't fed for so long?"

I nodded. "Being the second generation of vampires, their blood is stronger than a modern vamp's. Every human they feed it to will become one of us." While our blood had weakened over time, theirs was still chock full of alien nastiness.

"What can we expect to face over the next few days?" the general asked.

"Based on what I've seen and heard so far; carnage," I replied and both men flinched. "Do you know the exact number of villages that have been attacked yet?"

Sanderson inclined his head. "We've heard of three more villages roughly of this size that have been cleared out. That brings the total of missing people to over a hundred."

I shuddered at the thought that there would shortly be a hundred or so rabid vamps running around desperately hunting for food. The first villagers to be attacked would already have risen. Each night that passed would only add to their numbers. "Do you have a map of the area?"

The general leaned over to pick up one of the laminated pieces of paper and spread it out on the table. The villages that had been targeted were far apart. It would take several hours to reach them on foot. It was disturbing to see just how many small villages were scattered around the area. If we were going to first contain then put down this threat then we had to try to anticipate where the next attack would take place.

"It appears that these creatures have been heading northward, attacking any villages they encounter,"

Sanderson said and pointed to the tiny towns that had been circled. "We haven't examined the other three villages that have been targeted yet, but we expect to find more of what we found here."

"Dead children who are missing their hearts and their parents nowhere to be found," Merwe intoned. He was staring at me as if I were personally responsible for the attacks. In a way, I was. If I hadn't killed the First, his disciples wouldn't have been unleashed on the earth. Then again, if I hadn't killed the First, his imps would have wiped out most of the population on the planet. It was a case of damned if you do and damned if you don't. I doubted anything could convince the general that I wasn't at fault. Expecting him to trust me would be asking for too much.

Studying the map, I noted the next closest villages to the north. There were several roughly the same distance away from the last town to be targeted. We would have to split our forces up to cover them all. "It looks like these three communities are the most likely to be attacked next." I pointed at them and received a nod from Sanderson and a grudging one from his associate.

"The General and I had come to the same conclusion," the American soldier confirmed. "We have more troops on the way, but I've had difficulties negotiating how many of my men are allowed into the country." The general frowned, but didn't deny the veiled accusation that the leaders of his country were being difficult. "We should have our troops ready to move in a couple more days."

"The disciples will already have moved on and increased their numbers by then," I pointed out. "We have to move quickly if we want to stop them from spreading." I'd hoped the soldiers would have been able to help, but I had the sinking feeling that the humans would only get in our way. "You'd better leave this to my friends and me."

"Wait a minute," Sanderson said when I stood. "Don't you need our help to take them down?"

I shook my head regretfully. "You humans won't be able to match these vamps. They'll be too fast for you to shoot. It's going to be up to us to wipe them out."

Standing, Sanderson rested his knuckles on the table. "I'm not going to let you and your people wander around Africa on a vigilante mission."

General Merwe stood as well. "Some of our soldiers will accompany you, or we will order our men to shoot you and your 'friends' on sight."

I noted their mulish expressions and heaved an internal sigh. *Men! They never listen.* When their soldiers came back dead, maybe they'd understand just how dangerous their new foes were. "Fine. Pick ten men you want to sacrifice. Our best chance of success will be to sneak up on the vamps. Humans make too much noise to sneak effectively and more than ten will pretty much guarantee our failure."

Sharing an affronted look at my estimation of their men's lack of stealth, the pair left the tent, calling for their soldiers. Each chose five men from their ranks and ordered them to accompany me. "They'll need transportation," I advised Merwe, since he had more men and more equipment on hand.

We barely had enough room for our people without adding to our numbers. The general signalled to one of his men and the soldier jogged over to a truck. It rumbled to life and the other nine soldiers climbed into the back.

Canvas sides had been rolled up, but could be lowered to offer shade, if required.

Yeah, that'll offer effective protection against a hungry mob of fledgling vampires, my subconscious observed sourly.

"Our men will keep in touch with us and give us regular progress reports," Sanderson told me.

"Don't count on them keeping in touch for long, Colonel," I replied grimly. "They'll most likely be dead by this time tomorrow."

Ignoring my warning, Sanderson offered his hand. "Good luck and Godspeed."

I shook with him, being careful not to accidentally crush his hand. I was pretty sure God was keeping out of this one. If Gregor was right, then we were an abnormality that needed to be corrected. Why would God care if we lived or died? We couldn't even say his name out loud anymore. Surely that was a sign that he had abandoned us to our fate.

Climbing into the passenger seat of the truck, I directed the driver to head back down the heavily traversed track. Turning left, we angled towards our convoy. My friends had listened to the conversation I'd had with the two rulers of the armies and were already waiting for us with their engines running. Even on foot in a dense jungle, they'd been far faster than the lumbering army truck.

Igor was behind the wheel of the van and Luc had taken the passenger seat. I waved as we squeezed past them on the narrow track. Luc offered me a strained smile and Igor nodded. They would have to follow us, since I was the one in possession of the only map.

My dark skinned chauffeur drove with his shoulders up around his ears with tension. He cut frequent nervous sideways glances at me. He was probably expecting me to sprout fangs and turn on him. He gradually relaxed when I didn't turn into a blood hungry monster. "Do you know the area very well?" I asked him.

Jumping at the unexpected question, the vehicle swerved. One of the American soldiers in the back cursed, then thumped on the glass dividing us from the back. The driver grinned sheepishly and turned his attention back to the road. "I know area ok," he replied in stilted English.

"You can speak in your native language if you want, I'll be able to understand you."

Turning an astonished look at me, the driver looked back at the road when I pointed at the windscreen to remind him he was supposed to be driving, not gaping at me. "I have heard that vampires have many mysterious talents," he said in his natural tongue. "I did not know that understanding foreign languages was one of them."

"I'm the only one with that particular talent," I replied as I studied the map. So far, at least. For all I knew, there were dozens of vampires even weirder than me scattered around the world. *Don't count on it,* my subconscious sneered. *We both know you are one of a kind.* I had the distinct impression that its observation hadn't been meant as a compliment. "Do you know the quickest way to get to these villages?" I held the map up and he switched on the interior light to squint at the laminated paper.

"Yes. I have family nearby and know the roads well."

You mean you had *family nearby,* I noted darkly. His family were either dead or had been turned into vampires by now. "The night is wasting so you'd better step on it," I warned him.

Turning his concentration back to the road, the soldier accelerated as I flicked off the light. The track was narrow, badly maintained and full of potholes. The men in the back bounced around, complaining about the battering they were receiving. The only complaints I could hear from my friends in the van behind us was Geordie whining that one of them should have been with me for protection. I smiled at his indignation that I was alone with the soldiers. As far as I knew, I was the only creature on the planet that couldn't be destroyed. Protection wasn't something I needed.

My smile froze, then disappeared when I sensed a small group of vampires somewhere close by. The driver made a noise of alarm as he caught sight of a figure standing on the dirt track ahead. I had a bare second to take in my first sighting of a fledgling before it launched itself at us.

Chapter Nine

Our vision was suddenly obscured as the fledgling landed on the front of the truck. Screaming shrilly in terror, the driver madly spun the wheel to the left and right. Sprawled on the windscreen like a gigantic bug, the filthy, dark skinned vampire swayed from side to side, but didn't fall off.

Wearing only beads and a loincloth, he was about as primitive as you could get. Blood stained his fangs and caked the lower half of his face. More of the dark liquid had splattered across his chest from his recent feeding frenzy. Mindless with hunger, he grinned at the driver, then drew his fist back to punch it through the glass.

Regaining a modicum of intelligence, the driver stomped on the brake. The rabid vamp lost his grip and sailed through the air. Landing on his back on the road, he left a five foot long skid mark in the dirt.

I was out of the truck and was running towards him before he managed to scramble to his feet. Eerily fast, he dodged away before I could grab him. His fists swung wildly and landed a punch on my jaw. My ears rang for a second or two, but I caught his next punch. His bloody grin of triumph turned to puzzlement, then fear when he couldn't pull away from me. He threw another punch and I caught that as well, capturing both of his hands.

Locking eyes, he flinched at what he saw in mine. He began to scream when I unleashed the power of my twin holy marks. His hands melted away and he was left with bubbling stumps. Even minus his hands, the fledgling was still dangerous and needed to be finished off.

Clamping my hands on his head this time, it disintegrated from the power of the dark magic that resided within me. Like so many of his kind before him, he was reduced to a watery stain on the ground.

Gunfire erupted behind me. Bright flashes of light illuminated a pack of frenzied, near naked vampires closing in on the truck. Soldiers were screaming either in pain, or terror as they tried in vain to gun down the attacking creatures. Wiping melted vampire flesh onto my jeans, I ran to their rescue.

Witnessing a frantic soldier being pulled out of the back of the truck, I wasn't quite fast enough to save him. The vamp had her teeth buried deep in his neck, muffling his screams with a hand clamped over his mouth. I peeled her off him then twisted her head around until it was facing the wrong way, momentarily forgetting that it wouldn't kill her. She bared her dripping fangs at me and her head wobbled sickeningly on her shattered neck. My holy marks quickly finished her off.

Using my bare hands was proving to be too slow. I needed my swords.

"Natalie!" Luc shouted as if he'd read my mind. My friends had caught up to us and were spilling out of the van and trucks. I caught the unsheathed weapons when Luc tossed them to me and started slicing the fledgling vampires apart.

Even with my enhanced speed, they were almost too fast for me. Unluckily for the humans, their attackers were more concerned with food than with survival. They made no move to attack me and concentrated on reaching the remaining soldiers.

Six of the soldiers were dead, or badly injured. My driver's throat was a mangled ruin. His eyes stared up at the night sky in frozen anguish. Merely four of the soldiers were still alive and unharmed. They stood back to back in the truck, staring wildly into the trees and shooting anything that moved.

Most of the canvas had been torn away, leaving them exposed and vulnerable. A rabid vampire burst out of the shadows on the far side of the truck and landed amongst them. A quick thinking soldier managed to blow half of the vamp's head off, screaming all the while. The fledgling fell backwards, turning to slush just before he hit the ground.

Ishida's people swarmed into sight. They were black clad killing machines who were experts with their weapons of choice. I saw my instructor cut down two vamps and was amazed at his grace and speed. I'd only seen him in battle once before, on the night he had helped me to cleanse the Japanese nation of their damned. I would have to thank Ishida for allowing his best warrior to teach me my skills.

Igor had a more direct approach at taking down the fledglings. He picked up a discarded machine gun and cut down five of them when they took another run at the truck.

Luc had taken down a few by coolly stabbing them through their hearts. Geordie stayed out of the fray, shooting an occasional crossbow bolt at our newly made kin. Gregor's tweed suit was splattered with blood as he chopped the head off a feeding vamp with a meat cleaver.

Being a newly made vamp, the fledgling's blood was still bright red. It took months, if not years for our blood to thicken into the diseased ooze that was normal for our kind. Mine had been transformed far more quickly due to the fact that there was nothing normal about me at all.

I noticed that Nicholas made no move to attack, or to help defend the humans. His arms were crossed and he wore an expression of mild annoyance.

The battle lasted for only a few minutes, but it had felt much longer. When the last of our new kin died beneath my swords, I sensed someone watching me. Glancing up, I spied a distant, vague outline of a vampire through the trees.

"You must be the presence I sensed several nights ago," he called in what I assumed was an ancient form of African.

Ishida motioned for his soldiers to be still and Gregor did the same for our friends. They wouldn't understand what the man was saying, but they knew I'd be able to translate.

"You must be the Second," I replied in English, not sure whether he could understand me or not. The two soldiers who were still alive were both American. None of the African soldiers had survived the attack to relay what I was saying to my new nemesis.

"Who, or what are you?" he asked. His tone held curiosity, but very little anger that we'd just mowed down his freshly made servants.

"I am Mortis." It still felt ridiculous saying that out loud.

"I am unfamiliar with that word."

He'd been banished long before the legend that was me had been prophesized. He'd also never heard anyone speak Latin before. The language had been invented and had become all but obsolete long after he'd been interred. "It means 'death'."

There was a short pause while he pondered this. "Tell me, Mortis, why do your eyes glow the colour of fire?"

I hadn't realized that they were, but it made sense. Thanks to the imp blood in my system, I tended to be taken over with battle lust when I was embroiled in fights. Having orange eyes was the only side effect that I'd noticed so far. Hopefully, it would be the only side effect to crop up.

I opted to ignore his question. "You have to stop creating new vampires," I told him, striving to sound reasonable. "You'll endanger us all if you increase your numbers too quickly and send your servants out in a mindless feeding frenzy."

After a thoughtful silence, the Second's response was unnerving. "It is my right as the Second to create as many servants as I see fit. It is the right of my brothers to do the same. Who are *you* to tell us what we can and cannot do?" He paused to examine my friends and Ishida's people. "Our kind has grown weak with the passing of years," he observed. "It is long past time for us to become what nature intended." With that, he disappeared into the trees.

Grimacing at his pronouncement, I turned to find myself the centre of attention. "What did he say?" Ishida demanded. Kokoro stood at his shoulder, looking grave and drawn. With her ability to read minds, she knew exactly what the Second had said.

"He thinks modern vampires are weak and that its time for our kind to become what nature intended for us."

"Don't tell me," Geordie said wearily. "He wants to try to take over the world just like the First." I didn't argue with him. "Why do all ancient vampires have megalomaniacal tendencies?" he asked plaintively.

Ishida cut the teenager a narrow eyed glance, but decided not to take offence at the comment. "Do you believe he sent his servants to attack us as a test, Natalie?"

Gregor answered for me. "It is very likely." Dabbing at the blood on his tweed coat with a handkerchief, he gave up on trying to clean the stain with a rueful wince. "The Second seems to be quite intelligent for a being that should still have been fairly primitive."

"He can't read minds as well as Kokoro can, but I think he was picking up knowledge from the closest humans as he was trapped beneath the ground," I said. "He understood what I was saying well enough."

"Are we going to stand around talking about him, or are we going to hunt him down and kill him?" Igor grumbled. One of the things I liked about him was his no nonsense directness.

"You are quite correct, Igor," Ishida said with a bow in the Russian's direction. I was surprised that the child king had bothered to remember my friends' names. Maybe he didn't think they were beneath his notice after all. "There is still plenty of night left for us to track him and his brothers down."

One of the two remaining American soldiers clumsily jumped down from the back of the truck. Trembling with shock, the other man sank to his haunches. His eyes roamed the darkness, expecting another attack at any moment.

Striding over, the American veered around the moist patches of dead fledglings and the bodies of his fallen comrades. "You mean you're going after them?" Blue eyes wide with fright, he looked at one of his deceased friends lying on the road a few feet away. The man's throat was a jagged ruin and he was covered in blood. "I hope you don't expect us to go with you."

Luc put a soothing hand on the man's shoulder and he flinched at the contact. We might be allies, but how could the humans think of us as anything other than monsters after seeing our ravenous kin in action? "We do not expect you and your friend to join us in our hunt. But perhaps you had better tell your Colonel what has just transpired."

As the soldier fumbled for his radio, we gathered around to survey the damage. This was just the beginning of what would happen to the soldiers if we weren't there to assist them in this fight. The vamps had melted to slush, but the same wouldn't happen to the humans.

Gregor gestured towards the eight dead uniformed men "We should burn their bodies to prevent them from rising and becoming our enemies." It was difficult to tell if any of them had been fed vampire blood or not. It was best to err on the side of caution.

"Wait," the soldier said when he overheard the suggestion. "Colonel Sanderson wants to talk to you."

I assumed he meant me since he was looking right at me. My friends listened in as I took the radio he proffered. "Natalie? Are you there?" Sanderson asked.

"I'm here, Colonel."

"Was my soldier's report accurate?" I could hear the disbelief in his tone. Unless he'd witnessed the carnage for himself, it would have been difficult to believe.

"Every word was true." I hadn't actually listened in on the report the shaky soldier had given his boss, but I doubted he'd lied.

"He says you want to burn my men's bodies." The colonel's tone turned angry. "I forbid you to desecrate any of our soldiers."

"They aren't your men anymore, Sanderson," I told him as gently as I could. "They've been bitten and possibly fed vampire blood. There is a good chance that some of them could rise as the undead."

His silence was heavy and brooding as he contemplated the possible consequences of not burning their corpses. "Leave them where they are. I'll send some men to take care of them." He clearly either didn't believe me, or he was in denial of the possible fate that awaited his men.

Gregor shook his head in warning, but it wasn't necessary. I knew all too well what would happen if we didn't act now. "We can't do that, Sanderson. They'll rip your men to shreds as soon as they wake and then we'll have to put them down as well." It was best to take care of them now instead of waiting for three nights to see what would happen. I didn't trust him to do what was necessary.

Breathing was all we heard from the other end as the colonel tried to get himself under control. "Leave one of them intact," he said in clipped tones. "Send his body back with my two remaining men. I'll see that he is kept in a secure area. If he rises, I'll put him out of his misery myself."

I could understand that Sanderson didn't want to think his and the general's men would rise as creatures of the night, but he had to be practical. In order to keep our relationship cordial, I conceded to his request. Knowing how savage the fledglings were now, surely they would be able to contain one lone monster, if he did rise as one. "Fine. We'll send one of them back, but you'll be responsible for what happens if he turns."

"Understood," snapped the colonel. "Keep the radio and the weapons. Let me know if we can offer you any further assistance." His tone was cold and he signed off curtly.

We didn't interfere as the two surviving soldiers chose a body to take back to their base. Apart from the holes in his neck, the man looked like he was sleeping. Only his utter stillness and pallor indicated that he was beyond saving. Interestingly, the holes were showing no signs of healing. Maybe that only happened to live humans.

After their dog tags had been collected, the other soldiers were stacked in a pile on the side of the road then doused with fuel. The blue eyed soldier held the tags tightly, bowing his head in silent prayer. I wanted to ask him why he'd gathered the tags, but he didn't seem to be in the mood to answer questions. Maybe they'd be returned to the families of the deceased.

Igor struck a match and tossed it onto the bodies. As the flames rose I was strongly reminded of the cavern of doom. Once again, humans were being roasted in a fire. This time there weren't any imps to chow down on them. It was the only blessing in an otherwise horrible situation.

Chapter Ten

We'd lost our African guide during the attack, but we were close enough to the next village on the map for Igor to get us closer without becoming lost. I opted to ride in the back of the van and sat beside Geordie. Since we were both narrow of shoulder, we had plenty of room.

Sitting directly across from me, Nicholas wore an expression that I couldn't read as he voiced a suggestion. "We should swap positions so we have more space." He and Gregor were crammed in hip to hip and shoulder to shoulder.

Geordie immediately tensed and opened his mouth to retaliate, but Gregor spoke first. "That is an excellent idea, Nicholas. Geordie, if you'd be so kind as to swap with me?"

Geordie didn't want to sit next to Nicholas, but he also didn't want the overly muscled vamp to sit next to me. Mumbling ungraciously, he swapped places with the once dapper and now blood stained former Court lord. Gregor sent me a sardonic look as he shifted, deftly hiding his expression from our newest team member. None of us liked, or trusted Nicholas. So far, he was making no effort to get along with anyone. If anything, he seemed to be deliberately trying to annoy us.

"Why didn't you help us fight?" I asked him. Sitting beside Igor up front, Luc shifted his head slightly, indicating he was also interested in hearing the answer to my question.

Shrugging his massive shoulders, Nicholas managed to bump Geordie's head into Igor's seat. "It did not seem necessary, my...Natalie."

Rubbing his head, the teen glowered at Nicholas, suspecting he'd been knocked into the seat on purpose.

My eyes had stopped glowing shortly after the battle had ended, but I felt as if they should have been blazing with anger. "Do you have any intention of helping us at all, or are you going to continue to be a pain in my butt?"

The ex-courtier's lips twitched upwards at my poor choice of words. His flesh hunger burst into life and invaded the back of the van. He raked his gaze over me, pausing on my chest. "Believe me, Natalie, I would love nothing more than to be a pain in your-"

Luc cut him off before he could finish the sentence. "I would be very careful with the next words you choose if I were you, Nicholas." He turned and I shivered at the rage he was barely suppressing. "If you speak one more word of disrespect to Natalie, or the rest of us, I will end you myself."

Shaken, Nicholas slumped and his flesh hunger abated. Unfortunately, mine didn't. "I thought this was supposed to be a democracy," he mumbled.

"Perhaps you have forgotten the concept of common courtesy," Gregor said dryly. "It is a desirable trait in any democracy. Respect is not given automatically, but must be earned. You have not displayed a penchant for gaining respect from any of us thus far."

Showing that he was at least pretending to listen, Nicholas bent his head in a short nod. "I apologize to you all," he said stiffly and was affronted when I didn't acknowledge him. I was too busy trying to suppress my flesh hunger. If I'd still been able to sweat, it would have beaded my forehead at the strain.

Igor stopped several kilometres short of the first village on the map. As we exited the van, Ishida and his people joined us. The young emperor motioned to one of his men and he handed me a package. "I almost forgot to give you this," Ishida said. I opened it to find four black leather suits and one pair of matching boots. "Kokoro said you wouldn't need the red suit anymore and that black would suffice."

I'd loved the red suit I'd worn when killing the First, but it did tend to stand out. The suits he'd just presented me with were the typical ones worn by his female soldiers. "Thank you, Emperor Ishida." We bowed to each other and I climbed into the van to change. As always, I had to contort myself to do the laces up at the back. The suit was a perfect fit and contoured to my body as if it had been made to suit my exact measurements.

I drew stares when I exited the van for the second time. Luc lifted an eyebrow in approval and Nicholas unconsciously licked his lips. Geordie playfully batted his eyelashes at me as I settled the twin sheaths into place across my back. "Let's go," I said and took off into the jungle.

With the flesh hunger still raging through me, I wanted to sprint and try to put it behind me. That would mean leaving my friends and allies behind as well, so I matched my pace to Luc's. He sensed that I was troubled and what was troubling me. "Can you hold on until after our next battle?" he asked.

Nodding, I didn't trust myself to speak. Sensing vampires ahead, I narrowed my focus to the job at hand as we burst into a clearing. A quick glance around the tiny village told me we were too late. Most of the humans had already been mostly drained and lay on the ground. Their normally dark skin was pale with blood loss.

Fledgling vampires only wanted food at this stage of their creation. It would take several days before their flesh hunger would also rise. Since several women had been used to feed someone's flesh hunger, I knew that at least one of the disciples had to be somewhere nearby.

Ishida motioned his men and women into action and they began to attack the still feeding vampires. My head snapped around when I heard strangled human screams and I ran towards a hut at the far end of the village. Monstrous, muffled chuckling came from within.

Ducking to enter the hut, I was confronted with three dead children, a drained man and a weakly struggling woman. I paused in shock at my first glimpse of one of the disciples. His flesh had withered away from starvation and he was just a skeleton wrapped in grey skin. Clumps of long, matted hair clung to his skull.

Despite his prolonged entombment and lack of nourishment, he was still far stronger than a human. He'd regained enough strength to be able to feed both of his hungers at the same time from the poor human.

Sensing that he was no longer alone, the vampire stood with dreadful speed. Whirling around, he held the naked, bleeding human in front of him as a shield. His cheeks were hollow and his eyes were dark caves as he peered at me around her. "You must be the one my brother warned me of," he gurgled around his last mouthful of blood. "Have you come to kill me then? I, who am greater than you shall ever be? I am the Fourth and you," he looked me up and down with a sneer, "you are less than nothing."

I lunged forward, not bothering to wait for him to issue any more insults. My sword took him through the right eye and he dropped his meal in surprise. In most modern vampires, the injury to his brain would have been fatal.

Our kind really has weakened over time, I observed. He grasped the blade, slicing his hand to the bone and tried to yank the weapon out. I speared the other sword through his chest and he jerked back a step.

Dropping his uninjured eye to the blade, he looked back up at me in bewilderment. "But...you can't," he whined.

"I just did," I replied and pulled both weapons free.

He might be fifty thousand years old, but the Fourth was as susceptible to death as any of our kind, barring me of course.

His victim was still breathing, but she was close to death. Scared and full of pain, her eyes drifted up from the bodies of her family. They found mine and beseeched me wordlessly to end her suffering. Fulfilling her silent request, I ended her life with a quick thrust of my sword. She would join her family in whatever afterlife they were destined for, if such a thing truly existed.

Outside the hut, the sound of humans screaming and fledglings feeding triggered something inside me. My flesh hunger evaporated and battle lust descended. I left the hut in search of prey.

With their overwhelming need to feed their blood hunger, the fledglings didn't even seem to realize that their maker was dead. *Maybe the Fourth wasn't their maker. Any of the ten disciples could have created them.* One thing seemed certain, the ancient vamps had separated and no longer remained in one group. They would now be able to hit multiple villages in the same night.

If we didn't put a stop to it, there would be an infestation of our kind in a matter of weeks. *It's like fighting the First and his minions all over again.* My thought was full of despair that was mixed with weary resignation. I couldn't remember signing up for this job, but I was somehow stuck with it.

Wading into battle, my mind emptied and my hands took over. It dimly occurred to me that this attack might have been a diversion. The Second had proven he was intelligent by splitting his forces up. He might also be crafty enough to cause a delay to give himself enough time to build a bigger army.

When the last of the fledglings was dead, we were left with the unenviable task of checking for survivors. I found a small family huddled together in a hut on the outskirts of the village.

Twin toddlers clutched their mother's legs, screaming in fright and confusion. Shaken and bleeding from a wound in her neck, she flinched away from my glowing eyes. She hadn't been drained of her blood, but Kokoro's warning echoed in my mind. Every human that had been bitten could eventually turn into a monster. Her mouth was free of bloodstains, but I couldn't take the chance that she'd been infected. At least her kids were spared the sight of my blade sliding into her chest. Hopefully, they would be too young to remember this night of horror.

A mere handful of humans had survived the slaughter. Gregor checked each of them carefully for wounds before deeming them to be ok. "I found a couple of kids in that hut," I pointed at the tiny dwelling I'd just left. "I don't think they were bitten, but someone should check them over."

Gregor chose one of the surviving women and attempted to escort her to the hut. Sobbing in terror, she resisted him as well as she could, but her pitiful struggles were no match for him. He kept his expression neutral, but I could tell that he regretted causing her further fear. The survivor ceased her struggles when she spied the children. She disappeared for a few seconds as she ducked inside before emerging with the toddlers in her arms.

The remaining villagers huddled together, uncertain of what we expected from them. We weren't equipped to deal with them and I could think of only one solution to our problem. I'd left the radio in the van, so jogged over and retrieved it. "Sanderson, are you there?"

"I'm here, Natalie," he replied almost instantly. "Did you reach the village?"

"We did, but it was already under attack."

"Were there any survivors?" he asked with an undertone of bleakness.

"We found five uninfected adults and two children. What do you want us to do with them?"

"I'll send a team to pick them up. What's your next move?"

My next move was to wash the fledgling blood off my shiny new suit. My blood hunger began to rise at the smell that was coating me. Fledgling blood was too close to human blood for my liking. "We'll head for the next village as soon as we finish up here." We should have time, if we hurried.

Sanderson paused before speaking. "What's wrong with your voice?"

"Nothing," I lied through my fangs that had descended from my increasing hunger. "I'll give you an update soon." Throwing the radio onto the seat, I turned to find Nicholas standing right in front of me.

Staring down at me, he ran a finger down my arm, then licked the blood off the tip, proving that it hadn't yet turned diseased and deadly. His flesh hunger had risen again and now mine rose to meet his, driving the blood hunger away. My body couldn't decide which hunger it wanted to feed more. He moved to touch my cheek and I snarled at him in warning.

"Tell me what you would have of me, my Queen," the muscled vampire said softly. "Name it and it is yours."

"I want you to leave me alone," I said and it came out as a throaty growl. The orange glow of my eyes was reflected in his. He bent his head towards me and my sword was touching his neck before I could order my hand to move.

Before I could shove the weapon home, Nicholas was yanked backwards. He went sailing through the trees and landed with a crash somewhere in the distance. Luc stared after him, then turned his gaze on me. He was furious, but his ire wasn't directed at me. Sensing my need, he took my hand. "Gregor, get everyone moving towards the next village. Natalie and I will catch up to you shortly."

"Where are they going?" Geordie asked plaintively. We moved out of range before I could hear Gregor's explanation for our sudden disappearance.

I raced with Luc through the trees, easily dodging or jumping over obstacles in my path. Activity was what I needed to drive the hungers that were assailing me away.

We couldn't run forever and Luc eventually stopped at a wide stream. I halted beside him with my diseased blood all but thrumming in my veins. Dropping the swords and sheaths to the ground, I plunged into the water to wash off the gore. The picture of Nicholas licking the red liquid off his fingertip played over and over in my mind. I wanted fresh blood and I wanted it now.

"What is wrong, Natalie?" Luc asked. He was watching me carefully from the bank.

Slicking my drenched hair back from my face, I shook my head. "I don't know why, but my hungers seem to be getting stronger."

"Do you think it might have something to do with the imp blood that you were forced to drink?"

It seemed obvious as soon as he mentioned it. Thanks to the new infusion of alien blood, I was now imbued with the imp's battle lust. It had also apparently strengthened my blood and flesh hungers. My thoughts trailed off when Luc shrugged off his jacket, then pulled his t-shirt over his head and dropped it to the ground. Nicholas had a beautiful body, but it was just too bulky for me. Luc's physique was perfect. Lean and muscled, he had a light dusting of hair on his chest that did nothing to hide his torso.

I'd left the creek without even realizing it and fumbled for the laces of my suit. Luc stepped behind me and brushed my hands away. With a few tugs, the top of my suit came free. Strong hands slipped around me and cupped my breasts. Luc was hard against me and my dead heart tried to lurch in my chest in excitement.

Spinning me around, Luc's mouth descended on mine. He paused long enough to strip my suit and his pants off before reaching for me again. A haze came over me and we were on the ground, grappling and rolling, fighting for dominance. Then he plunged into me and I threw my head back and voiced a scream of intense pleasure.

He moved with the blinding speed and strength that I craved. I anchored myself with my hands on his shoulders and my legs around his waist. Sliding over the edge, my body bucked and Luc's bones snapped. He swore in pain, but kept going until he reached his own release and finally collapsed on me.

Tracing a finger over the unnatural bumps on his shoulders, I winced in sympathy when the broken bones popped back into place. Rolling onto his side, he rode out the healing process with his usual equanimity.

"How many was it that time?" I asked him guiltily.

"I believe it was only four," he said with a definite smile in his voice.

How can he smile after I caused him so much pain? "Which ones?"

"My femurs and both clavicles."

Putting my hands over my face, I willed away the lump that wanted to form in my throat. Almost every time we were horizontal together, I broke something in my one true love's body.

"I do not mind, Nat," he told me. Luc's rare usage of my nickname made me drop my hands and turn to view his face. He took my hand and planted a kiss on the holy mark on my palm. "It is a small price to pay to be with the woman I love."

Threading my fingers through his, I leaned over and kissed him gently, as if that could somehow make up for the agony I'd caused him. Deep in the back of my mind, I wondered how much stronger my hungers would grow and whether I'd lose control of them entirely.

Chapter Eleven

Dressing quickly, we retraced our steps to the village. A gigantic bonfire had been built in the centre of the clearing. Bodies of the fallen humans had been piled high. The smell of pork that wasn't really pork lay thick in the air and made me want to dry heave.

Sanderson's men hadn't arrived yet and our friends and allies had already departed for the next township on the map. It was easy enough to follow their tracks. We moved far more quickly along the rugged dirt road than the lumbering vehicles could.

Hearing the sounds of battle ahead, we put on a burst of speed. Luc was at my side, sword in hand when we entered the next village. This time, far more humans were still alive. Curiously, only a small number of fledglings were attacking them. For a moment, I thought I sensed one of the disciples nearby, but the sensation rapidly faded.

One of the fledglings launched herself at a fleeing human. A bolt struck her in the back, piercing her heart and halting her in mid-flight. She hit the ground and lay there, unmoving. Only when the bolt was removed would she turn to slush. Geordie, clearly terrified, reloaded his weapon. His head swivelled in search of another target.

Igor emerged from a hut, cleaning his long knife on a filthy piece of fabric that had probably once been a loincloth. His stoic expression belied the fact that he was in the middle of a warzone. I spied Gregor slicing the throat of a hissing vamp that was trying to sidle around him to reach a cowering trio of children.

Ishida held a stained sword in one hand and motioned imperiously at a quartet of fledglings, inviting them to engage him in battle. The child king, along with several of his guards, was shielding a family from attack.

Intent on feeding, the fledglings scuttled forward, ignoring the danger. Ishida proved he'd been well trained when he moved with fluid grace to intercept them. He ended their lives with controlled thrusts and slices. His expression remained blank and almost bored. I could tell by the way he moved that we'd shared the same instructor.

Every one of our friends and allies were defending the villagers. Except for Nicholas. I couldn't see him anywhere. Anger began to stir, but I willed it away. I couldn't allow my hungers to rise each time I fought our rabid new kin or I'd be perpetually hungry for either blood or sex.

Luc and I joined the fight, hacking apart any vamps that weren't on our side. With far fewer fledglings to face this time, the battle was fairly short. A lot of the humans had fled from the village. I hoped they would return when Sanderson's soldiers arrived. Some of the escapees may have been bitten. I'd have to warn the colonel to check them for fang marks before they faded to faint spots that could be mistaken for insect bites.

I finally saw Nicholas emerge from one of the huts. Blood smeared his clothing and mouth as well as the machete he'd appropriated from somewhere. He sent me a burning look and I gave him a bland one in response. Taken aback at my lack of reaction, he hesitated. Luc put a hand around my waist and our overly muscled ally's face darkened. He used his sleeve to wipe the blood from his lips.

"I am going to kill Nicholas one day," Luc said mildly.

"Not if I kill him first," Geordie muttered as he joined us. "I was worried about you, *chérie*. Are you well?"

"I'm ok. My hungers were getting out of control, so Luc helped me to take care of them."

Gregor ambled over in time to hear my explanation. "The imp blood is taking its toll, then?"

"What was that about imp blood?" Igor queried as he joined us. Nicholas wasn't far behind him.

"It seems to be making my hungers stronger," I explained when they had all gathered.

"Has Kokoro had any visions in relation to the imp blood in your system?" Gregor asked. The seer had appeared just after the battle ended and stood beside Ishida. Either reading our minds or feeling our gazes on her, she touched the child king on the shoulder and they started towards us.

"I have not had any specific visions in relation to the new blood that has invaded Natalie's system," the prophet said when they reached us. She'd plucked the thought out of our heads and didn't require a verbal query from me.

"Did you know about the four imp shadows I had following me around?" I asked her. They had been quickly killed off by my vampire shadows before the final four had then turned on each other. They'd managed to whittle their numbers down to three, I'd killed two of them and then I'd been back to having only one again.

Once I killed the First, my original shadow had lost its sentience and had thankfully reverted back to normal. That had been a great relief to me. Especially after I'd discovered that they'd been able to see, hear, taste and feel everything I did. That included my bedroom antics with Luc. I hadn't told him about that yet and wasn't sure I ever would.

"I knew their presence would not harm you and that they would be with you only temporarily," was Kokoro's serene reply. I wanted to be angry that she'd known what I'd be faced with, but couldn't dredge up the emotion.

Did I really want to know every weird thing that fate had in store for me? *Hell no!* If I did know, it might cause me to give up on all hope that I'd ever have a semblance of a normal life again. As it was, I barely knew what 'normal' was anymore.

Nicholas was staring at the seer as if she were a bug that he'd like to squash. "What other information have you been hiding from us, witch?" he demanded.

Ishida's eyes widened slightly at the insult and his guards reached for their weapons. Kokoro put a soothing hand on her leader's shoulder and gave Nicholas a chilly look. "I have been called far worse by better men than you, servant of the Council."

Rage flickered over the only recently appointed and already ex courtier's face. He clearly despised being reminded of his former lowly status as a guard. *Good one, Kokoro,* I thought at her and received a tiny nod in response. Nicholas wasn't going to live much longer if he kept antagonizing everyone. I sure as hell wasn't going to object to it when someone staked him to death.

"Dawn is drawing close," Gregor reminded us. "I suggest we finish up here while Natalie informs Colonel Sanderson of our progress."

Giving Gregor a mock salute that he returned with a small grin, I turned towards the van. From the corner of my eye, I saw Nicholas take a step after me. Luc stepped in front of him, blocking the path. "I'm sure you wish to assist with removing the bodies from the huts, Nicholas," my beloved said smoothly. It wasn't a request and the newest member of our team knew it. Maybe we didn't have much of a democracy after all.

Reaching through the open window of the van, I picked up the radio. "Are you there, Colonel?"

"I'm here." His voice was gravelly with fatigue. He was going to have to adjust his sleeping pattern if he wanted to keep up with us. Until this was over, he and his men would all become nocturnal.

"We're at the second village and there are a lot more survivors this time."

He was immediately suspicious. "What are the disciples playing at?"

I shrugged, then realized he couldn't see the gesture. Maybe I also needed to get some rest. "I think this was a diversion. If I were the disciples, I'd split my forces up and attack several villages at once. They'd be able to make a lot more servants fairly quickly if they do."

"Do you believe that ten villages will be attacked each night from now on?" Sanderson was as appalled at the idea as I'd been when I'd thought of it only a few moments ago.

"I took one of the disciples down, so that should lessen the attacks slightly." *Yeah, only nine villages instead of ten will be attacked.*

"Can't the new vampires attack without one of the disciples in charge?"

Remembering that I'd sensed one of their leaders briefly, I thought this was most likely the case. "I don't think so. Without someone organizing them, they'd just scatter and attack people indiscriminately."

"As opposed to what they're currently doing," the colonel muttered sarcastically.

"They've been pretty organized so far," I argued.

Sighing heavily, Sanderson battled a few moments of frustration before speaking again. "I'll start moving our forces closer to your location. We might not be of much use fighting the creatures, but we can at least help the survivors."

Turning to eye the terrified mob of humans that were huddled together, I had an idea. "Do you have anyone with you who could communicate with the survivors?"

"Probably. Why?"

"Because none of us speak their language and I'd like them to know that help is on the way."

"I'll see if I can rustle someone up." The radio went dead. While we waited for him to return, my friends and allies rounded up the deceased and placed them in a pile. Igor set them on fire, doing his best to ignore the bereaved keening of their surviving kin.

"Are you there, Natalie?" Sanderson said a few minutes later.

"I'm here."

"I've found someone who speaks the local language. Hand the radio to one of the villagers."

Striding over to the mob of survivors, I chose the oldest man, thinking he'd be the best person to take the call. Dressed in feathers and beads, he wasn't used to modern contraptions, but he got the hang of the radio quickly enough. An African soldier explained that we were the good guys and that help was on its way. Babbling gratefully in his native language, the village elder handed the radio back to me.

I found myself examining his neck and quickly turned away. Normally, I could go for a few days without feeding. Then I realized it had been a few days since I'd last had a meal. If I was hungry then the rest of the group must be suffering as well. I hadn't put much thought into what we were going to eat while hunting the disciples down.

Finished burning the dead, we gathered at our vehicles again. "Does anyone have any ideas about what we're going to do for food?" I asked hopefully.

Several of the Japanese guards glanced back towards the villagers then looked away guiltily.

"If Colonel Sanderson is serious about offering us aid, I suggest you request that his soldiers offer us their blood," Gregor said.

That thought had crossed my mind, but I'd dismissed it quickly. I just couldn't see any of the soldiers volunteering to feed the very creatures they'd been sent to eradicate. "Can't we just feed from animals?" I asked. "The jungle must be full of them." I'd noticed several types of monkeys swinging through the branches, watching us curiously, but keeping their distance.

Almost identical looks of disgust swept through the group. "Our kind does not drink from animals, Natalie," Ishida said in the snobbiest tone I'd heard since the brief time I'd spent at the Court.

Well excuse me for being uncouth, hovered on my tongue, but I swallowed the sarcastic remark down. "Fine. I'll ask the Colonel for food. What do we do if he refuses my request?"

"Tell him that we will refuse to hunt our own kind down and leave the job to him and his soldiers," was Nicholas' vote. Luc's expression told me that he wanted to argue, but he nodded reluctantly. Even Kokoro agreed and gave me a small nod.

"I suggest we begin to search for somewhere safe to spend the daylight hours," Gregor proposed. "Natalie can broach the subject with Colonel Sanderson when we rise." *As if I'll be able to sleep with this hanging over my head.* It wasn't a conversation I was looking forward to.

It was decided that Igor would take the lead again and Geordie cheekily scrambled into the passenger seat of the van. I didn't feel like arguing with him about it, so climbed into the back beside Luc. Even with my eyes closed, I felt Nicholas staring at me. I was going to have to decide what to do with him after this was all done. That was another conversation that I'd be happy to skip.

If he continued to annoy everyone, then I wasn't going to let him stay with us. The ex-courtier had three alternatives; if he behaved himself he'd get to stick around, he could strike out on his own and spend the rest of his nights lonely; or he could go back to the Comtesse and beg her for forgiveness for deserting the Court. The last choice would end in his immediate death, so I didn't think he'd be choosing that one. *Pity,* my subconscious roused itself to say then subsided again.

Chapter Twelve

Pulling over when dawn drew close, we parked nose to tail on the edge of the muddy, seldom used track. Igor debated about attempting to hide the van, but deemed the ground to be too soft. The vehicle would just sink into the soil and we'd have to struggle to pull it out again. Ishida's trucks were too large to even think about taking them off the track.

Being in a remote area deep in the jungle, few humans would be likely to stumble across us anyway. Most of the people in the area had already been either killed, or were in the process of being turned. Any that were about to become fledglings would be of no danger to us during the day.

Ishida and Kokoro disappeared into the back of one of the trucks, joining an already crowded group of their guards. Without curtains to keep the sun out, our van wasn't ideal to bed down in. Unless we wanted to cram into the back of the refrigerator trucks with our allies, we'd have to get creative and find somewhere else to spend the day.

After being hacked apart and buried, you'd think I'd be afraid of tunnelling beneath the ground. It didn't disturb me in the slightest and I found the idea to be almost comforting. Deep in the earth, I'd be safe from the sun and hidden from my enemies.

"Where are we expected to sleep?" Geordie asked crankily. "Beneath a pile of leaves?" He kicked at the ground, sending a clump of dirt and twigs flying.

"You're such a prima donna, Geordie," I accused him with a smile. "Haven't you ever had to dig yourself a nest for the day?"

"No," he said sulkily. "I've always had my cell to sleep in."

I grimaced at the memory of the tiny, bare place that had been his to call home. Both he and Igor had lived in the catacombs beneath the Court mansion in France for far too long. "It's not that bad," I reassured him. "I've done it a few times now."

Nicholas curled his upper lip at my plan. "Do you really expect us to dig out a burrow as if we are insects?"

Geordie sniggered. I heard him mutter 'Ladybug' almost too quietly to be overheard. I cut a glance at him and he smiled innocently, pretending he hadn't been laughing at me.

Dropping to my knees, I thrust my hands into the soil and responded without looking at the ex-courtier. "I really don't care what you do, Nicholas. Stay out in the open and burn to death if you want to, but I'm digging myself a lair."

Kneeling beside me, Luc efficiently helped me to widen the hole so he'd also be able to fit inside. His lips were pressed together tightly and I assumed that was to contain his amusement. His eyes were crinkled at the corners, a dead giveaway that he found this to be funny.

Grumbling quietly, Geordie moved a short distance away and was soon waist deep in the ground. He might not be happy about it, but he was efficient at digging. Igor and Gregor moved off to hollow out their own temporary shelters. Nicholas glowered at me for a few seconds then stalked off into the trees when I continued to ignore him. The sun would be up in minutes, so he would have to dig fast if he wanted to survive.

Burrowing out a lair roughly fifteen feet beneath the earth, Luc and I lay on our sides facing each other. "Are you all right, Geordie?" I called.

"I am fine, *chérie*," was his muffled reply. "Covered in dirt, but fine." He had resigned himself to spending the day in conditions even worse than he was ordinarily used to.

"Igor? Gregor? How are you going?" They both replied in the affirmative. I hesitated, but forced myself to check on the final member of our team. "Nicholas?"

His reply took even longer and came reluctantly. "I am well, my…Natalie."

Luc exaggeratedly rolled his eyes and I was suddenly muffling laughter. "What is so funny, *chér-*" Geordie's question was cut off as the sun made its appearance and he succumbed to its spell.

One by one, my friends surrendered to the sun's pull until only me, and several of Ishida's guards were still awake. Just like any normal human, even I had to sleep eventually. Snuggling against Luc's chilly body, I closed my eyes and was drawn into thoughts that I instantly knew came from the Second.

Resting in the nest I'd dug, surrounded by humans that would soon rise and become my servants, I resisted the urge to slide into unconsciousness. My brothers were too far away for me to feel. I felt a strange sense of loss after being able to reach out to them for so many thousands of years. It had seemed prudent to split our forces. We would now have a far greater chance of creating more of our kind at a far greater pace.

I was intrigued and disturbed by the female who hunted us. She was unlike any vampire I'd ever encountered before. After being banished for so many thousands of years, I had no way of knowing just what kind of creatures roamed the planet now.

My brothers and I were outnumbered and were being hunted by our own kind. If I had been the First instead of the Second, our existence would have been so very different. Bitterness flowed through me that fate had been so unfair.

Casting my mind back, I remembered the night my life had changed forever. The First had been a thug and a braggart who I'd hated since we'd been children in the same cave. I had long ago forgotten the names that we had been born with. I did, however, remember why I'd despised and wanted to murder the First. He had attracted the attention of the woman I'd hoped to pair myself with.

Desperate to stop him from stealing my female, I followed my adversary on his next hunt. My intention was to kill him and finally put an end to our rivalry. Thanks to a recent drought, game was scarce and our hunting trips took us further and further away from our cave. I knew that I would have plenty of opportunity to stalk my prey and that no one would witness the deed.

On the second night of my hunt, I waited until it was very late and snuck up on my enemy only to find that he was not alone. A gigantic, grey skinned creature with red, glowing eyes towered over him. It spoke a crude form of our tongue and offered the First everlasting life. I watched with angry jealousy as my opponent drank from the creature's wrist and became the first of our kind.

As if feeding the First had taken the last of its energy, the grey creature stumbled away, presumably to die. I lost sight of it as my enemy writhed in pain, howling his agony to the stars. With some strange new instinct, he burrowed beneath the soil, hiding from the sun just before it rose.

Disturbed by what I had witnessed, I decided it would be best not to approach my adversary alone. It was impossible to predict what changes might have happened to him after drinking the blood of the strange grey creature.

I returned to the cave and gathered some of the other warriors together. Once they saw what had become of my nemeses, I was confident that they would help me to destroy him. It took three nights to run for help and return to the campsite.

How my enemy had changed when I saw him next. He was faster, stronger and infinitely more evil than he'd been as a human. I was his first victim, thus becoming the Second. He drained me of my life, then dribbled foul tasting blood into my mouth from his torn wrist. From that moment, I was doomed to be his slave and to obey his every command. How it galled me to be Second to someone who was so intellectually inferior to me.

Three nights later, my nine brothers and I rose and became bound to the First. Being the only creatures of our kind, we were forced to rely on our strange new instincts. It took months to learn how to control our hungers.

During that time, my brothers and I created hundreds of our kind. As my intelligence returned, I began to worry that we would eradicate our food source. The First seemed not to care. After making us ten his slaves, he had opted not to create more. Even back then, at the beginning of our creation, he had been paranoid and had little trust for the creatures he had created.

Eventually, I persuaded our hated master that we must stop making more of our kind. Finally seeing the wisdom of my words, he agreed. At his direct order, my brothers and I could no longer create creatures like ourselves. We didn't need to restrict our servants from swelling our numbers. They were aware of how close to starvation we had all come. When desperate, we fed from animals, but humans would always be our preference.

As the millennia passed, the First became secretive and withdrawn. I began to notice something strange about his shadow. It almost seemed to be alive at times, but perhaps that had merely been my imagination. What wasn't my imagination was the change in the First's skin. It had lightened from dark brown to an ashy grey. I became afraid that he was turning into the very creature that had been the father of us all.

My nine brothers, who I had doomed by bringing them with me to hunt down the First, were almost as unhappy as I was at our fate. I pointed out the changes that were occurring in our master's body. They became convinced that he was turning into an even stranger monster than we already were. It was reason enough for us to plot his demise. Sensing our unrest, our master had banished us to our earthy graves in revenge and punishment before we could instigate his death.

Now that he had been vanquished, it was finally time for me to become all that I was meant to be. I wouldn't make the same mistakes that the First had. I would build my army of servants quickly, sacrificing as many as it took to slow the enemy down. As I'd planned, the ploy had already worked tonight.

Soon, I would engineer the disposal of my brothers, ensuring that I would have no competition for my ultimate plan. Within months, I would have control of the country that they were now calling Africa. With millions of our kind thirsting for blood, the humans would be forced to submit to me, or risk the complete annihilation of their species.

Fate had erred when I'd been made Second. It was time to correct that mistake. I would achieve my destiny and become what I was meant to be; ruler of a vast vampire nation with humans as our cattle.

Waking from the dream that was really just a disturbing trip through the Second's power hungry thoughts, I lay beside Luc without moving. The sun was still high in the sky and my beloved was dead to the world.

What is it with ancient vampires being obsessed with ruling the planet? I was arguably the strongest, most powerful of our kind that had ever existed and I had no designs on ruling mankind at all.

At least I now had confirmation of the Second's plan. I'd caught a glimpse of where he'd sent his remaining eight brothers and their servants. If I was correct, they had begun to spread out in a wide semi-circle.

With a total of only sixty vampires on my side, we were going to be hard pressed to stop them from spreading like a contagion.

Chapter Thirteen

Luc's elbow nudging me in the side woke me just after
dark. We dug our way back up through the loose soil of
the tunnel we'd made the previous night. I could hear the
others also digging their way free. One by one, we emerged
from the ground like zombies in a low budget horror
movie.

Geordie was the last to dig his way out. Igor grabbed his
flailing hand and hauled the teen to his feet. Shaking dirt
out of his hair, Geordie grimaced at his stained clothing. "I
would not like to make a habit out of spending the day
beneath the ground," he complained. "Give me a pallet on
the floor any time."

My suit had kept most of the dirt out and the soil just
didn't seem to stick to it. Luc's clothes were dark enough
to hide most of the new stains. Igor and Gregor both wore
earth tones that were even earthier now.

Nicholas sauntered into view, pulling his too tight t-shirt
over his head, making sure I had a good look at his abs

and chest as he did. His clothes were as clean as they'd been before he'd gone into the ground. "If you'd had even a scrap of intelligence, you would have stripped off before digging out your little burrow," he informed Geordie.

"Thank you kindly for pointing that out to us all, Nicholas," Gregor said dryly. His tweed suit was showing definite signs of wear and tear.

Realizing he'd made a gaffe, Nicholas tried to backtrack. "I did not mean to imply that you lack intelligence."

"No, you just meant that *I* lack intelligence," Geordie said with more than a hint of belligerence. His lower lip was beginning to pooch out, a sure sign that he was about to descend into a sulk.

"I believe a change in clothing is in order," Gregor said to forestall a fight. Our belongings were stashed in the back of the van. I didn't bother to change, my suit would last through another night. The dunking it had sustained in the creek last night had washed all of the bloodstains out.

Ishida and Kokoro joined me while the others were changing. My friends and Nicholas reappeared as I retrieved the radio from the front seat of the van. "Are you there, Colonel?" I asked.

Sanderson was waiting for me on the other end. "What news do you have?" he replied immediately, forgoing a greeting.

I really wasn't looking forward to this conversation, but with my friends and allies surrounding me, I had little choice. "We're going to have to split into nine teams if we want to take down the remaining disciples and their servants."

He was aware of how many of us there were and did the sums. "That will leave you with fairly poor odds," he said doubtfully. "Do you think it's time my men assisted you? We might not be as fast as your kind, but I'd like to see a vampire try to outrun a flamethrower."

Gregor nodded at me to accept the offer, not that I needed the urging. I was well aware of the needs of our group. "We do need your help and we'd appreciate the extra weaponry, but there's something else we require from your soldiers." To my credit, I didn't sound nearly as uncomfortable as I felt at broaching the subject of food.

Sanderson's breath was indrawn when he came to the only possible conclusion to my inference. His voice dropped to a bare whisper so his men wouldn't overhear him. "You want me to order my soldiers to let you drink their blood?" I could almost picture the veins pulsing in the American's temple in fury at the very idea of it.

"We won't be able to keep up the hunt if we're weak from starvation," I pointed out reasonably.

Keeping his voice low, the colonel couldn't hide his anger. "What if my soldiers refuse to be sheep for you and your kind?"

I had an answer prepared because, if I were him, I wouldn't have been very happy at forcing my people to offer their blood either. "Then you'd better get used to the idea of having a vampire overlord."

Ishida almost cracked a smile at my quip. Geordie clapped a hand over his mouth to smother a giggle. I wasn't the least bit amused after spending some time inside the Second's thoughts. Maybe it was time to reveal what I knew about him. "Colonel, the creature in charge of these attacks isn't just a mindless, blood crazed vampire. He's smart, he's ambitious and he's adaptable."

Swallowing an angry tirade before it could escape from him, Sanderson's voice rose slightly in volume since we had switched topics. "Give me the bottom line, Natalie. What exactly are we facing here?"

Since he was being blunt, I decided I might as well be, too. "He plans to build an army of rabid fledglings that will number in the millions. He will then force you humans to submit to his authority. If you don't, he'll wipe out everyone on the planet." All amusement faded from my friends at the news.

"How can you possibly know his plans in such detail?" Sanderson asked suspiciously.

"Because I'm Mortis," I reminded him. "I'm different from the rest of my kind. I have dreams that come true nine times out of ten and that is what I saw." Kokoro's white eyes gazed directly at me. I wasn't quite alone in the things that I saw. She and the Romanian prophet were both given flashes of our fate. I wondered uneasily if this made me some sort of prophet as well.

"I can't make this decision alone," Sanderson said curtly. "I'll get back to you after I've spoken to General Merwe." With that, he broke off our contact abruptly.

"I think that went well," Geordie said tentatively and offered me a weak grin.

Nicholas naturally disagreed. "They will never agree to allow us to feed from their men." Standing with his arms crossed, he looked down his nose at the teenager.

"They might not like it, but they'll agree," Gregor countered. "They are intelligent men and they will quickly realize that they have no choice."

Nicholas was about to make another snide comment when one of the Japanese guards went on the alert. She'd heard something in the jungle and motioned for us to be quiet. It was faint, but I heard a group of people moving with complete lack of stealth in our direction. *Great, what now?* I chose not to voice my internal whine out loud.

Ishida's guards melted out of sight and the rest of us did the same. Luc and I crouched down behind the van, swords in hand and ready for battle. I wanted to send out my senses to see if it was vampires approaching, but it might be another diversion from the Second and I didn't want to tip him off that I knew he was there.

"I think they're just ahead," a male said quietly. "I'm sure I heard people arguing a few seconds ago."

He was speaking in French and Luc stood as he recognized the voice. It was familiar to me, but it wasn't until the group stepped out onto the track that I recognized them.

"Lord Lucentio," Aventius said and offered my beloved a short bow. "I am glad we finally found you." The aged vampire and his small band of followers had discarded the black robes they'd been wearing the last time I'd seen them. They had swapped them for normal clothing that would help them to blend in with humans. Then again, with his sunken cheeks, black bags beneath his eyes and fangs that were too prominent, Aventius would have trouble fitting in anywhere except with other vampires.

"We've come as you ordered," snapped a young man that I had no trouble recognizing. "Now what do you expect us to do?" He directed the query at me, looking me up and down insultingly. "Build a tree house so you can rule over us in the middle of nowhere?"

"Joshua," Aventius reprimanded his servant gently. "We swore our service to Mortis. Show her some respect."

Turning still mostly green eyes on me, Joshua ignored the warning and sneered at my outfit. "Who do you think you are? Batgirl?"

Outraged, Geordie strode forward and did something totally unexpected. His hand connected with the back of the young vamp's head with a slap that echoed around the area. Igor nodded his approval at his apprentice's actions. Joshua stumbled forward a step and fumbled for the knife he'd shoved through his belt.

I could see this escalating into a free-for-all and made a decision I'd been hoping I'd never be forced into. "If you pull that knife, I will turn you into a slimy puddle of ooze," I said to Joshua bluntly. His hand was on the hilt, but he didn't pull it. Aventius put a shaky hand on the young vamp's shoulder.

"None of you seem to realize that we are in a crisis situation here." I met the eyes of each newcomer then turned to rake my gaze across the rest of the group. Ishida looked mildly affronted that I'd included him in my tirade, but he allowed me to continue without interrupting. "I'd hoped we could all work together to take down the First's disciples and their growing horde of servants. I see that's not going to be possible without someone in charge."

They could see where I was going with this and uneasy glances were exchanged. Some of the looks came from within my tightknit group of friends. I felt a stab of hurt at Luc's fleeting doubt that he quickly masked. *Fabulous, even Luc doesn't think that I can pull this off.* After all we'd been through together, I'd hoped that he would have had at least a modicum of faith in me. *Why would he when he knows you better than anyone,* my subconscious roused itself to mutter. It was one more treachery I didn't need.

"What are you saying, Natalie?" Ishida asked. His young face was as bland as usual, but I detected a hidden frown.

"I'm pulling rank," was my blunt reply.

"You have no authority over me," Ishida shot back. "I am the Emperor of the Japanese empire. I have been ruler for over ten thousand years." Arrogance poured off the kid in palpable waves and he drew himself up so we were a match in height.

"Yeah? Well I'm Mortis and no one on this planet can top that." He withered slightly beneath my glare. "Until we have killed every last disciple and their servants, I am now in charge." Not even Nicholas was quite brave enough to challenge me openly. He quailed beneath my glare just like everyone else.

Kokoro placed a hand on Ishida's shoulder in a show of support. Then she surprised us all and pulled the rug out from beneath him completely. "If we wish to survive as a species, we must follow Mortis' command."

"Who are you?" Joshua demanded then cringed when I narrowed my eyes at him.

"I am an oracle," Kokoro replied calmly. "I have foreseen the fate of our kind and what will transpire if we do not follow Natalie."

Aventius darted a glance at me before risking a question. "Perhaps you had better explain what will transpire."

Casting her blind stare at the former Court Councillor, Kokoro's answer was simple. "Death and then darkness." She'd been keeping that little gem a secret, but we were in dire enough trouble that she felt she had to be honest.

"What would you have us do, Mortis?" Ishida's tone was formal and I mourned the loss of our friendship. *Mourn later,* my subconscious ordered. *Survival is more important than friendship.* If I'd had the time, I would have argued the point. What use was it to survive if you didn't have friends to share your life with?

At a quick count, we now had an army of just over one hundred vampires. Aventius had scooped up the small band of vamp's we'd freed from their possessed master in Russia. They were a snaggle-toothed bunch of less than attractive specimens of our kind. He'd also found others that I didn't recognize. All were frightened and uncomfortable with the idea of mingling with their hated Japanese adversaries.

"I'm going to split us evenly into nine groups. Don't bother arguing with me, or trying to swap around," I warned them. "Just do as I say and I won't unleash my holy marks on anyone."

I chose Ishida as a team leader first simply because his people would revolt if I caused him any further insult. Kokoro automatically went with the teen, keeping her dainty hand on his shoulder as a guide. The emperor crossed his arms and stood very straight, pointedly not looking at me. His way of sulking was different from Geordie's, but it was just as annoying.

Luc, Gregor and Igor moved to the spots I indicated. My one true love didn't argue, but his jaw clenched when he realized we would be separated. *Maybe if he'd believed in me for even one second, I'd have kept us together,* I thought bitterly. If I wanted to be completely honest, he was a far better leader than I was. We'd have a greater chance of success if we split up.

I chose Aventius to be leader for the next group and he bowed his head in gratitude. As a Councillor of the Court, he was well used to being in charge. He'd be able to follow my orders and keep his band together.

My weapons instructor became the next leader. He inclined his head in acceptance and we exchanged polite bows. I chose two more of the Japanese guards I knew to be intelligent and clear headed. There were mutters from the Europeans at my show of favouritism, but no one objected to my decision.

Geordie waited in an agony of suspense until I directed him to join Igor. His smile of relief lifted my spirits a little. Nicholas wore an expression of icy disdain that thawed slightly when I beckoned him to my side. Having him close wasn't something I was looking forward to. I just didn't trust him to be on any of the other teams. Luc's jaw clenched again, but he didn't embarrass me by arguing with my decision.

In just a few minutes, I'd split the teams up evenly. "I'm sure Colonel Sanderson will have radios for us so we can all keep in touch," I told the unhappy groups. "We'll need to coordinate our attacks if we want to take down all of the fledglings quickly."

With excellent timing, Sanderson spoke through the radio I'd clipped to my belt. "Natalie, are you listening?"

"I'm here." I kept my eyes on the uneasily shifting groups, watching to see if anyone would be stupid enough to disobey me and try to swap teams. I sincerely hoped they wouldn't because I hadn't been bluffing. I really would end the unlife of anyone who wasn't on board with my plan. It would be regretful and I'd be sure to feel guilty for a while, but they had to learn to work together. The human population might not know it yet, but they were counting on us to end this disaster.

Sanderson updated me with the verdict on my demands. "General Merwe and I agree that our soldiers will feed your people on the condition that you will allow a thousand of our men to join your hunt."

One thousand soldiers would help, but more would be even better. I had a feeling that their survival rate would be low. "Make it two thousand and you've got a deal."

He nearly spluttered in surprise, but quickly recovered. "Agreed. What is your current location?"

I estimated how many kilometres we'd travelled from the last village that had been attacked and advised him. They just had to follow the tracks we'd left and they'd find us easily enough. I didn't need to request radios, his men would be equipped with them when they joined our ranks.

"Stay where you are and we'll join you shortly," Sanderson said curtly then his voice cut out. An awkward silence descended. No one seemed to want to brave my wrath.

"May we ask questions, Mortis?" Ishida said a few minutes later. "Is that at least permitted?" His tone was cool, verging on icy. *So much for being afraid of my wrath.*

Feeling the weight of fate or destiny pressing down on me, pushing me away from the people I cared about, I teetered on the edge of running away again. *Why did this have to happen to me? I'm just a clothing store manager!* How could I be responsible for the fate of both vampires and humans? Not for the first time, I wondered if someone or something had made a terrible mistake when they had picked me to be Mortis.

Unexpectedly, Geordie came to my rescue. "You might be a ten thousand year old Emperor, but you're acting like a spoiled little brat! Do you think Natalie wants to be in charge?" The teen cast a hand at me and Ishida unwillingly studied me. "She *hates* the idea of being a ruler. She's doing this to try to save us all, so you can cram your snotty attitude right up your imperial butt."

Our small army was poised on the edge of imploding until Ishida cracked a tiny smile. "Tell me, Geordie, have you ever killed a zombie?"

Thrown by the change of topic, Geordie was momentarily baffled. "Everyone knows that zombies aren't real." Despite his claim, he seemed uncertain.

"I am speaking of electronic zombies," the child king clarified.

Recognition dawned and Geordie shook his head. "I have never played any kind of computer games."

"When this is all over, you may visit our island if you wish. I will teach you how to master the art of computer gaming," the emperor invited him.

Geordie stared at the other teenager with his mouth open in surprise. Igor nudged him discreetly and his apprentice graciously accepted the offer. "I would be very pleased to visit your island." I wasn't so sure the inhabitants of the island in question would be particularly happy to have him there, but it wasn't my call to make.

Chapter Fourteen

Engines rumbled in the distance and slowly drew closer. Sometime during the day while we'd been sleeping, the soldiers had relocated the survivors to safety. Not that anywhere on the continent would be safe unless we worked fast to curb the outbreak of new vampires.

Sitting behind the wheel of a jeep, Colonel Sanderson led the convoy. General Merwe was in the passenger seat beside him. Their expressions were grim as they pulled over. I moved to meet them as they climbed out. A long line of army vehicles parked behind them in orderly lines. Most of the American and African soldiers remained in their trucks. I caught frightened snippets of conversation. They were all centred around one theme; they were petrified at the thought of being bitten by vampires.

Sanderson nodded at me in greeting and flicked a curious glance at the nine teams standing behind me. The general didn't bother with even a modicum of politeness and glared at me contemptuously. In any other circumstances, he'd have tried to kill me. When this was all over, he probably would.

To him, I was an abomination that had no right to even exist. After everything I'd been through and after all of the vamps and imps that I'd killed, I wasn't sure that I disagreed with him.

"Do you and your people want to feed from our soldiers now?" Sanderson asked. From the sweat beading his forehead, he was also terrified at the idea, but he hid his fear better than his men.

No time like the present. The sooner they saw we weren't going to tear out their jugular veins, the quicker we could get on with our job. "Now would be best." I didn't want to weaken my standing with either soldier by consulting with the team leaders that I'd chosen. Everyone had to think of me as their ultimate leader, or we'd lose cohesion and fall apart.

"You will feed from me," Merwe stated, pointing at me and meeting my eyes squarely. Usually, men automatically fell to my evil charms when they stared into my eyes. I made a conscious effort not to ensnare him. If his men saw their leader becoming a mindless minion, they might react badly.

When Silvius had bitten me the first time, he hadn't put me under and the experience had been very painful. I hoped Merwe wouldn't suffer too much. If he started screaming and thrashing around in agony, his men would most likely panic and start shooting. While most of the soldiers were still in the trucks, enough heads poked out through windows for word to spread quickly when they witnessed the feeding.

"I'll try not to hurt you," I said to the general as I stepped closer. He very nearly backed away, but clenched his hands and controlled his fear. I was glad he was short so it wouldn't be quite so awkward to feed from him.

Merwe's eyes snapped shut when I put my hands on his shoulders and his breathing sped up. Gently tilting his head to the side, my fangs descended and cut through his skin. Inhaling sharply, Merwe made no further noise of protest as I drank enough of his blood to half fill the hole in my stomach.

His eyes fluttered open again when I stood back and released him. "Is that it?" He seemed incredulous at the lack of ceremony. Maybe he'd been expecting me to turn into a raging maniac. Seeing the aftermath of the fledglings' attacks, I couldn't blame him.

"That's it," I confirmed.

Exchanging glances, the leaders of the two armies reached a final decision and waved for their men to leave their vehicles. While they were organizing themselves, I returned to my teams. "We're all going to be able to feed, but be careful not to hurt them. Don't put any of them under, or they might think we're trying to control them."

Nicholas naturally had an objection. "I do not feed from men." His upper lip was lifted in a sneer. Joshua agreed with a silent nod and a sneer of his own. They might not look alike but, personality wise, they could have been twins.

"You have two choices here," I said to them both. "Feed from the soldiers, or go hungry."

"Why can't we feed from the villagers?" Nicholas shot back.

I flashed back to when he'd emerged from a hut with blood on his mouth. He hadn't been helping us kill the fledglings at all, I belatedly realized. He'd been feeding from the humans. "The villagers have already been traumatized enough by the attack from the fledglings and disciples. The last thing they need is us chomping on them."

Studying my face, Nicholas seemed confused. "They are only humans, my…Natalie. Why do you care about their wellbeing so much?"

Geordie stirred at the overly muscled vamp's continued annoying habit of addressing me so familiarly. He subsided when Igor flicked him a look. It was going to be extremely annoying having Nicholas on my team, but it would be unfair to inflict him on anyone else. I'd been the one to allow him to join us, so it was only fitting that I should be the one to have to put up with him.

I had to remind myself that Nicholas had been undead for over two thousand years. He probably couldn't even remember what it was like to be human. "In case you've forgotten, we were all human once. You might not remember what that is like, but I still do."

I still felt empathy for our food and had no wish for any of them to suffer. Most of the European vamps didn't seem to agree with me and stared at me askance. Nods told me that Ishida's people understood where I was coming from. They treated their food source with great respect.

"Humans are inferior to us," Joshua stated. "We have the right to treat them as we wish." Considering he'd only recently been made into a vampire, I thought his attitude was laughable.

Gregor took offense to the idiotic claim. "You have been a vampire for…two months?" he guessed. Judging by the way Joshua shifted uncomfortably, he was right on the mark. "You must feel superior indeed to have formed such an opinion about your former kin in such a short space of time. I wonder, if you were still human, how you would feel if one of us said something so preposterous to you?"

Tired of the arguing, I decided it was time to pull rank again. "I'll be watching you as you feed," I said to the group at large. "If any of you cause the humans pain or frighten them unnecessarily, I'll introduce you to the holy marks on my hands."

Holding my hands up, I let them all get a look at the crosses on my palms. Everyone knew what would happen if I used them. They'd either witnessed the power themselves or had heard the stories. To ignore my direction would end with them becoming a messy stain on the ground.

Sanderson and Merwe had brought a thousand soldiers each and quickly chose enough to feed my people. As I'd threatened, I watched the process closely as my teams took turns to feed.

Nicholas and Joshua stood firm and refused to bite any of the soldiers. Their resolve wouldn't last when hunger started clawing at their insides. Being so young, Joshua would falter far more quickly than Nicholas. He was probably already feeling half starved.

The process went smoothly and I didn't need to melt anyone with my holy marks. It had also taken time and the night was slowly trickling away. As the last team lined up to feed, the two leaders of the armies and I sat at a tiny table to discuss strategy.

Luc gave me a wink to indicate he'd keep his eye on the team for me. I smiled gratefully, already wishing I could relinquish the responsibility of being a leader altogether.

I spread out the map Merwe had loaned me and the humans squinted at the villages that had been attacked. "The Second plans to send his people out in a semicircle, attacking as many humans as they can," I explained.

"They can only attack at night, correct?" Sanderson said.

"Yes."

"What do they do during the day? Where do they hide?" General Merwe asked.

"My best guess is that they're digging out nests beneath the ground to keep the unrisen safe," I replied. That was the distinct impression I'd gathered from my unpleasant and unplanned trip through the Second's thoughts.

Sanderson pondered this then looked alarmed. "There could be dozens of nests with stockpiled newly made vampires around the area waiting to rise."

I hadn't even thought of that and nodded reluctantly. When they rose, they would have no one to direct them. They could scatter in any direction, much like cockroaches did when the lights were turned on. "You should probably call some more soldiers in to search for any freshly dug earth. Can you get your hands on equipment that lets you search for bodies beneath the ground?" I'd seen the gadgets on TV and knew they existed.

General Merwe looked doubtful, but Sanderson was already nodding. "I'll ask if the equipment can be shipped here from the US asap. I'll also ask for more reinforcements. Now that we know what we'll be facing, the African officials might be more amenable to allowing my soldiers into the country." The general hesitated before nodding, which didn't exactly fill me with confidence that his leaders would comply.

The Second had concocted a simple, yet brilliant plan. We had no way of knowing how many pockets of fledglings were waiting to rise, or where they'd been stashed. We would be fighting a never ending battle, running around in the jungle putting down each group that rose even as dozens more were being made each night.

Any soldiers that were bitten during the skirmishes could also become infected and become our enemy. I knew how reluctant Sanderson was to destroy the men who fell in the line of duty. He was going to have to suck it up and do the sensible thing.

"We'll split our forces into nine teams and join them with yours," the colonel was saying. "We'll send the teams out to the nearest villages and begin searching for the fledglings and for any survivors."

"We'll have to move quickly before they can spread too far across my country," Merwe said. "The sooner we get started, the more of my people can be saved."

Neither Sanderson nor I were about to argue with the general on that topic. We all had the same goal in mind and we all wanted to get this over with. "Let's move," I suggested and stood.

Shouting at his men to gather together, Sanderson split them into nine groups and the general did the same. After some shuffling, our groups merged together into nine less than comfortable units. Soldiers and vampires eyed each other with understandable mistrust. I hoped no 'accidents' would occur when we headed off towards our prospective targets. It wouldn't take much to make our people turn against each other.

I gathered my team leaders together and we huddled around the map to decide which villages we would each target. I nodded to the colonel when we were ready. Sanderson had a final message for his troops before we parted. "I know you don't like it, but from now on, these nine vampires are in charge of each team."

Heads swivelled to take in Luc, Gregor, Igor, Ishida, Aventius, my weapons teacher, the two Japanese vamps I'd picked and lastly, me. "You take your orders from them and are to follow their instructions. We have a job to do and that job is to put down the threat of vampire invasion and to save as many human lives as possible." His eyes swept across the small army of Americans, Africans, Europeans, Japanese and one Australian. "If we work together, we just might be able to pull this off. Good luck and Godspeed."

Ishida's eyes passed over me as if he didn't even see me as headed for one of the army trucks. They were far quicker than the refrigerator trucks his tame human had stolen. Kokoro smiled at me, but it was distracted and half-hearted. A polite American soldier placed her hand on his arm to help her to the truck. She accepted his assistance with a nod of thanks. She might look small and dainty beside the well-built human, but she could easily snap his neck with one hand if she wanted to.

My friends and allies had no time for proper farewells. Gregor waved before herding his team after the group of soldiers that had been allocated to him. Aventius nodded respectfully and dragged Joshua off before he could say anything to annoy me. My teacher and the other two Japanese team leaders offered me bows, which I politely returned.

Igor wasn't about to give up his beloved van or his independence. With a gruff nod, he ambled off to retrieve the vehicle. Geordie hesitated then launched himself at me. He hugged me tightly then kissed my cheek. "Take care of yourself, *chérie*. Promise me that we will win this battle and that we will be reunited again."

"I promise," I said solemnly and meant it. Relieved, the teen ran after Igor and clambered into the passenger seat.

When I turned, Luc stood in front of me. His black eyes seemed darker than usual as he stared down at me silently. I felt someone at my back and knew Nicholas had closed the distance between us. I didn't need to see his expression to know that it would be designed to annoy Luc.

My one true love didn't even seem to notice the over muscled vamp behind me. Tilting my head back with a finger beneath my chin, he lowered his mouth to mine and kissed me as thoroughly as possible. We didn't need to voice how we felt about each other, the kiss said it all.

With a final burning look over his shoulder, Luc joined his team and climbed into one of the army trucks. Now I was left with Nicholas and nine other vampires who I barely knew or who were complete strangers to me. Colonel Sanderson and two hundred or so of his men would be travelling with us.

Somehow, I wasn't surprised that the colonel had decided to stick with me. As the leader of the vampire army, he'd want to keep his eye on me to make sure we were sticking to the plan. I doubted he'd ever really be able to trust me or my kind. Why should he after two of the most ancient creatures on the planet had both launched a plan to try to take over the world?

Chapter Fifteen

Sanderson briskly led the way to his jeep and I was right behind him. Nicholas followed me almost too closely for comfort. From the disdainful looks he was giving everyone else on our team, he seemed to think he was my second in charge. I foresaw problems ahead, but would have to deal with them as they arose.

I climbed into the back of the jeep and buckled myself in automatically. Nicholas didn't bother with the seatbelt when he took the seat next to me. Spreading his knees wide in typical man fashion, he made sure his thigh brushed up against mine. When he received no reaction from me at all, he subsided into a sulk, but stubbornly kept his leg pressed against mine.

Our chauffeur, an American soldier, took off, following his colonel's directions. The young soldier kept throwing wide eyed glances at me in the rear view mirror. He would eventually either get used to the sight of my unnatural beauty, or he'd drive us into a tree. For his and the colonel's sake, I hoped he would snap out of it quickly.

The track we were on was infrequently travelled and was very nearly overgrown by the jungle in places. Our vehicles were almost overwhelmed by trees at one point and one of the larger trucks had to forge the way.

A couple of hours later, our small convoy drew close to the village we'd picked. Stopping only a couple of kilometres away, I heard no sounds of battle ahead. Jumping out of the jeep, I debated about the safety of sending out my senses then decided it would be worth the risk.

Gathering my consciousness, I sent it out slowly towards the village. Sensing nothing, I widened the search and caught the tail end of a group of my kind in the distance. *Damn it, we're too late!* "We might as well drive in closer," I told the colonel. "The village is empty of vampires."

"How could you possibly know that?" Sanderson asked me, perplexed by my knowledge.

"My…Natalie is capable of wonders you could not even imagine," Nicholas told the soldier haughtily. He stood at my right shoulder like an honoured henchman.

I resisted the urge to roll my eyes. "I can sense them," I explained to Sanderson.

"That would have come in handy when we were trying to locate the imps in Russia," the colonel said as he motioned his people back into their vehicles.

"The First blocked my ability to sense them when I was within a few hundred kilometres of him," I explained as I climbed back into the jeep again. "With him gone, I have no trouble sensing my own kind now." Unfortunately, my talent wasn't unique anymore and it might not be as great a help as it could have been.

He turned around to study my face. "You're not telling me everything."

Caught out, I had little choice, but to tell him the truth. "The Second can also sense our kind. He can feel it when I'm searching for him."

Musing, the colonel thought that over. "So, it will be difficult for us to sneak up on him if you try to search for him."

"He could easily set a trap for us if he knows we're on his trail."

Disappointed that my secret weapon was all but useless, Sanderson rode in silence. Nicholas nudged me with his knee and I moved away, crossing my legs so he would have to slide over if he wanted to maintain contact with me. I found his attention far more annoying than flattering.

As a plain, ordinary human, I'd have been invisible to a hot guy like Nicholas. Now that I had unnatural vampire beauty, he was drawn to me. I almost wished I could turn back to being ordinary again just so he would leave me alone.

Just ahead of us, the lead truck broke through into a clearing and pulled to a stop. I smelled blood thick in the air, confirming that we were too late. Sanderson and his men were grim as they surveyed the ruins of what had once been a thriving village.

This one was larger than the others. I estimated that at least a hundred people had once lived there. Now it was littered with the tiny bodies of children, all missing their hearts. The adults had been drained then stashed in their underground lairs.

As Sanderson's men searched the village for small bodies to be disposed of, I gathered my own troops together. My team consisted of five European vamps, including Nicholas, and four Japanese. "Spread out and see if you can locate any freshly dug tunnels where they might have hidden the fledglings." Nicholas obviously thought he was above following my direction and stayed by my side. "That includes you, Nicholas," I said pointedly. With a stiff nod, he turned and disappeared into the jungle.

"What's his problem?" Sanderson asked me quietly as he reached my side.

"His ego is even bigger than his muscles," I responded.

"Do you two have some kind of…thing going on?" He looked awkward as he asked the question.

I almost laughed, but kept it in just in case Nicholas hadn't moved out of earshot yet. "No. The only person I have that kind of relationship with is Luc."

"I'd watch out for Nicholas," Sanderson whispered. "He seems like trouble to me."

I indicated my agreement with a nod, glad he'd been discreet when warning me. Even people who had only just met the ex-courtier could see he wasn't a team player. Maybe Nicholas would calm down after a few more weeks of spent away from the Court. The prospect of dealing with his prickly attitude for any length of time was depressing.

One of the Japanese vamps returned at a run. Stopping in front of me, she gave me a quick bow. I returned it automatically as she gave her report. "I have discovered a tunnel, Mortis." She spoke in her native language, which I translated for the colonel.

"Show us," I told her and was on her heels when she took off. Sanderson and some of his men followed as best as they could. They were panting and out of breath by the time they caught up to us.

The Japanese vamp pointed at a spot that had recently been dug up. Sending out my senses, I could only feel about twenty fledglings beneath the ground. That meant there had to be more nests somewhere in the area. It would be time consuming to search for them all.

Debating about the dangers of the Second becoming aware of my location, I tried to decide whether it was worth trying to sense more buried fledglings. The more we destroyed before they rose, the fewer we would have to deal with later. *The more time you waste digging them up, the more vampires the Second and his brothers will make,* my subconscious argued. We weren't exactly in a win-win situation.

"We have a choice to make, Colonel." Being new to a leadership role, I figured someone who was far more used to it could make the decision. Sanderson raised an eyebrow at me, so I laid it out for him. "I can sense where the fledglings have been buried. We can either take the time to dig them up and destroy them, or we can advise your reinforcements and they can take care of them when they arrive."

Sanderson barely needed to think about his decision. "It will take four or five days for my men to be deployed. I vote we dig these monsters up and kill them now."

While I wasn't happy about my new kin being described as monsters, I agreed with his choice. Several of his men began digging the freshly turned earth up. Some carried flamethrowers, which would be an effective way to make sure all of the bodies were destroyed.

Sending out my senses, I located five more nests. It took us several hours to dig them up and eradicate all of the bodies. Apart from the one nest that the Japanese vamp had found, the rest of my team had been unsuccessful at locating them.

If we couldn't find freshly made tunnels with our enhanced night vision, then I hoped the humans would have better luck with their technology. The nests had been dug fairly close to the village, which was the only point in our favour. If the disciples kept up this trend, locating and destroying their servants would be a much easier task for us.

Finished with the village at last, we moved on to the next one.

Chapter Sixteen

Again, I sensed the tail end of a group of vamps when we were close to the next small township. It took time for the disciples and their minions to clean out even a small cluster of huts. Storing their victims in safe keeping slowed them down some more and we'd managed to close the distance between us considerably.

"I can sense a group of vampires ahead," I said to Sanderson. "I think they've finished with this village and are already moving on to the next one."

"How close are they?" he turned his head to ask. Our driver had grown used to chauffeuring a couple of vampires and only occasionally glanced at me in the mirror now. He held the wheel tightly, grimly intent on ferrying us to our next destination.

"They're just a few kilometres away." If we continued on our current route in the trucks, they'd be able to hear us shortly.

Studying the map I'd handed over earlier, the colonel considered our best course of action. "If we take this track, we can circle around and beat them to the next village." He stabbed a finger at a tiny squiggle on the page.

Nicholas and I leaned forward to examine the map. Dark brown hair tickled my face and the strands didn't belong to me. I'd decided the best way of dealing with Nicholas was to ignore him. It was either that, or kill him. Considering the numbers of vamps we'd be dealing with, he might come in handy eventually. *That's if he deigns to actually help us fight instead of terrorizing the victims even more by feeding from them.*

Following Sanderson's finger to the path, I saw where we would end up if we took the road. It would take us far enough away that our quarry shouldn't hear our engines before we doubled back to the township. "Let's give it a try," I decided.

It would be a race to see who would reach the village first. While our vehicles were big and slow, we had a path to follow. The vamps would have to fight their way through the jungle on foot. Being newly made, they would be clumsy and unused to their new strength and speed. It would take them a couple more weeks before they would become used to their new status as the undead.

Two hours later, we neared the village and pulled to a stop. Motioning his men to be quiet when they exited from their vehicles, Sanderson turned to me expectantly. My team of vampires took the lead and fanned out ahead. I kept my pace to a fast walk so the humans could keep up. Nicholas strode along at my side, making sure to brush up against me as often as possible.

Geordie had been correct in his assessment of the muscle bound addition to our group, Nicholas really did think he was pretty special. He either didn't realize it, or he refused to believe that I wasn't attracted to him. Ok, I found his body nice to look at, but it was the package inside the body that put me off. Alive or undead, I would never be drawn to arrogant men.

Most of the soldiers were breathing hard by the time we reached the outskirts of the village. Sweat ran down the colonel's face and stained his collar and armpits. It was from exertion rather than fright this time. Well, some of it would be from fright. He was about to have his first battle with my kind. He'd taken down his share of imps, but this would be different. This time his prey would be faster, more cunning and desperate to feed.

Reaching the edge of the village, I heard the tell-tale sounds of humans sleeping or talking softly. Without televisions, radios or telephones, they had no idea that unnatural creatures were stalking through their jungle. In just a few minutes their lives would be altered forever. Even now, I sensed my kin closing in.

I didn't think that the Second was with this band of fledglings. He would have sensed me waiting for him and would have figured out that this was a trap. The disciple leading this mob remained clueless about our presence. I wondered if the Second was sacrificing another of his brothers. We might be working in our adversary's favour, but we would still have to take the ancient vampire down.

Two hundred soldiers weren't quiet, even when they were trying hard not to make any noise. Most were hunkered down, readying their weapons for battle. My small team did the same. My swords were in my hands and

I didn't remember drawing them. It was freaky the way my body acted without conscious thought sometimes. From his crouch beside me, Nicholas drew his machete. Dried blood caked the rusty blade. For a former Court guard, he took lousy care of his weapons.

"They're close," I whispered to Sanderson. He made hand signals to his men that had them going still and quiet.

Peering through the trees, I spied the first fledgling as it arrived. Mostly naked and covered in the blood of her victims, she sidled up to the closest hut. "Wait!" a voice snarled in an ancient African dialect from the trees. Cringing, the female looked longingly at the opening of the hut, but obeyed the order. That told me the disciple in charge was her maker. If he hadn't been, she would have already been inside, feasting on the still oblivious humans.

A lone fire burned in the centre of the village. It didn't shed enough light to aid the soldiers and most had donned their night vision goggles.

Emerging from the tree line, an emaciated, grey skinned walking skeleton stopped and lifted his arms up high. At his gesture, dozens of his new servants scurried into the open. Even after almost a week of draining his victims dry, the disciple was still making up for tens of thousands of years of starvation.

Horribly thin, his teeth were far too prominent. If he'd been swathed in bandages, he would have looked like a mummy that had escaped from a museum. Blood caked his face and body as well as his filthy loincloth. Still stuck in the past, he hadn't gotten the hang of wearing clothes yet. Then again, most of the humans he'd attacked so far still wore primitive clothing. Maybe he didn't realize how behind the times he was.

Sanderson waited until the fledglings were clear of the jungle before signalling his men to attack. A quick count came up with over fifty targets. I didn't need to instruct the Japanese members of my team what to do. They stealthily circled around to cut off any possibility of retreat. I motioned to the Europeans to follow them, but stopped Nicholas with a shake of my head. I would be keeping a close eye on him. He smiled smugly, incorrectly assuming I actually wanted to keep him close.

Shouldering their weapons, the soldiers took aim and fired at the dozen or so fledglings that were poised at the entrances to the huts. I was on the move before the first bullet shattered the silence.

Whipping his head in my direction, the disciple drew back his wrinkled lips to hiss in fury. With prey so near, his servants turned into uncontrollable eating machines. Any that weren't cut down in the initial assault launched themselves at the soldiers, seeing them as food rather than a threat. A barrage of gunfire rang out, villagers screamed in terror inside their huts. My team of vampires attacked in spooky silence.

Bright orange flames lit the area as the first soldier fired up his flamethrower. Screeching in agony, a fledgling twisted and turned like a man possessed. He dropped to the ground and rolled around in an attempt to put out the flames. It was a useless endeavour and he was soon just a blotch of ooze.

"You," the disciple intoned in his ancient language and pointed a wizened finger at me. "You are responsible for this." He swept a hand at the soldiers who were moving in on his servants. An African soldier went down beneath three frenzied vamps. With forced dispassion, another soldier turned his flamethrower on all four of them.

"That's right," I agreed readily. "What are you going to do about it?"

Instead of attacking me, the disciple unexpectedly turned and took off into the trees. He was fast for a creature that looked like a mummy and he disappeared from my sight almost instantly. "Stay here and help the soldiers," I said to Nicholas, then took off after my quarry.

I blamed the continuing gunfire for masking the sounds of the ambush when I ran directly into it. One second the disciple was a barely discernible figure through the trees, the next he had stopped and turned to face me. I halted twenty feet away, wondering what he was up to. Grinning widely, showing off his bloodstained teeth, he shouted an order. "Kill her, my servants!"

Only then did I realize that I was surrounded by over a dozen fledglings. They'd armed themselves with weapons from the villages that they'd attacked. Spinning in a circle, I knew I couldn't fight all of them at once. Cutting the first crazed vampire down by chopping off his head, I winced when a spear was thrust into my back.

There goes another suit, I thought briefly before concentrating on defending myself. Brand new and unskilled in combat, only sheer numbers saved them from being cut down swiftly. They were eerily fast, but they couldn't move quickly enough to dodge my weapons.

More spears pierced my back and I turned to receive one through the stomach as well. Beheading the fledgling who'd dealt that blow, I saw that only four of his friends remained now. Their leader was watching me fearfully. He flinched when my glowing eyes landed on him.

At his urging, the remaining four came at me together. I blocked two spears, then stumbled back when a third one went through my heart. When the disciple crowed in delight, I realized he didn't know who and what I was. I'd grown used to my kind knowing that nothing could kill me.

Falling to my knees, I feigned death and crumpled to my side. As far as the disciple knew, that final spear had dealt me a death blow.

Just as I'd hoped, he was duped by my performance. "Well done, my children," he crooned. "She fell for my trap just as I knew she would." Moving closer, he came to within a few feet of me before making his final observation. "Even after so many thousands of years, it appears that women are still stupid."

Moving with the shocking speed that set me apart from the rest of my kin, I was on my feet before he could even flinch. Ramming one sword into his chest, the other sliced across his throat. "Who's stupid now, huh?" I asked him then pulled my swords free. His surprised expression melted along with the rest of his body as he turned to slush at my feet.

Keening with distress at the death of their master, the remaining fledglings made a final effort to kill me. I cut them down then contemplated the state of my suit. With five spears sticking out of me, it wasn't in very good shape.

Chapter Seventeen

I'd removed all but one spear by the time I jogged back to the village. The gunfire had ceased a couple of minutes ago. Either all of the fledglings were dead, or all of the soldiers were. At the murmuring of American voices, I figured at least some of the troops had survived the encounter.

Nicholas stood anxiously beside Colonel Sanderson in the centre of the village. Both men exchanged relieved glances when I joined them. Shell-shocked from their first battle with creatures they'd once thought of as mythical, the remaining soldiers checked the bodies of their fallen.

Some had survived after being bitten and they were the ones that worried me. If they had ingested any vampire blood, they would turn. Of course, if they fell unconscious when the sun rose, their fate would be pretty obvious. It was the people who had been drained dry that would be impossible to predict if they would rise or not.

"May I help you with that spear, my Queen?" Nicholas offered.

Sanderson realized a weapon was sticking out of my back and turned an interesting shade of green. The spear was positioned right in the middle of my back where I couldn't reach it. "Yes, thanks," I replied, ignoring the title he insisted on giving me. I turned and he yanked it out. The wound healed before I turned back to him.

Sanderson quickly counted how many of his soldiers were dead and shook his head. "I lost twenty men during that fight." His expression was a mixture of anger and sorrow.

I'd tried to tell him how dangerous the fledglings were, but he hadn't believed me. Now that he had witnessed their mindless need to feed for himself, he was aware of what we were facing. Maybe it was a lesson that had to be learned before he and his men could become more effective. They would have to learn to adapt if they wanted to eradicate this threat.

Terrified villagers were still huddled in their huts, reluctant to leave the dubious safety of their dwellings. At Sanderson's insistence, they emerged and gathered in a large group. At least we'd been in time to stop these people from being slaughtered or turned. There would be no underground caches of fledglings to locate and destroy this time.

"We still need to return to the last village the vampires swept through to search for both survivors and hidden fledglings," the colonel said, as if picking up on my thought.

It was getting late and we would be pressed for time if we backtracked. While we were cleaning up this latest mess, I'd bet that the remaining eight disciples and their minions were wreaking havoc in the towns nearby.

The attacks were drawing further and further apart, but at least the fledglings and their masters were still on foot. If they managed to find transportation, our job would become a lot harder.

Sanderson organized two of his trucks to transport the survivors back to their main camp several hours away. We torched the bodies of the fallen, then headed back to the village we'd bypassed earlier.

We found no survivors as we toured the area. There were plenty of children with missing hearts, but no adults. With Nicholas at my side like a faithful dog, I sent out my senses to locate the hidden caches of soon to be vampires. Dawn was near by the time I located the last batch.

Checking his watch, Sanderson motioned to one of the larger trucks. It was fully enclosed and didn't have windows in the back. "You and your people can sleep in the truck if you wish."

"I trust that no one will 'accidentally' open the door while we slumber inside?" Nicholas said snottily.

"*I* trust the Colonel with our lives," I cut in before Sanderson could respond to the barb.

The soldier's expression was tired and angry and he bit his words off. "Natalie has my word that she and her people will remain safe."

Nicholas opened his mouth to no doubt say something to further insult the American. I forestalled him by giving him a shove towards the truck. Stumbling several steps, he rounded on me, but I utilized my new way of dealing with him by ignoring him completely.

"Anyone who doesn't want to sleep in the truck is welcome to find their own place to spend the day," I said to my small team. "Sanderson plans to move ahead to the next village while we're resting. Anyone who doesn't sleep in the truck will be left behind and will have to catch up to us," was my final warning. There was always a chance that my team members might simply run off, but if they were that cowardly then we didn't need them on our side anyway.

Giving Nicholas and the soldiers nervous glances, the Europeans decided to dig their own lairs somewhere in the jungle. Trusting my judgement, the Japanese warriors leaped lightly into the back of the truck. Still ignoring Nicholas, I jumped up after them. I had the door half closed before Nicholas relented and joined our group. I'd almost hoped he wouldn't so I could have a break from him for a few hours.

There was plenty of room for the six of us to lie down without rubbing shoulders. I chose a spot near the door, since I'd have the greatest chance of survival if an accident should occur. While I trusted Sanderson to keep us alive, at least until the threat had been dealt with, I didn't trust his men. Most were afraid of us, especially since we would need to feed from them each night. Now that they had seen the fledglings in person, I could understand their reluctance to allow us to sink our fangs into them again.

Nicholas settled down beside me, close enough for our shoulders to touch. "You don't trust me," he accused me quietly.

"You haven't given me any reason to trust you, Nicholas," I pointed out. Politely pretending that they couldn't hear us, the Japanese guards conversed quietly at the far end of the truck. They were worried about their emperor and didn't like being separated from him. "You've been acting like a dick from the moment you joined us."

"I do not like your companions," he replied sulkily after a few moments of thought. For him, the reply was diplomatic.

"Why?" I asked with my usual bluntness.

"They barely knew that I existed when we were at Court. I was nothing to them." Bitterness crept into his tone. "Now that we are all supposed to be equals, they do not treat me as such."

"I repeat, you've been acting like a dick. You can't expect people to treat you well if you treat them like crap first." I was thinking of how Nicholas had treated Geordie in the past. Bringing it up now would only start an argument. If we ever had that conversation, I didn't want it to be in public.

Confused by my logic, Nicholas remained quiet. The sun was almost up before he commented again. "None of them are worthy of you, my Queen. You should surround yourself with powerful, ambitious people, not with the dregs that you have gathered." His lip was curled as per usual when he made this pronouncement.

Seconds later, the sun made its appearance and everyone in the truck but me succumbed to death. Studying Nicholas coldly, I was highly tempted to insert one of my blades into his heart. He obviously thought he was one of the people who I should be surrounding myself with. His jealousy and prejudice were growing worse.

Luc and Geordie had both stated their intentions of killing Nicholas. Right now I was toying with the idea of beating them to it.

Subsiding into a light doze, I listened to the soldiers bustling around outside the truck. Sanderson organized his troops when they were finished dealing with the hidden caches of soon-to-be vampires. During the day was our best chance of catching up to our quarry and possibly preventing more attacks from occurring. If we could evacuate as many humans as possible from the area, it would help to keep the numbers of fledglings down.

Sanderson spoke into his radio as he climbed into the front of the truck, rousing me from my near slumber. Men from each of his other eight teams were reporting in. My blood tried to run cold when I heard of a single casualty amongst my people. "Repeat that, soldier," the colonel snapped after a stammering young man passed on the bad news.

"One of the African soldiers accidentally killed one of the vampires who was on our side, Colonel," the soldier repeated.

"Which one?"

"Uh, I don't know, sir. One of the Europeans, I think," was the nervous reply. My dead heart lodged somewhere in my throat at the news.

"Find out who the casualty was and get back to me asap," Sanderson ordered.

I spent the next few minutes in tense agony, trying not to imagine the worst. Losing anyone on our team was bad, but if it was one of my close friends then God help Sanderson and his men. Our alliance would be null and void and they would become my enemies.

He seemed to be aware of the danger and answered his radio quickly when the soldier reported back. "Did you find out who the casualty was?" the colonel snapped.

A trifle more sure of himself now, the soldier had an answer. "It was a French vampire from their Court." That narrowed the list down considerably. Only Gregor and Geordie were French from my team, apart from Nicholas. Aventius had brought a number of French vampires with him. My fingers were crossed that Joshua had met a timely end. Frankly, the world would be better off without him.

"Does this vampire have a name?" Sanderson asked with a hint of impatience.

"Her name was Marie, sir."

I knew that name and who they were talking about. Marie was one of the vamps that we'd freed in Russia. Her leader had been possessed by his shadow and had been taking the group to the First's cavern of doom. It seemed ironic that we'd saved her from being turned into an imp, but hadn't been able to save her from dying at the hands of our allies.

I'd placed Marie in Luc's team after recognizing her by her very short auburn hair, overlapping teeth and prominent nose. She hadn't been a courtier, but a member of a rogue pack. Antony had enjoyed taking his servants to the mansion in France to show them what they could never be part of. Marie might not have been beautiful, but at least she'd had character and guts.

Relieved that my close friends were unharmed, I closed my eyes. I'd need to rest if I wanted to be at my best. I allowed myself to slide into sleep to the sound of tyres travelling over the damp, muddy ground and branches scraping against the metal sides of the truck.

Floating in a void, I was surrounded by darkness. Remembering that I'd had this dream before, I opened my eyes. A dull silver metal wall stretched out to either side. It was cold when I brushed my fingertips across it.

Something suddenly bumped into my back. Floundering, I managed to turn around and started back at a face only inches away from mine. Aged, pinched and wrinkled, there was something familiar about the shape of the jaw. Lifeless dirty hair hung limply over the person's brow. Frost coated his face.

Reaching out, I touched the ancient cheek lightly, wondering how I knew this vampire. His eyes cracked open slightly. "Help us, Natalie," the wizened creature croaked.

I didn't know who it was, but I knew it was imperative that I save him.

Chapter Eighteen

Struggling out of the dream that I still couldn't make any sense of, I woke to the unlovely sounds of screams. Nicholas was crouched beside me, machete in hand and apparently ready to defend me from attack. The sun had fallen only minutes ago and all of the vampires in the truck were awake.

From the gurgling sounds of pain coming from somewhere nearby, someone was being mauled to death. *Gee, I wonder who could possibly be responsible for this attack?*

My subconscious was more sarcastic than usual, but it was correct. I could only sense one other vampire in the immediate vicinity and I was positive it wasn't one of my European team members. Even sprinting full tilt, it would take them some time to catch up to us after spending the day in their temporary underground burrows.

I pushed open the truck door and jumped to the ground. Moving as a unit, Nicholas and the Japanese warriors surrounded me to protect me from danger. I appreciated the sentiment, but none of us were likely to be attacked. Our blood was dead, diseased and tainted by a long dead alien. We couldn't feed the blood hunger of the creature that had just risen.

Pushing my way through the crowd of soldiers, I stopped at the sight of three dead men and the newly risen fledgling that was crouched over them. Sanderson stood several feet away from the former soldier who he had insisted be brought back intact. Just as I'd feared, the man had been fed vampire blood and was now my kin. The back door of an armoured truck hung crookedly from one hinge, indicating it had been the supposedly secure site where the undead soldier had been stored.

"Jackson, do you recognize me?" the colonel said to the blood soaked vampire.

Jackson had been stripped down to a plain white t-shirt and boxer shorts. The lower half of his face had turned red and his t-shirt was splattered with blood. Cocking his head to the side, the fledgling contemplated the tall, thin, blond man before him. There was no reason left in his still mostly pale blue eyes. The former soldier snarled and hurled himself at his former superior.

I was already on the move before the fledgling launched himself into action. Crossing the distance, I pushed the colonel out of the way and crashed to the ground with the ravenous vamp on top of me. The former soldier sank his teeth into my neck, tearing through the skin and into the vein.

His blood hunger was so extreme that he didn't even realize his mistake at first. Jerking back from me once he actually tasted what he was ingesting, the fledgling stared at the rapidly healing wounds in my neck in confusion.

Instead of bright red, my blood was sluggish, black and highly unappetizing.

Standing unsteadily, Jackson took a step towards the colonel then coughed. Sanderson scrambled to his feet and several of his men hauled him out of danger. Encircled by flamethrower wielding soldiers, the fledgling was far too sick to worry about being barbequed.

Gagging, he clutched his throat and turned to me as if seeking an explanation for what had gone wrong. I'd been told that drinking the blood of our kin meant death, but I'd never actually seen it for myself. Two imps had tried to snack on me and had died horribly as a consequence. This guy was about to suffer the same fate.

Jackson's face began to change colour as my blood spread through his system. Instead of pale white, he was soon a dusky grey. For a few horrible moments I thought my blood was turning him into an imp. Then I realized it was altering his blood from its usual red to black as his veins swelled and bulged.

Doubling over as the blood surged towards his heart, he let out a groan of agony and collapsed to his knees. Jerking spasmodically, he fell to his side and proceeded to have a fit. Now I knew what I'd looked like the night I'd first been bitten. Silvius' blood had turned me into the undead, but my blood was having a far worse effect on the already unliving fledgling.

The black, acrid substance that had originated from my body ate its way through the former soldier's skin. He shrieked in agony, writhing in the dirt as his skin began to melt. Sounds of disgust and superstitious dread issued from both humans and vampires.

Flesh disintegrated from his mouth and neck, leaving a raw open wound. Stains blossomed on his clothing as my blood worked its way through his digestive system and ate its way free. Hypnotized with horrified wonder, I watched as he died slowly and in intense agony.

Sanderson roused himself and took action. Stepping forward, he drew his handgun and pumped several bullets into Jackson's head. The screams cut off and what remained of his trooper's melted body disintegrated.

"So, that's what happens when we drink each other's blood," I said in astonishment.

Nicholas shook his head and was echoed by the four Japanese guards. "I have never seen anything like that before, Natalie." They were nearly as afraid as the humans and darted disturbed glances at me.

"You mean that wasn't a normal reaction?" This time I received five nods and they unconsciously edged away from me. "What usually happens when we drink vampire blood then?"

One of the Japanese warriors answered me. "Normally, we just…die. That," he pointed at the blotch that used to be the soldier, "has never happened before."

Remembering the times that Luc had come close to breaking my skin with his fangs during sex, I barely held in a shudder. I doubted he'd try that again once he heard of this new development. "I guess it's just part of the awesomeness of being Mortis," I said lamely. There were already enough differences between my kin and me, I didn't need any more cropping up.

Shaky and whiter than usual, the colonel directed his men to dispose of the bodies of the three soldiers who had just been mauled to death. I had no desire to launch into a lecture that I'd told him this might happen. He'd learned his lesson and the mistake wouldn't be repeated.

He drew me aside when the bodies were ablaze. "You saved my life," he pointed out needlessly.

"Believe it or not, I still believe in the sanctity of human life." How could I not when I still felt human myself sometimes?

"You have my thanks, Natalie." In a very manly gesture, he held out his hand. I shook with him solemnly, knowing that I could trust him just a bit more now. Honour and integrity were a large part of his makeup. It would go against his nature to turn on an ally, unless he was forced to.

Our moment of understanding was interrupted when his radio crackled. Luc's voice came through. Being Italian originally, he had a faint accent that had been altered after seven hundred years of living in France. "This is Lucentio," he said formally. "I wish to speak to Natalie."

Sanderson handed me his radio, but made no move to give me privacy. "Hi, Luc. What's up?"

"I have some bad news." His tone was grave and warned me to brace myself.

I already had a pretty good idea why he was contacting me. "Is it about Marie?"

His silence was startled, but momentary. "I only just found out myself that she was killed last night. How did you find out?"

I went with the truth. "I heard the Colonel speaking to one of his men about it."

Sanderson frowned as he realized I'd been awake and listening to him in the back of the truck. He gave me an apologetic look, but my expression warned him that there would be questions.

"I think it would be wise for us to keep in regular contact to ensure that our people remain safe," my most favourite companion suggested.

"I agree," I replied while looking Sanderson in the eye. "I'll make sure to check in with the team leaders myself. If any more of our people die due to an 'accident', we'll pull out and let the soldiers deal with the disciples and their fledglings themselves."

Sanderson understood my warning and flushed at the threat, but he didn't argue the point.

"Agreed. Stay safe, *chérie*." I could hear the smile in Luc's voice as he used Geordie's nickname for me.

"You, too." I was smiling as well, but it dropped off my mouth as soon as Luc was gone.

Holding up his hands to forestall my angry tirade at being reminded of Marie's death, the colonel talked fast to save himself from my ire. "If you overheard that conversation then you must have heard me contacting all of the groups and warning them that there would be severe consequences if any more mistakes occurred." His posture was defensive, but not particularly alarmed so I assumed he was telling the truth.

"Actually, I fell asleep and missed that part."

Searching my face, Sanderson wasn't reassured. "I swear to you that Marie's death was an accident. She stepped in front of one of General Merwe's men as he opened fire. No one could have prevented her death."

I'd have to question Luc's team to see if any of them had witnessed this episode, but it would have to wait for now. Sadly, our task was too important to seek justice for just one unlife. "We'll talk about this later," I decided. "What is our current situation?"

Relieved to be let off the hook, the colonel pulled out his trusty map. Even with the lamination protecting it, the map was beginning to look worn. "Our teams have cleared out a number of villages in the area while your people slept." He indicated a few green circles on the map. The red circles of villages that had been attacked far outnumbered them.

On the downside, the villages were turning into actual towns the further away from the heart of the jungle they became. It would take longer for the vamps to reach them on foot, but their numbers were swelling with each attack. Soon, they would have enough fledglings to carry their victims away rather than burying them beneath the ground. I could only hope that the Second was unaware that we were digging up and eradicating anyone he left behind.

"As you can see, the villages are getting bigger and are becoming more numerous." Sanderson pointed to the groups of dwellings that led outward in an expanding circle. I nodded impatiently. "General Merwe and I believe that our best course of action is to get ahead of the enemy." He indicated an area that left a few villages within the danger zone. "Our intention is to evacuate these towns and work our way into the centre." They must have worked out this plan while I'd been sleeping.

"This reminds me of back burning to prevent a fire from spreading," I murmured. It was a common practice in Australia during the bushfire season. The only problem with that scenario was that sometimes the fires had a habit of turning on the people that had set them.

Many humans would be sacrificed if we went with this plan, but desperate times called for desperate actions. "Let's do it," I said and sealed the fate of everyone who lived inside the kill zone.

Chapter Nineteen

While Sanderson contacted General Merwe to coordinate our plan, I checked on my people. Sanderson had given us our own frequency to use to keep in contact. I hoped someone was listening in from each of my teams.

"This is Natalie," I said into the radio. "Come in, Team One."

One of Ishida's female guards answered. Her ruler was either still pissed at me, or he thought he was above using the device. Probably, it was a bit of both. "This is Team One, Mortis."

"Have you had any casualties so far?" It was the most diplomatic way I could think to ask whether any of our people had died under suspicious circumstances.

"Not so far, Mortis," was her crisp reply. If anyone from the army was listening in, they'd have no idea what her response was, unless they understood Japanese. "We are all well, but several human lives were lost."

"Did you see any of the disciples during the scuffle?"

"Several of our people caught a glimpse of an ancient, withered vampire, but he disappeared before we could catch him."

I was disappointed, but unsurprised. The disciples would all be aware that they were being hunted by now. "The disciples are our main priority," I told her. "If you spot him again, take a team, hunt him down and kill him."

"Understood, Mortis."

One by one, I contacted the other teams. I skipped team two because I'd already spoken to Luc. Gregor answered when I called for his team. "Natalie, it is good to hear from you."

"I'm glad you're ok, Gregor. How is your hunt going?"

"Quite well," he replied warmly as if we were discussing a party he'd recently thrown. "We lost only a few soldiers and managed to destroy all of the fledglings." He'd been listening in during my discussion with the female from team one. "We didn't spot any of the disciples, but we will heed your orders that they take priority."

I contacted Igor's group next. "Come in, Team Four."

"I'm here, *chérie*!" Geordie said excitedly, not to mention loudly.

Wincing, I jerked the radio away from my ear. "Hi, Geordie. Is everything ok in your team?"

"We are fine, but I have good news. We killed one of the disciples!" he crowed. "We cornered him while he was feeding his flesh hunger." His joy was dampened slightly and his voice lowered when he continued. "I'm very glad that we killed him, Natalie."

"Why?" There had to be another reason apart from the obvious, that he was one of the bad guys.

"He hungered for the flesh of children."

My mouth opened, but my disgust was so strong that at first I had nothing to say. "Who killed him?" I asked at last.

"Igor had that honour. He heard the little boy screaming and went to investigate. The disciple was distracted with mauling the child and didn't even know Igor was there until his knife pierced his body."

"What happened to the boy?" Grief for the poor little kid welled up because I knew what the answer would be.

Geordie's answer came reluctantly. "We had to destroy him. The disciple had fed him his blood."

My lips wrinkled back from my teeth as I realized that the perverted disciple had intended to make the child his sex slave. Nicholas had wandered over during the conversation and laid a hand on my shoulder. His expression was disturbed at the idea of a child vampire. "Tell Igor that he did the world a service," I said.

"I will, *chérie*. Take care of yourself."

Nicholas still had his hand on my shoulder when I called for the next team. Pretending I was having trouble hearing, I moved away a few steps. Unfortunately, he ignored my hint and stayed by my side. At least he kept his hands to himself. Crossing his arms, he stared at the side of my head moodily.

Aventius himself responded to my call and advised that all was well with his people. Next, my weapons instructor replied gruffly that no accidents had occurred with any of his team and that they also had spotted a disciple.

"Everyone, listen up," I said and knew that the people appointed to radio duty would be paying attention. "Be wary of being led into a trap by the disciples. Don't chase them alone. Make sure you have a team with you. Take some of the humans along if you have to."

"Are you speaking from experience, Mortis?" the Japanese leader from team eight asked.

"Yes." Even to myself I sounded sheepish. "He led me right into an ambush of a dozen fledglings. Luckily for me, I can't die from being staked, speared, sliced or shot through the heart."

"That is an interesting fact," a strange voice said in an ancient African dialect. "I wish I had known of this sooner. I wouldn't have wasted the Fifth by sending him to kill you."

"Who is that?" Geordie asked in bewilderment, unable to understand the language being spoken.

"That's the Second," I responded calmly, despite the thrill of alarm that raced through me. *How did he get his hands on a radio?* Even as I asked myself the question, I knew the answer. "Team Nine, is anyone there?"

"Regretfully, your people are indisposed at the moment, Mortis." A monstrous chuckle sounded from the radio and I was tempted to smash it. The Second's voice on the radio meant that we'd lost ten vampires as well as a couple of hundred soldiers.

"What did he say?" Gregor asked.

"Team Nine has been destroyed." I couldn't disguise the bleakness in my tone.

"Do not fear for them," the Second crooned. "The soldiers will soon rise to join my army."

"Yeah, that's a great comfort." I didn't bother to hide my sarcasm. "What about our kin?"

"Regretfully, they refused to serve me. As my enemies, I naturally had to dispose of them."

Nicholas' hand settled on my shoulder again when I tensed, warning me against saying anything rash. "None of us are ever going to serve you," I told the ancient monster coldly. "Our purpose is to kill you."

After a lengthy silence, the Second's tone was arctic when he responded. "If you and your people persist in defying me, I will kill every last one of you. Know this, Mortis, it is not I who will die."

"You know," I said thoughtfully, "you're a really lousy poet."

With a snarl and a crunch, the Second crushed the radio to death. If he truly had taken down team nine, then he would have access to more radios.

Nicholas remained by my side as I sprinted to Sanderson. The five European members of our team arrived just as I issued my warning. "The Second has managed to get his hands on some radios."

Sanderson looked at me in surprise. "How did he manage that?"

"Have you had any contact with Team Nine lately?"

Reaching for his own radio, the colonel futilely attempted to contact his people. Giving up after receiving no response, his expression was worried. The lines in his forehead seemed to deepen with each night that passed. "Do you think the Second is aware of our plans?"

I shrugged. "I'm not sure, but I hope not. Where was Team Nine located?"

Out came the trusty map again and we huddled together to study it. That particular team had been to the east. Luck was on our side because they had the fewest number of villages and towns in the area. We would have to spread our teams out further in the hopes of containing the disciples and their growing army.

I wished my team could head off the Second personally, but we were to the north. Aventius and his people were the next closest group to team nine. With the Second monitoring our frequency, we couldn't formulate any plans over the air.

"We will have to stick to our original plan and hope for the best," Sanderson decided, echoing my thought.

"What has happened?" one of the European vamps asked. One of the Japanese members filled them in on the way to our transportation.

"I think we should stay close in future," the European muttered to the others. "It will be safer if we stick together." I couldn't fault his decision and nodded my approval, not that they actually sought it. I'd feel better knowing where they were at all times.

Sanderson rounded up enough soldiers for us to feed, but I declined the offer. Munching on someone whose eyes were rolling wildly in terror did nothing for my appetite. The rest of my team weren't as squeamish. Even Nicholas relented and fed from one of the men. He cut a glare at me before closing his eyes and taking a bite. Remembering my warning, he caused the man as little pain as possible. The Japanese people bowed to their meals and the bemused soldiers bowed back. Once they'd been fed from, their fear abated. Our method of feeding was far gentler than the fledglings'.

It was a long ride to our next destination. The sun came up and the undead settled down to sleep. I closed my eyes, but my slumber was shallow and unsatisfactory. I woke every time we hit a bump or a branch screeched down the side of the truck.

Sanderson stuck to the plan and we drove right through the day and into the early night before we reached the town that was at the outer edge of the kill zone. We made enough noise with our arrival to wake the entire town.

Instead of mud huts, I was surprised to see wooden buildings when I jumped down from the back of the truck. Frightened townsfolk, wearing colourful dresses or plain shirts and pants, gathered to protest our arrival. Holding up his hands to indicate we came in peace, Sanderson attempted to calm them. One of the African soldiers acted as a translator.

The town held several hundred people, including over a hundred children. They citizens didn't have enough vehicles to transport them all to safety and we couldn't spare our trucks. "Do you really expect us to believe that monsters are roaming around in the jungle?" the village elder asked after the translator had finished laying out the problem.

Sanderson caught sight of me through the crowd and motioned me over. Nicholas was on my heels like an unwanted shadow. "Can you please demonstrate who and what you are for these people?"

Glancing around, I found all nine of my team members behind me. At my nod, they all turned to face the townspeople. Almost as one, we opened our mouths and allowed our fangs to descend. Screams of fright rang out and someone brandished a cross.

The others flinched back, but I stepped forward and took the proffered piece of jewellery. "We mean you no harm," I said, wishing I could speak foreign languages as well as understand them. "But the creatures on their way intend to kill your children and turn every last adult in this town into monsters."

I handed the cross back to the elderly woman who had attempted to drive me off with it. Taking it with a shaky hand, she spoke rapidly to the village elder. "We must leave this place immediately if we wish to save our people."

Nodding his agreement, the elder instructed his townsfolk to gather only a few belongings each. Within minutes, he'd organized the sick, elderly and very young and herded them to their few vehicles. Everyone else would have to hike to safety.

As the exodus went underway, Sanderson contacted his team leaders for updates. Aware that they were probably being monitored by the enemy, they spoke cryptically of latitudes and longitudes. Only by looking at the map could I determine that our process of evacuating the area seemed to be working.

By widening our net and working our way inwards, we would hopefully be able to contain the threat of vampire invasion. The next town was fairly close and we headed there next, hoping to save as many humans as possible.

By dawn, we had cleared several more towns. Sanderson kept in regular touch with his men to make sure our teams remained on track. My people and I retired for the day while the colonel's men continued to evacuate the towns and villages. Sleep was a long time coming and when it arrived, it took me on another trip into the Second's mind.

Chapter Twenty

My plan was working even better than I'd hoped. While the enemies hunting us were technologically advanced, they were no more intelligent than the humans I'd encountered before being banished to my underground tomb so very long ago.

Still, the female vampire who named herself after death itself worried me. While she was also not particularly intelligent, she was tenacious. Despite my threats to end her and her people, I was certain that she would continue to plague me. It infuriated me that a creature so inferior thought she had the capability or the right to end my life.

If the female would only agree to serve me, she could become one of my concubines. Despite being so pale, she was attractive. I'd have to see her unclothed before making my final decision whether to kill her, or keep her.

I'd been amused when overhearing her preposterous claim that nothing could kill her. Even the red eyed, grey being that had first created us had been susceptible to death. Making such a ridiculous statement was probably designed to bolster her people's morale.

I would have an interesting next few nights ahead as I battled wits with this Mortis. She was mistaken if she thought she and her tame soldiers would be able to stop my servants from spreading. Nothing on this earth would be able to keep me from my destiny.

Waking to the sounds of a mental chuckle, I stared up at the ceiling of the truck. *The Second is planning on turning me into his sex slave.* The thought was more amusing than scary. One thing I knew for sure was that I would never be anyone's slave. He'd been alive for so long that he couldn't really conceive of the thought that he might one day die. If he knew that I had been the one to best his maker, then he might have rethought his evil scheme.

Nicholas had shifted closer to me during the drive and was now pressed up against my side. All vampires, except me of course, were incapable of waking up until nightfall once the sun had set, so he hadn't moved closer deliberately.

Checking my watch, I saw that the sun wasn't due to set for another couple of hours. All nine of my team mates were still dead to the world and no one was awake to observe me. Using my feet, I shoved the over muscled vamp several feet away. His head lolled to the side, facing me. It almost looked like he was staring at me coyly through his lashes except his eyelids were shut.

Feeling just the tiniest bit creeped out, I stretched out, wiggled my boot beneath Nicholas' cheek and flipped his head until it was facing the other way. It landed with a dull thud that I hoped the human passengers up front didn't hear.

We were on the move again and I wondered how well our own plan was working so far. Knowing that the Second was currently awake and was probably listening in on the radio, I didn't bother to call any of my teams to check in with them.

If the truck's walls hadn't been so thick, I would have yelled out to Sanderson to request an update. I could hear him speaking to the driver clearly enough, but my voice would be muffled and unintelligible to him.

Quickly growing bored with having nothing to do but bounce around in the back of the truck and fend off Nicholas' shifting corpse with my feet, I took a chance and sent out my senses. As far as I knew, the Second was somewhere off to the west, so I swept my search to the south first then to the east.

Passing over the tiny pockets of vampires that were most likely my teammates, I strained to my limits and found a large number of my kin near the centre of the trap we were laying. It was difficult to estimate how many fledglings we would be facing. I only hoped that we would have enough resources to wipe them out.

We'd begun the hunt with two thousand soldiers and still had about nineteen hundred left. Each time our teams faced the fledglings, we lost men to their feeding frenzy. I didn't like our odds if we were to face hundreds of our newly made kin in one group, but it looked like that was going to be the most likely outcome.

Trapped in the back of the truck, bored and feeling lonely being the only one awake, I waited impatiently for the sun to fade from the sky. We stopped a short while later at yet another village and the soldiers instantly began the evacuation process. I listened to the action, unable to leave the safety of the truck until the sun went down.

Confused, frightened and unable to understand why they were being tossed out of their homes, the villagers refused to leave. Sanderson's translator was having no luck explaining the situation to them. The colonel's voice rose as he began shouting at the villagers. "You need to get your people out of here now!" I assumed he was yelling at the village elder.

"We're not going anywhere!" the elder screamed back after Sanderson's words had been translated.

"Don't you understand that you are all going to die if you don't leave this place?" The colonel didn't bother to hide his frustration at the villager's continued stubbornness.

I didn't need to check my watch to know the sun was finally about to abate. My body felt the killing rays of light recede. Sanderson and his men might not be having any luck, but I was pretty sure I'd be able to persuade the villagers to leave.

With one shove, I pushed open the heavy metal door as darkness descended. The villagers had gathered in a group to argue against being ousted. They were all talking at once, vying to be heard. *Perfect, I won't have to round any of them up. Now to convince them to leave.*

Mentally rubbing my hands together, I allowed my fangs to grow and let out a snarl. I'd heard plenty of howls, grunts, gibbers and growls from the imps, so it wasn't difficult to improvise.

All sound ceased as heads turned. Wrinkling my lips back so my teeth were displayed, I jumped to the ground and stalked towards the suddenly terrified group of villagers. Turning my hands into claws, I increased my pace and the volume of my snarl.

"Uh, Colonel?" one of the American soldiers said nervously. "Is this for real, or is she just acting?"

Shifting his hand to his gun, Sanderson was almost ready to pull his weapon when I met his gaze and subtly rolled my eyes. "It's an act," he replied then turned to yell at the translator. "Get these people out of here!"

Frantically flapping his hands and screaming instructions with completely unfeigned terror, the translator finally managed to get the villagers moving. Sanderson pulled his gun and fired a shot that deliberately went wide of me. I let out a fake scream of pain and stumbled to one knee. The villagers stampeded, shooting frightened looks back over their shoulders.

Most of the soldiers had their weapons trained on me when I stood and sauntered over to the colonel. He motioned for them to put their guns and flamethrowers down, but hesitated for a moment before putting his own weapon away. "You had us fooled for a minute there." His smile was forced and didn't ease his men much.

"If I really did turn evil, do you think I'd give you any warning?" I pointed out.

"Probably not," he conceded after a moment of thought.

Still the object of mistrust by everyone in the area, I decided it was high time to pass on some good news. "Our plan seems to be working. I can sense a large number of fledglings near the centre of our kill zone."

Frowning at my description, the colonel followed it up with a grim smile. "Then we shouldn't waste any time clearing out any more villages and head directly for the threat instead."

While I wasn't happy about having innocent humans in the line of fire, I had to admit that wiping out the fledglings and their masters was more important than saving a few hundred souls. If we were lucky, we could put an end to this whole shebang tonight.

"I'll let my people know," I told him and reached for the radio. My entourage had woken and left the truck to form a guard around me while I spoke. Nicholas stuck to my side, pretending to be my right hand man. Maybe he was, in his own mind.

"This is Natalie," I said into the radio. "Is everyone there?" Someone from each team responded quickly. I was relieved to hear from all of the remaining teams. "There's been a change of plans and you are all to head directly for the target zone asap."

Our target was a tiny village roughly at the centre of the large circle our teams had formed. By tightening our advance, we'd forced the disciples to band together instead of branching out.

Somewhere in the back of my mind, I was worried that this seemed a bit too easy. The Second had seemed so smug when I'd taken a peek inside his mind. He clearly thought he was far cleverer than any of us. If this was the case, then surely he wouldn't allow himself to be caught in our trap so easily.

"What is the plan, exactly?" Geordie asked on behalf of all of the team leaders, or those in charge of the radios as was his case.

"Shoot, stab or slice anything with fangs. Keep shooting, stabbing and slicing until they turn into a slushy puddle," I told him.

"It shall be as you say, Mortis," Aventius said formally.

For an ex-Councillor, I was surprised at how well he was assimilating with our cause. I'd expected him to at least protest some of the orders I was handing out. Unlike Nicholas and Joshua, he did as I asked without complaint. "I'll see you all in a few hours." I hoped I sounded more cheerful than I felt. A nagging sense of doubt tugged at my mind.

I wasn't the only one who was worried. Nicholas wore a heavy frown that almost made him look ordinary instead of gorgeous. "I do not like this plan, my...Natalie." His tone was concerned rather than flirtatious, yet the term still irritated me.

"Stay behind then," I said carelessly, knowing he wouldn't take me up on the offer. He'd chosen to be on my side and at my side he would stay.

"I am not a coward, my Liege," he said stiffly.

"Then quit whining and get in the truck." Going by his narrowed eyes and flared nostrils, I'd offended him. The rest of my entourage sent him cautious glances then followed my directions.

Sanderson was motioning his people into action. He raised his eyebrows at me when I shut the door of the truck without climbing in. I seriously needed a break from Nicholas and decided to ride up front for a change.

There wasn't enough room for three people in the front, so the colonel waved his driver away and slid behind the wheel. I was already buckled in by the time he was seated. Taking a look at my brooding expression, he wisely chose to remain silent. It would take us several hours to reach the target area and a bit of peace and quiet suited me just fine. It was a pity the silence only lasted for five minutes before arguing broke out in the back of the truck.

"Keep your distance, Asian scum," Nicholas snarled to one of the Japanese vamps.

"Who are you to call us scum, European dog?"

"At least we are civilized and live in a mansion rather than squatting in caves like cockroaches," the ex-courtier countered.

Even with the engine rumbling, I heard the sound of swords sliding free from their sheaths. Turning before any black ooze could be shed, I pounded my fist on the wall that separated us from my team members. "Sit down and shut up. Don't make me come back there!" *Christ, I sound like my mother!*

With a few mutters too low for me to make out, they complied and silence descended again.

Throwing me a sympathetic glance, Sanderson couldn't quite hide his smile. "What?" I asked grumpily.

"Is ruling a race of vampires turning out to be as much fun as you'd anticipated?"

"It's worse than I could have possibly imagined," I complained, not caring if my kin overheard me. "I can't wait for this to be over so things can go back to the way they were." What I meant was that I could return to being a nobody again and have zero responsibilities.

Sanderson's expression was slightly pitying this time and I wasn't sure he even knew it. "Do you really think anything can ever be the same again?"

In the short time that I had become one of the undead, the world had irrevocably changed and I was to blame.

Almost every human on the planet now knew that we existed. I was kidding myself if I thought we could ever return to our former obscurity again.

Chapter Twenty-One

We didn't bother to come up with a detailed plan during the journey. Like I'd told my teams, our goal was simple; take down anything that wasn't human. It was impossible to plan for every eventuality that might be thrown at us until we came across it anyway.

Sanderson checked our coordinates regularly to make sure we weren't straying from our path. The track we were on was narrower than usual and one of the armoured trucks was pushing its way through the dense jungle ahead. Our pace wasn't exactly swift and I was beginning to worry that we would be the last to arrive to the party.

"We're nearly there," the colonel reassured me after I'd glanced at my watch for what had to be the fiftieth time.

As planned, we stopped a couple of kilometres away from the area that I'd termed as the kill zone. Three villages were on the outskirts of the zone and one of them was just ahead. Instead of evacuating the townsfolk, we crept quietly past their dwellings on foot. Sanderson had called for radio silence so that our arrival would hopefully be a surprise to our enemies.

By now, most of our troops should be in place near the village that was central to our plan of eradication. I didn't have to send out my senses to know that a large number of fledglings weren't far away. I could feel them and the terrible hunger that drove them. Some of the older fledglings were mature enough for their flesh hunger to have risen by now.

My hackles began to rise as we drew closer to the mob of undead. Touching Sanderson on the arm, I indicated that he should give the signal to attack. At his nod, one of the Americans raised a flare gun and pulled the trigger. At the bright red burst of light overhead, our troops rushed towards the next village.

As soon as I saw the fledglings, I knew why the Second had been so smug. They hadn't fallen into our trap at all, but had allowed us to herd them to this spot. They were all armed with some kind of weapon, whether it was just a crude rock or a rusty spear. Facing outwards, a few of the vamps on the outer edge of the circle carried guns.

"Take them down!" Sanderson screamed and bullets began to fly. As per the plan, my vamps stayed back to avoid friendly gunfire from our soldiers in the initial attack. Grenades were tossed into the mob and vampire parts rained down.

Hundreds of fledglings huddled together, protecting the disciples hidden in their midst. The ones with guns fired wildly, managing to take down a couple of dozen soldiers, but not making much impact otherwise. With dismay, I realized that the disciples were just waiting for the soldiers to close with them before they launched their own attack.

Before I could shout a warning, the fledglings were suddenly let loose. Deranged with hunger, they sped towards the soldiers. Too fast to track with a human eye, they dodged bullets, leaped over flamethrowers and began to feed.

"Move in!" I shouted to my entourage. Nicholas hesitated then reached for his machete.

Sanderson wisely stayed back, uselessly ordering his men to retreat. His soldiers were either screaming in terror, or were firing at the oncoming vamps. The noise drowned out his commands.

My worst fears were coming true; the soldiers were being overwhelmed. They would soon become the very things they were trying to eradicate if my people didn't put a stop to it.

Passing General Merwe, I shouted at him to pull his men back. Wild eyed, he gave no indication that he'd heard me and shot a fledgling point blank in the face.

My swords went into action and fledglings fell. Battle lust descended and I chopped, sliced and diced any vamp that came within my reach. A strange and not completely unwelcome thrill raced up my spine with each death that I doled out.

Nicholas did an adequate job of keeping up with me, but he wasn't doing a great deal of damage to the enemy. He only attacked when he was directly threatened. The rest of my entourage did a far better job. The ten of us cut our way through to the centre of the circle to what turned out to be a lone disciple.

Luc and Igor had already beaten us there and were engaged in combat with several fledglings. Geordie screeched from somewhere in the crowd. It was a scream of triumph rather than pain, so I turned my attention to the disciple and started towards him.

"You dare to attack me?" he sneered. "You are a lowly dog and should bow down to one who is far greater than you."

"You're not greater than me," I contradicted him. "You're just really, really old." He was also less skeletal than the last two disciples I'd seen. He'd fleshed out a bit. And he didn't quite look as mummified as the others. His skin was more brown than grey.

Drawing himself up, he gestured me forward. "If you think you are a match for me then come, face me in battle." Armed with a spear, he twirled it to show me that he was skilled with his weapon of choice.

I could have twirled the swords flashily in retaliation, but chose not to. "This one is mine," I said to my friends. They had finished off the closest fledglings and had gathered to assist me. "See if you can help the soldiers."

They reluctantly turned their attention to the rabid fledglings. Luc tipped me a wink and I gave him a smile. Even when my eyes were glowing orange, he was still attracted to me. Unfortunately, so was Nicholas. He ignored my order and remained a few steps behind me.

The disciple moved around me in a slow circle. I copied him, studying his movements as I'd been taught. I was ready for it when he suddenly lunged forward. His spear missed me by inches, but my sword scored a slash across his stomach. Rage flared as his intestines bulged out through the seam I'd just made. He healed almost as quickly as I did, pushing the slimy, stinky innards back into the slit first.

Not quite as cocky now, he made a feint then went for my face. He might be fast and have thousands of years of fighting practice behind him, but he was doomed to failure. He had only one weapon while I was armed with two. It would have been satisfying to draw the fight out, but there were still dozens of fledglings to eradicate.

Slicing the blade of his spear off with one sword, the other opened a wound across his throat. Proving just how fast he was, he leaped backwards before I could slice all the way through his spine and sever his head completely. For a second, he looked at me in shock then his head tipped backwards until it was hanging by a flap of skin and a couple of veins.

"Oh, gross!" Geordie complained. He'd stumbled his way through the fight in time to witness the near decapitation.

Groping blindly, the disciple grabbed his head and set it back on his shoulders. The wound healed and he was as good as new again in seconds. His grin of triumph turned to a look of surprise when a crossbow bolt appeared in his chest. He stared at Geordie, amazed that the teen had dared to shoot him. My young friend's aim had been slightly off and he'd missed the disciple's heart.

Switching his gaze back to me, the disciple realized he was facing someone even more skilled with a weapon than he was. He turned and ran and I was on his heels instantly.

Dodging and weaving like a rabbit attempting to outrun a fox, he made it as difficult as possible to keep him in sight. I was impressed with his speed even as I was annoyed by my inability to catch him.

"Screw this," I muttered and put my swords away. Sparing a moment to concentrate, my left hand came free at my mental command and I lobbed it at the fleeing vamp like a grenade.

Glancing backwards, he caught sight of Lefty about to descend on him and his mouth opened in a scream. Landing on the disciple's face, Lefty didn't give him a chance to utter his terror and clamped down hard. I unleashed the power of the holy mark before my hand could be torn away.

Giving a bubbling screech, the disciple hit the ground and Lefty leaped clear. Scrabbling around in a circle on his side, the ancient vampire tore at his melting flesh. Both holy marks working together was the only way my power could end a vampire's life. One on its own just caused intense pain and horrible disfigurement.

Planting a boot on the writhing creature's chest, I leaned down to allow Lefty to reattach itself. The terrified black eyes of my quarry beseeched me to end his pain. I complied, but not because I felt any pity for him. It was my duty as Mortis to end the creature's life. Placing my hands on the disciple's head, I released the power of both holy marks this time. His head imploded and I stepped aside to avoid being splattered.

Four down, six to go, I thought grimly. I wondered just how far away the other disciples had managed to travel while we'd fallen for the Second's crafty distraction.

Chapter Twenty-Two

I'd run quite a distance away from the kill zone during my pursuit of the disciple. By the time I returned, most of the fledglings were dead. So were a great many of our troops. Sanderson's face was tight with grief and fury as he directed his men to encircle four fledglings. Shrill screams of pain rang out as their flamethrowers were switched on and orange fire scorched undead flesh.

General Merwe had relinquished all pretence of control and was firing two pistols simultaneously at anything with fangs. Unfortunately, this also included the vampires who were on our side. Gregor narrowly dodged a bullet and hurriedly moved his team to a safer location.

I spied Ishida off to one side, battling a pair of fledglings. His young face was almost bored as he defended himself from their clumsy attacks. Kokoro stood nearby, guarded by two female warriors. Her expression was serene, but she was tense with worry for her ruler's safety.

Growing tired of playing with the pair, Ishida ended the fight by brutally beheading one of the vamps and stabbing the other through the heart. His gaze turned icy as it passed over me.

"He will come around," Luc said from beside me and I started. He could move very quietly when he wanted to.

"I never wanted to be in charge," I complained quietly. I looked for Nicholas, positive he'd hurry to my side as soon as he saw me with my beloved. I spied Gregor speaking to the ex-courtier, either purposefully, or accidentally giving us a moment alone.

"You have done very well organizing us into a cohesive unit, Natalie." I hadn't been expecting his compliment and was momentarily thrown. "Far better than I had expected," Luc admitted with a tiny frown of apology.

He must have known I knew he didn't think I would be an effective leader. Hearing him admit that he'd been wrong lessened the hurt. "Thanks, Lucentio."

One side of his mouth lifted in a half smile. "I actually think I prefer it if you call me Luc." Now that was an admission that I'd never expected to hear. "I have grown used to it," he admitted quietly. *I knew he'd come around eventually,* I thought smugly.

He bent to kiss me as Nicholas finally broke free and jogged towards us. "My Liege," the overly muscled courtier said and I lifted a finger to delay him until Luc was finished. He took his time and I wasn't about to complain. Luc was easily the best kisser I'd ever had the pleasure of locking lips with.

"That's so sweet," Geordie said as he joined us and bit back a sentimental sob. "You can tell that they really love each other." I was pretty sure he added that last bit just to bait Nicholas.

Luc finally pulled back and I discovered we were surrounded by our friends and allies. Hiding my embarrassment as best as I could, I was glad the blood couldn't rush to my face anymore.

"How many disciples have been dispatched now?" Gregor asked.

"Four that I know of," I replied.

"Then there are six still remaining, including the Second, who seems to be far cleverer than I'd given him credit for." Gregor gestured at the carnage surrounding us. "Does anyone else feel that this was just an elaborate diversion staged to waste our time?"

Ishida's head turned to survey the damage, passing over hundreds of mauled soldiers stonily. He'd lost some of his warriors and so had the Europeans. None of us had forgotten that team nine had been wiped out entirely. The child king's expression was as blank as ever, but I detected signs of rebellion in the depths of his midnight coloured pupils. I hoped he wasn't rethinking the wisdom of allying himself with me. The aid of his warriors would be crucial to ending this threat.

Colonel Sanderson's voice rose, cutting through the moans of survivors and shocked chatter of his soldiers. "*How* many are missing?"

Geordie sidled over to me, forcing Nicholas to take a step back. "This doesn't sound good," he murmured as he slipped a hand around my waist.

The colonel was too far away for us to be able to hear the reply. A hand came up to cover his mouth, which was a bad sign. Signing off, he searched for General Merwe, swivelled his head until he saw me then was clearly undecided who he should go to first.

I solved his problem by motioning him to head for the general. My entourage and I met the two men on the edges of the battleground.

"What has happened?" Merwe demanded. His face and uniform were speckled with blood. Equally splattered, his hands were still shaking from a combination of adrenalin and terror.

"Apparently all of this," the colonel circled a hand to include the whole area, "was just a diversion." Gregor nodded as his suspicions were confirmed. "A large town was attacked while we were busy being annihilated here."

His tone was bitter and I could understand why. I'd warned him that his men would be no match for the blood crazed fledglings and I'd just been proven correct. A bare third of their troops remained. Out of two thousand soldiers, only six or seven hundred were still well enough to fight.

"Which town was attacked?" Merwe asked. His skin had taken on an unhealthy shade of grey at the news.

Pulling the map out of his back pocket, Sanderson unrolled it and pointed to a town a few hours to the north. While we had been hastening southwards to set our trap, the Second had been sidling around us, neatly avoiding it.

"How many humans lived in this town?" Luc asked. We all picked up on his usage of the past tense.

"Somewhere between four and five thousand," the general replied.

Silence descended as we contemplated the awful news. The Second had enough fledglings with him to take an entire large town in one night. In three nights, thousands of new blood thirsty monsters would emerge from wherever he'd stashed them. It would take us a whole night just to reach the town. In the meantime, he would be attacking even more people and increasing his numbers.

Ishida chose that moment to voice his displeasure. "What is your plan now, Mortis?" I met his angry gaze. "You insisted on being in charge and you have led us to disaster."

His accusation cut deeply because he was right. I had no experience at being a leader and I clearly had no idea what I was doing.

"What would you have done differently, Emperor Ishida?" Gregor asked the teen curiously. "I myself would have done almost exactly what Natalie, Colonel Sanderson and General Merwe have done." I appreciated his reminder that I hadn't made all the decisions alone.

"Do you want to be in charge, Ishida?" I asked the kid bluntly. His people threw affronted looks at me for not using his title.

Lifting his chin snottily, Ishida opened his mouth to reply, but Kokoro cut him off. "I mean no disrespect, Emperor, but that would mean disaster for us all."

General Merwe seemed to see Kokoro for the first time. He was instantly entranced by her and she wasn't even looking in his direction. "Explain your reasoning, please." Sanderson did a double take at his colleague's sudden politeness.

Kokoro touched Ishida's shoulder lightly. He allowed it, but kept his expression stony. "My visions tell me that only Mortis can save our people from total destruction."

Joshua felt it was necessary to put his two cents worth in. "I guess that means we're all screwed then." Aventius frowned at him and received a sulky, green eyed glower.

Nicholas took a step forward so he became the focus of the rough circle of people. "I think we should contact our kin at the Court and request their assistance."

My upper lip instantly curled at the idea of asking the Comtesse and her cronies for their help. Luc frowned slightly and I slid my arm through his. The last thing either of us wanted was the praying mantis to come within close range of him again. One word from her could turn him into her slave again and he would be helpless to resist her commands.

Aventius looked even more horrified at the idea than I was. Once the Comtesse caught up with him, his chances of survival were limited. His followers gathered around, offering him their silent support. Joshua patted his leader on the back, murmuring something comforting.

"While your suggestion is repugnant to us all," Gregor said, "it has merit." His tone was apologetic at causing us more distress.

Sanderson, desperate for a solution, grasped at the idea. "You're talking about the group of vampires who escaped from the cavern in Russia?" I nodded unhappily. "Do you think they will agree to assist us?"

I shrugged uneasily and Gregor had a more detailed reply. "If it is made clear just how dire our futures will become, perhaps the Comtesse may see reason."

Luc and Aventius exchanged a look of dread before they nodded after reaching a mutual agreement. "Call the mansion," Luc decided quietly. "We need to put aside our personal grievances until after we have succeeded in killing the remaining disciples and their minions."

Gregor took out his phone, but found he had no reception. Sanderson handed him a bulky phone that had a much thicker than usual antenna. I recognized it to be a satellite phone. Gregor dialled the Court mansion and was answered after a few short rings.

"You have reached the Court," a cultured female voice said in French.

"This is Gregor McIver," Gregor announced. "I wish to speak to the Comtesse about a matter of grave importance."

The voice on the other end became hushed, as if she were covering her mouth in an effort not to be overheard. "Is this about the vampire uprising in Africa?"

"It is."

After a short pause, the servant reached a decision of her own. "Please hold while I speak to the Comtesse."

None of us were surprised when the praying mantis made us wait several minutes before deigning to speak to us. At last, her voice came through the radio. "Lord Gregor, what is it you wish of me?" I wasn't the only one to cringe at the sound of her voice.

"Comtesse, thank you for taking my call." Gregor could be very formal when he had to be and proved just how diplomatic he was. "Have you heard of our fledgling kin attacking villages in Africa?" We knew she had, the servant who had answered our call had confirmed it.

"I have been advised of the matter," the praying mantis said icily.

"What you may not be aware of is that they were created by the First's ten disciples."

"What are you talking about?" she snapped.

"When Mortis killed the First, ten followers he created and later banished were freed from their forced captivity. Their leader, known as the Second, has intentions of ruling the world." Gregor's tone was dry and barely reflected our urgency.

Clearly unwilling to embroil herself or her people in our mess, the Comtesse remained silent for long enough that I thought she wasn't going to help us. "How serious is this threat?" she asked at last. I breathed a silent sigh of relief that she hadn't simply dismissed our call. I might hate her guts but, like it or not, we needed her help.

"Being the second generation of our kind, the disciples' blood is far more virulent than ours," Gregor explained. "Their fledglings are stronger, faster and more vicious than any modern day vampire's. In less than two weeks they have created hundreds, if not thousands of our kind. We have just learned that they have attacked a town containing five thousand souls."

She might be evil, but the Comtesse wasn't stupid. Grasping just how quickly the fledglings would begin to spread if left unchecked, she reached her decision. "I will send as many of my people as I can spare immediately."

Gregor allowed his relief to show. "Thank you, Comtesse. Your assistance is much appreciated."

"I wish to speak to Lord Lucentio, if he still lives," she said haughtily.

I was on the move before Luc could even start in dismay. Snatching the satellite phone out of Gregor's hand, I put on a burst of speed to get out of earshot before she could order Luc back to her side. "I'm sorry, but Luc's not available right now," I said to her in a sickly sweet tone.

"I suppose I am now speaking to the anorexic servant?" she said with utter disdain.

"You suppose correctly."

Mutual malevolent hatred flowed from both of us. "He will belong to me again," she declared softly in heavily accented English.

"He will never belong to you," I contradicted her.

"You are quite wrong about that, servant. From the first moment I saw Lucentio in Italy so long ago, he was mine. When you are nothing but dust and a memory, he will be mine again."

"Why do I get the feeling you aren't this possessive of all your sex slaves?" She'd made over a thousand of them over the millennia, both male and female. Despite the many other servants she had at her beck and call, she'd latched onto Luc like a terrier with a rat and wasn't about to let him go without a fight.

"Lucentio, as you are probably most aware by now, is special." I didn't like the suggestive smugness in her tone. "He is quite a…vigorous lover. He is the sort of bed partner that one never tires of."

Red crept into my vision and my hand tightened alarmingly on the bulky phone. "You will never get your remaining hand on him again. I promise you that."

The praying mantis lost all shred of pretend calm at my barb. "And I promise you that I will make sure that you lose everything and everyone you care about. If I can't have Lucentio, then no one will." Her tone was vicious and she reverted to speaking French in her fury.

"If any of my people are harmed by you or your servants, I will hunt you down and make you wish you had never been bitten by whatever idiot made you in the first place," I promised her in return.

I switched the phone off before she could retaliate then spent a few moments trying to regain control of my temper before heading back to my friends, allies and Nicholas.

Chapter Twenty-Three

Sanderson crooked a finger at me when I emerged from the jungle. The dead were already being seen to. The smell of burning hair and flesh was never lovely. Most of the men wielding the flamethrowers wore makeshift masks to block the fumes.

I handed the colonel back his phone when I reached him. "I've arranged for more soldiers to meet us at the last town that was attacked," he told me. Tired and splattered with blood, he looked like he could use a solid twenty-four hours of sleep.

"How many soldiers did you manage to round up?"

"Five thousand of my countrymen will be here within two days," General Merwe said. He looked just as weary and grim as his American counterpart.

"I have another three thousand of my men on the way," Sanderson said.

"I hope some of them will be sent to wipe out any caches of fledglings we might have missed."

Rubbing his forehead in frustration, he nodded. "They're bringing the equipment you suggested, as well as weaponry that should be more suitable for taking down these creatures."

"What type of weaponry?" Geordie asked suspiciously as he reached my side. The rest of my friends ambled over as well with Nicholas trailing along behind them. Both Igor and Gregor were interested in the colonel's response. Luc was more interested in my state of mind after my private conversation with the praying mantis. I smiled to show him I was fine and he relaxed minutely.

Sanderson's answer was vague. "They're brand new, highly experimental guns and explosive devices that we haven't tried out in the field as yet."

Astute as always, Gregor jumped to an accurate conclusion. "These weapons have been designed specifically to destroy our kind, I take it?"

Put on the spot, the soldier was clearly reluctant to dig himself a hole that he wouldn't be able to claw his way out of.

"We can't exactly blame them for creating weapons designed to eradicate us," I said as he struggled to find a response. Sanderson shot me a grateful glance. "After seeing the imps in action and discovering that vampires really do exist, they're naturally going to upgrade their weaponry." Hadn't any of these guys ever watched a vampire movie? Humans always came up with something nasty to take us down. We were lucky no one had whipped out an ultra violet light and tried to fry us to death.

"We should get moving," Igor interjected. "It is a long drive to our next destination."

He had a valid point and Sanderson agreed. "We have plenty of vehicles to spare if you and your people wish to borrow any of our trucks." He made the offer with only a hint of bitterness that so many of his men were now deceased.

"Thank you, Colonel," Gregor accepted graciously. He and Igor headed to the convoy to decide which mode of transportation would best suit us.

We had just over a hundred kin left and all would need suitable cover during the day. Ishida stood with his back to me, sulking about basically being just one of the gang instead of an exalted leader. Kokoro was gazing in my direction. If she sent me any thoughts, I didn't pick up on them.

Aventius had taken charge of all of the Europeans. They clustered around him, glad that someone was stepping up to keep them together. I wondered why Nicholas didn't join them and insisted on sticking with me. I almost felt sorry for him at the mistrustful glances he was receiving from pretty much everyone. My pity was squashed when he dropped his eyes to my chest.

Catching the glance, Geordie stepped in between us. When his eyes also dropped to my chest, I took a look at what was so interesting down there. An expanse of white skin and the swell of both breasts were revealed through a long cut. Embarrassed at being exposed, I was glad my breasts weren't actually popping out of the suit. "I'm going to change," I told the small group around me.

"You do not need to change on my account," Nicholas said with what was probably supposed to be a sultry smile.

"I'm not," I told him bluntly. "I just don't want you guys ogling my chest." Geordie had the grace to look abashed, but immediately ruined it with a giggle.

Luc matched his steps to mine as I headed back towards the truck where I'd left my gear. "One escort will be enough, Nicholas," he said coolly as the muscle bound vamp tried to follow us.

I didn't bother to look over my shoulder to see Nicholas' expression. It would be sulky and annoying, as usual.

"Are you all right?" Luc asked me as we jogged through the now deserted village.

"I'm fine," I lied. Stress had worked its way up my spine and into my shoulders. I was so keyed up that I was worried I'd stab anyone who accidentally surprised me.

"What did you and the Comtesse talk about?"

"You, of course." He arched a brow at my short and undetailed reply. Hearing humans ahead, I slowed down and he adjusted his pace to mine. "She wants you back because you're so good in the sack and there's apparently no one else like you in the whole world."

Studying my unhappy expression, Luc took my hand and planted a kiss on my knuckles. "I would rather die than return to her bed. I might be the best lover she has ever had, but you are the best that I have ever had."

Both of my eyebrows tried to climb up past my hairline in surprise. As far as I knew, I wasn't particularly all that talented in bed. "Why?" I had to ask.

"Because I love you," was his simple, yet touching reply.

I felt a smile lifting the corners of my mouth. "The Comtesse told me she found you in Italy. Where were you when she nabbed you?"

Thrown by the change of topic, he frowned lightly. We reached the truck and found a soldier about to drive off with it. "I'm heading back to the main group if you want a ride," the American offered. I nodded and leaped into the back of the truck. Luc joined me and I swung the door shut.

"I have long tried to forget the night that my life was torn from me," Luc said softly as he took a seat.

"You don't have to tell me if it's too painful for you."

Taking my hand again, he ran a fingertip over the cross embedded in my palm. "I was the spoiled youngest son of a wealthy land owner. My life was extremely frivolous and mainly centred around drinking and wenching."

I sniggered at the picture of barely clothed barmaids his archaic term dredged up then sobered when he shot me a look. "Go on," I invited him.

"My friends and I were in the local tavern, having a contest of who could drink the most without losing consciousness." His eyes went far away as he remembered back seven centuries. It didn't surprise me how little men had changed since he'd been turned. "I was very drunk and had to step outside to relieve myself. One moment I was standing in the alley behind the tavern and the next I was deep in the forest." I knew full well how frightening it was to black out and wake up somewhere else. I squeezed his fingers, but remained silent, afraid I'd shatter the mood if I spoke.

"It was dark, but I knew I was not alone. A small white hand suddenly reached out to touch my chest. I jerked out of reach, but found the creature behind me instead. " I could just imagine the Comtesse cruelly toying with her newest servant.

Unrolling my fingers that had clenched into a fist, Luc threaded his fingers through mine. "When I refused to run from her, she quickly tired of the game." His face tightened at the seven hundred year old memory. "I never saw her face as she bit into my flesh. It was only when Monique took me to the Comtesse's white palace that I knew it was she who had created me."

"I wish I could wipe that memory away for you," I said in a low voice. Tears were threatening, or as close as I could come to tears.

"Each night that I spend with you lessens the centuries of torment I suffered at the Comtesse's hands."

It was utterly dark in the back of the truck, but my night vision was strong enough to read his sincerity. "How would you like to lessen the torment a bit more?" I offered and waggled my eyebrows. My eyes dropped to his talented mouth and it quirked up in a smile.

Chapter Twenty-Four

Since my suit was ruined anyway, Luc tore it off me then lowered his mouth to my flesh. His teeth grazed my skin and I shuddered in both pleasure and alarm. "Be careful," I said as he teased my nipple. "One of the fledglings was stupid enough to bite me and it didn't end well for him." Unfazed, Luc sucked as much of my breast as he could into his mouth. He stopped momentarily when I clarified my point. "My blood ate through his flesh like acid."

Halting what he was doing, Luc pulled back and stared at me intently. I was afraid to meet his eyes in case I saw fright or revulsion. Taking my chin in his hand, he angled it so that our eyes met. Instead of revulsion, I saw a hint of awe coupled with trust, as if I could somehow will my blood not to kill him in such a horrible manner. "Do not fear, Natalie, I am very practiced at this."

A frown furrowed my brow at the reminder of his four centuries of sexual bondage, but it was smoothed away when his mouth came down on mine. All thought fled and my flesh hunger became paramount.

Grappling and tearing at our clothing, we were finally naked. I barely even felt the cold metal floor of the truck against my back. Luc speared me with his gaze and then with his body. Drawing my legs back, I wrapped them around his waist as he plunged inside me.

His teeth nuzzled my neck as if I was a human he was dying to feed from. He nipped me just hard enough to almost break the skin and I moaned in response. Turning his attention back to my breasts, his cold mouth closed over the tip and began to suck.

As always, I was catapulted towards the edge of ecstasy with each stroke. Luc felt my body begin to tighten and increased his speed. A human would have been torn apart at the force he used, but my moans just increased in volume and intensity.

Reaching my peak, my legs bore down and several bones snapped. Luc gave a shout of pain mingled with pleasure and collapsed beside me.

"Oh my," I heard Kokoro murmur from somewhere nearby. Geordie sniggered, then he and Ishida were howling with laughter.

Turning my head in horrified embarrassment, I discovered Luc attempting to hide his smug smile as his bones realigned themselves and popped back into place. I'd been so lost in the moment that I hadn't realized we had reached the base again.

"Kill me now," I said to him quietly. Outside, Geordie shrieked even louder with laughter.

"How do you suggest I accomplish that?" Luc asked me while trying to keep his face serious. "You are impossible to kill."

I rolled my eyes at the reminder then scrambled for a fresh set of clothing. Still embarrassed, I refused to leave the truck and face everyone who'd heard us having a not so intimate moment. Understanding my distress even if he didn't share it, Luc opened the door just wide enough to toss everyone's belongings out.

"Aren't we going to travel with you?" Nicholas complained.

"Natalie wishes some time alone," my beloved replied.

"She's just embarrassed because we heard her voicing her pleasure," Geordie said cheekily. Ishida sniggered in agreement. Igor's hand connected with the back of first one head and then the other. Silence immediately fell, but it didn't last for very long.

"You dare to strike the ruler of the Japanese empire?" Ishida asked in a hushed tone that spoke of immense rage.

"Someone needed to," Igor responded without any sign of fear in his voice.

"I am ten thousand years old! No one has ever dared to lay a finger on me before." Ishida's voice quivered just like any twelve year old that had been embarrassed in front of friends and strangers.

"Congratulations," Igor said dryly. "If you were five thousand years older, we would be the same age." My mouth dropped open at the revelation that Igor was fifteen thousand years old.

Ishida wasn't impressed with the Russian's age. "I demand your life for the insult you have given me."

Enraged by his snotty tone, I pushed the door of the truck open. Heads turned and eyes widened at whatever they saw in my face. Jumping to the ground, I stalked towards the gathering. Even Geordie quailed away from me instead of rushing to my side as he normally would.

Coming to a stop in front of the child king, I stared at him until he caved in and tilted his head back to meet my eyes. "I travelled to your island to learn from you and your people because I'd heard how wise and powerful you were."

I hadn't heard that at all, but it served as a reminder that he was supposed to be civilized. "During the four months I spent with you, I thought we had become close to being friends." His eyes flickered, but didn't drop. "Now I see the truth, that you consider us all to be beneath you. You want to kill one of my best friends because he did to you what he does to Geordie every time he acts like an idiot."

Geordie stirred at that, but Igor's glare prevented him from protesting. "I was wrong about you, Emperor Ishida." My tone was sad rather than irate as my anger leaked away. "You're not wise at all. You're just a spoiled little kid with more pride than sense."

Words trembled behind his tightly pressed lips, but Ishida refused to let them out until he'd regained control. "When this business is finished, Mortis, so are we. While I am ruler, our nations will never again be on speaking terms."

"Just give me a second to call home and tell all the other Australian vampires about your decision. Oh, wait, I'm the only one," I said with heavy sarcasm, reminding him I wasn't European. "Since I am the only one, I think I can live with your choice."

Turning on my heel, I headed back to the truck. Wisely, the humans had stayed out of our tiff. Sanderson quirked an eyebrow at me and I waved him to get the show on the road. Vehicles had been leaving at a steady pace and nearly half were already on their way to the last town that had been attacked.

Luc joined me in the back of the truck, but no one else was game to. A human took the wheel of our vehicle so I assumed our friends had found alternate transportation.

Sliding his arm over my shoulder, Luc hugged me to his side as our truck rumbled to life and lurched into motion. "You have my gratitude for saving Igor's life."

Swiping a hand beneath my un-runny nose, I struggled not to subside into tearless sobs and failed. Due to my intervention, I'd saved Igor's life, but I had also effectively destroyed relations between the Japanese and European nations forever.

"Do you know how m-m-many zombies we killed together?" I wailed when my will not to cry broke completely.

"No. How many?" Luc asked to humour me.

"T-t-thousands!" Sobbing some more, I struggled to articulate my sorrow. "I thought Ishida cared about me. I thought we were friends." Dry sobs overwhelmed me and cut off my ability to speak for a few moments. "I mean n-n-nothing to him at all!"

"I know, Nat." Patting my back soothingly, Luc did his best to comfort me. One part of me was disgusted at my behaviour. *You're acting like a schoolgirl who has just been dumped for the first time,* my subconscious observed snidely. *At least I've had boyfriends,* I thought back nastily. *What have* you *ever had?* Then I realized how completely absurd my mental conversation was.

"I just want this to be over," I said mournfully when my sobs subsided.

Luc squeezed my shoulder. "Everything will work out in the end." His smile was reassuring, but I had trouble believing it. No matter how this ended, Ishida and I would never be friends again. The two vampire nations would go back to killing each other on sight. The time I spent on the Japanese island might as well have never happened.

Chapter Twenty-Five

Our convoy stopped briefly an hour before dawn so my people could feed from the soldiers who were unlucky enough to be chosen to be our meals. Luc sent me an enquiring look and I just shook my head, pretending I wasn't hungry.

Are you going to stay in the truck with Luc and sulk for the entire journey? My inner voice sounded amused as it asked the question. *That's the plan,* I responded snidely, daring it to make an issue of my decision.

As always, my plan didn't turn out as I hoped. As the convoy rumbled to life again, the door of the truck was thrown open and several bags were tossed inside. Geordie was the first to leap inside. He sent me a stricken look, then busied himself claiming a spot in the far corner.

Gregor was the next to enter. He nodded amiably then picked up his bag. It was worn and battered and no doubt contained at least a couple of his favourite natty tweed suits.

Igor came straight to me when he entered. Dropping to his knee, he held his hand out. Put on the spot, I grasped his hand. Instead of shaking it, he simply held it. "I owe you my life," he said gravely in barely understandable English.

"You're my friend, Igor. I wasn't about to let anyone kill you just for slapping a snotty little brat up the back of the head."

Geordie snivelled, then clapped his hands over his face and subsided into tearless sobs. Igor squeezed my hand then released me. "Geordie feels responsible for your fight with the Emperor," he said gruffly.

"So he should," Nicholas said as he leaped lightly into the back of the truck. "If not for his childish antics, our nations would not currently once more be on the verge of war."

Luc joined us and closed the door, shutting off the light. "Geordie cannot be blamed for our nations being on the verge of war. They have been so for many thousands of years."

Nicholas had an answer ready. "My...Natalie had won the Japanese scum over to her side. We could finally have had peace."

I wasn't in the mood for company at all let alone to have to deal with everyone's problems. Luc nudged me with his foot and pointed to Geordie. Huddled in the corner, the teen looked utterly heartbroken and even younger than usual.

When Luc drew his foot back to deliver a not so subtle kick to my side, I fended him off and stood. I knew I was being selfish and childish, but it would have been nice to wallow in my misery for just a bit longer.

Dropping down beside Geordie, I wrapped an arm around his shoulder. He tried to cringe away, but was trapped against the truck wall and had nowhere to go. "This is all my fault, *chérie*," he said in a small, broken voice.

"No one blames you, Geordie," I told him and pulled him to my side.

"I do," Nicholas said with a sneer in our direction. He quailed under the looks Luc, Gregor and Igor gave him.

Peeking at me from between his fingers, the teenager seemed hopeful. "You are not angry with me?"

"No. I'm angry with myself." If anyone was to blame for this fiasco, it was me.

Nicholas flicked a glance at Luc then me. "If you two were able to control your flesh hunger then this collapse between relations might have been delayed."

Gee, it didn't take him long to switch the blame. "If you'd been fed the blood of four imps, you might have trouble controlling your hungers as well, Nicholas," I pointed out. "Oh, no you wouldn't because you'd be dead. Pretty much every shitty thing that has happened to me would have killed any other vampire on the planet." My voice was rising and I couldn't seem to stop it. "Who the hell are you to lecture me about controlling myself when you have no idea about the crap that I've been through?"

Ducking his head to break eye contact, Nicholas slumped his shoulders. "Forgive me, Natalie. I was merely jealous of your relationship with Lucentio. It is obvious that you care for each of your friends deeply." He snuck a glance at my face to judge my reaction before dropping his eyes again. "I have been friendless for two thousand years and crave the ability to trust others."

"Maybe if you stopped acting like such a douchebag, people might actually want to be your friend," Geordie said nastily. The hand he slipped around my waist was curled into a tight fist.

"Perhaps you are right, Geordie," the muscled vamp said almost humbly. Luc narrowed his eyes in automatic distrust and I found myself emulating him. Nicholas had rubbed everyone up the wrong way from the moment he'd become part of our group. Gaining our trust was going to require a substantial shift in his personality, possibly even a brain transplant.

Ignoring Nicholas, Geordie turned to me. "Do you think you can repair your friendship with Ishida?"

"I don't know." I didn't think it was possible, but I wasn't about to shatter his hopes and send him spiralling into a depression again. "I'll worry about that after we take down the Second and his five remaining brothers." Not to mention the horde of fledglings that would be rising over the next few nights.

When dawn struck a few minutes later, Geordie became limp and heavy at my side. I laid him down gently then moved back to my usual spot. Everyone had opted to die for the day, so I was truly alone for at least a few hours. I was in a brooding mood, so I sat beside Luc's prone form instead of lying down beside him.

What if Gregor's hunch about our fate is correct? Once we put down the latest uprising, would another one simply pop up somewhere else? It seemed counterproductive for fate to allow thousands, or possibly millions of fledglings to be created if it truly planned on eradicating us.

Then again, our numbers were slowly being whittled down with each confrontation we had with the fledgling minions. By the time we defeated the Second, would there only be a handful of us left? Could whatever it was that was pulling our strings really be that ruthless?

Settling onto my side next to Luc at last, I closed my eyes, dreading to fall asleep and see what my dreams would bring me this time.

Lying amongst the freshly drained bodies that would soon rise to become my servants, I felt the sun burning high overhead. We had spent too long in cleaning out the last town and hadn't managed to get very far before daylight had driven us underground.

Somewhere out there, death was chasing me. I could almost feel her prying at my mind, attempting to steal my very thoughts. I almost wished that she could so that she could see what I had planned for her.

One night not far from now we would meet face to face. When we did, she would be at my mercy and she would pay for killing so many of my fledglings. She wouldn't die slowly. I had plans for Mortis, plans that would make her scream if she knew about them.

Grimacing at the mental pictures the Second had conjured up, I was revolted, but didn't even come close to screaming. Sitting up, I attempted to wipe away the images of me being mauled by the still wizened old mummy. I'd seen far too many horror movies to be terrorized by his juvenile fantasies.

Igor was the first to wake when the sun went down moments later. As usual these days, he'd slept with a knife in his hand. He tucked it into the waistband of his brown woollen pants. Moments later, Gregor woke. Flicking dark blond hair back from his face, he smiled at me and nodded at Igor. Nicholas roused next, followed shortly by Luc. Geordie remained dead to the world for another few minutes.

"How is it that you wake so early when you are still so young, my Liege?" Nicholas asked.

"Because I sleep instead of falling dead when the sun comes up." My friends were used to how weird I was, but Nicholas was still struggling with it.

"How is this possible?" Staring at me curiously, Nicholas reached for a bag that someone had given him and pulled out a change of clothes. I averted my eyes while he stripped off down to his undies. Luc smiled wryly, aware that his over muscled rival was still doing his best to attract my attention.

Gregor answered the question for me, which I appreciated since I had no idea how to answer it. "No one can fathom the mysteries of Mortis. Even the Prophets were given only snatches of information about her, enough to give us hope and little more than that."

"You are familiar with the prophecies that were written about Mortis?" Switching his attention to Gregor, Nicholas pulled a green t-shirt down over his wide chest. The camouflage pants fit his butt tightly and barely contained his thighs. One of Colonel Sanderson's larger troopers must have donated the clothing to him.

Inclining his head, Gregor searched his pack for a clean jacket. "I have copies of all the Romanian Prophet's ramblings."

"I have heard only rumours about the fate that is waiting for us," Nicholas said as he sat across from me. I drew my legs back as he stretched his out towards me.

"One part that I remember stated that most of us would die once Mortis rose. If that is the case, then why are there so many fledglings being made now?"

His thoughts echoed the ones I'd had before I'd fallen asleep. Geordie woke, rubbing his eyes like a cranky kid as Gregor put his own theory forward. "Whatever it is that sends the Prophet's their visions only allows them to see so far into the future. I am unsure why these current developments weren't prophesized."

I wasn't the only one who was disconcerted that the smartest person out of all of us had no idea what was going on. Gregor cut his gaze to my face for a moment then quickly looked away. *He's lying,* I realized. *He has a theory, but he's scared to voice it.* No doubt, it would be more along the lines of the mysterious powers that created us were trying to wipe us out to make up for their mistake.

The radio I'd clipped to my belt next to a set of throwing knives crackled. "Natalie, are you awake?" Sanderson asked.

Unclipping the radio, I responded. "I'm awake."

"I've just heard that another large town is currently under attack."

Concern painted each of my companion's faces. "How far away is it from the last town that was attacked?"

"About an hour's drive."

"They've found transportation," I said with a hollow feeling in my stomach.

"Why do you think that?"

"Because I dreamt my way inside the Second's head again. He was worried they hadn't made it far enough away from the last town before being driven underground by the sun."

Ignoring the fact that I had a telepathic link to the leader of the fledgling army, Sanderson jumped straight to the main concern. "Should we head to the next town, or stop at the first to eradicate any hidden caches of fledglings?"

"Both," Gregor suggested. "We should split our forces up so some can concentrate on wiping out the caches and the rest can go on ahead."

Sanderson wasn't happy about weakening his troops, but he'd already come to the same conclusion when I repeated Gregor's suggestion. "I'll arrange for two thirds of our soldiers to meet us at the second town," the colonel said. "Do you have a preference of which teams to leave behind?"

"Leave Teams One, Seven and Eight behind." They were the teams run by Ishida, my weapons instructor and the final remaining Japanese team leader. The fourth leader had been wiped out along with the rest of our ninth team.

"Copy that," Sanderson said crisply. "Our remaining forces will continue straight through to the next town then. It will take us another seven hours to reach it."

"Emperor Ishida will not like being relegated to a clean-up crew," Gregor guessed shrewdly.

"Ask me if I care," I said with a dismissive wave of my hand.

"Do you care?" was Geordie's sly response.

"Nope."

Seeing through my charade, the teen looked sad. "You are just trying to distance yourself from him so he doesn't hurt your feelings again."

Nicholas was baffled by the insight. "Why would my...Natalie care what the Emperor of a rival nation thinks of her?"

Geordie studied Nicholas to see if he was being serious. Just last night he'd told us that he didn't have any friends. He must have had some when he'd been alive, but maybe he simply couldn't remember what it felt like to lose them. Igor shook his head to warn the teenager not to bother trying to explain it. It would probably just lead to another argument.

Chapter Twenty-Six

Seven hours later, we reached the latest town to be raided. It was much larger than the last, with nearly ten thousand people inhabiting it.

When I first jumped down from the back of the truck, I thought we were in the wrong place. No hysterical survivors were gathered on the street corners. There were no blood splatters or any other tell-tale signs of vampire attacks. I didn't spot any child sized corpses with missing hearts crumpled in the streets. Most telling, there didn't appear to have been a mass exodus from the town.

Curious heads were poked out of windows at the noise the soldiers made and were hastily withdrawn again when they saw the armed men. A police car pulled over and several officers disembarked.

General Merwe and Colonel Sanderson stepped forward to question them. "Tell us exactly what you saw," Merwe said to a badly shaken cop.

"At first, I thought my eyes were playing tricks on me," the man said in his native language. A translator converted his words into English as the man continued. "I saw half naked men and women entering a building as I drove past. I thought they must be going to a strange party, so I paid them little attention. But as I patrolled, I saw more and more of these people and realized what they must be."

"How many buildings have been infiltrated?" Sanderson queried.

"We do not know as yet," a man who had to be the police chief responded. His uniform was flashier and he wore half a dozen medals on his jacket. "We have searched over a dozen so far. All of the children were killed and their hearts were removed. The adults are missing."

I was amazed that the fledglings had kept their attacks quiet enough that the townsfolk hadn't erupted into a panic. It seemed that the survivors didn't yet know that their town had even been targeted.

It had been a blitz attack that had been well orchestrated and carried out silently. The Second had proven just how clever he was. They'd moved on hours ago and could have hit one or even two more nearby towns without anyone knowing yet. Come morning, word would begin to spread that the vamps had struck again.

"They could be anywhere by now," Colonel Sanderson muttered.

Everyone who was aware of my abilities turned to me. Without needing to be asked, I closed my eyes and sent out my senses. Almost directly beneath our feet, I detected a large number of fledglings. Almost completely drained of their blood, they would remain unconscious until they rose in three nights.

Sending out my senses further, I encountered another large group of my kind to the west. A third group was moving rapidly away to the north. I had little doubt that the vamps that had been left behind were yet another way to distract us. Without their maker to direct them, they would rise and feed blindly, unless we took care of them.

Opening my eyes again, I was about to report what I'd found when Sanderson's radio came to life. "Colonel Sanderson," one of Ishida's people said. "We have destroyed the caches of fledglings. What are our orders?"

"I can sense a large group somewhere to the west of here," I informed the colonel. "They've hunkered down and must have already found somewhere to hide for the day."

Sanderson relayed the orders for Ishida and his people to head west then turned to me. "I take it we have a welcoming party ready to wake up in a few nights somewhere in this town?"

I pointed at my feet. "We're standing on top of them right now."

"Did you sense anything else?" he asked and unconsciously shifted his feet.

"A third group is heading north rapidly." We all knew it had to be the Second. He was scurrying away from the latest mess he'd made, knowing we would have to waste time cleaning it up before we could follow him.

"The Comtesse's people are on their way to meet us," Gregor reminded everybody. "What if we ask them to try to cut the Second off?"

Sanderson grasped at the idea with the desperation he was barely managing to hide. "General Merwe and I can send a convoy ahead to attack them from behind." Merwe nodded his agreement with the plan.

I seconded Merwe's nod. "Let's do it."

Timing was everything when dealing with vampires. The night was more than half over and it would take many hours for us to catch up with the group heading north. My hope was that we would catch them with their pants down, so to speak, during daylight hours.

Even the Second was subject to the restrictions the sun forced upon us. He would have to hide somewhere and all I had to do was find his temporary lair. *Unless he has a tame human to drive him around,* I reminded myself. If that was the case then he could stay ahead of us indefinitely. Only when he stopped to make more of our kind would we be able to begin catching up to him.

Gregor took out his phone and dialled someone he knew from the Court. It was doubtful that the Comtesse had left the comfort and safety of the mansion in France, but he moved out of earshot just in case she was near. He didn't want Luc to fall into her clutches any more than I did. She'd made it clear to me that she was going to try to get him back. To avoid causing Luc any worry, I'd kept that particular piece of information to myself.

General Merwe organized some of his men to search beneath the town for the cache of fledglings. They were armed with flamethrowers and machine guns. Sanderson hastily rounded up the fastest vehicles in our convoy. A mixture of American and African soldiers were chosen for the vital mission.

Gregor returned wearing a worried frown. "The Comtesse's people are changing their course and will land somewhere to the north within the hour."

"What's wrong?" I asked.

"She has sent only fifty of her courtiers and guards to aid us," he replied in a low voice.

"She would not allow herself to be placed in jeopardy by sending more," Igor grumbled.

The last time I'd seen her, she and about a hundred of the courtiers had been held captive by their shadows in the First's cavern of doom. I actually thought it was almost generous of her to have split her forces in half. An extra fifty seasoned vampires would be a great help to whittle down the fledglings.

We climbed into a much smaller and faster armoured truck with Sanderson behind the wheel and General Merwe in the passenger seat. The windows had already been blacked out and a thick black curtain had been installed to protect us when the sun made an appearance.

There were ten comfortable seats facing sideways to choose from. I took the seat closest to the front with Luc beside me. Gregor sat across from me and Igor sat across from Luc. Geordie and Nicholas took the next pair of seats, neither was happy about being seated across from each other.

Ishida's people checked in by radio when we had been on the road for a couple of hours. They were bypassing me and were reporting directly to Sanderson now. Apparently, they had been confronted with a disciple as well as several hundred fledglings.

Ishida had lost ten people, a third of his force as well as over half of the soldiers during their battle. Instead of attacking the soldiers blindly, some of the fledglings had targeted the emperor's warriors as directed by the disciple. The newly made were beginning to regain the ability to think, which meant they would become more of a threat to us. They were far easier to deal with when they were mindless with hunger.

Just as I'd read in the Second's mind several nights ago, he was sacrificing his brothers in a bid to slow us down. His ultimate goal was to have absolute rule, but his brethren hadn't clued in to that fact yet. There had been ten to start with and their numbers were down to just five now.

I should have been confident at our chances of success, but a niggling feeling of doubt remained. The Second had outsmarted us every step of the way so far. Would he allow himself to be caught so easily now?

The sun was close when I felt the vamps that were somewhere ahead of us stop. We were still some distance away and wouldn't reach them before they found somewhere to hole up for the day. Drawing the curtain aside, I advised our chauffeur of the latest development. "They've stopped somewhere ahead. It feels like they're still a couple of hundred kilometres away."

Nodding, Sanderson didn't slow down. We were at the head of the convoy and there were very few cars on the narrow, ill kept road. The colonel concentrated on watching the road. We were in a fairly deserted area and had left the jungle behind at some point. The trees had become more scarce and the scrub more prevalent.

I wondered if we were heading towards a desert and wished I'd paid more attention to the documentaries of Africa I'd watched over the years. One thing was for sure, there were no human cities for the Second and his fleeing army of fledglings to hide in out here.

Chapter Twenty-Seven

Daylight arrived with the suffocating heat that I was used to and that no one else seemed to feel. Geordie succumbed to it instantly and slumped forward. Nicholas grimaced when the teen's face headed straight for his crotch. Igor caught his apprentice by the back of his jacket and buckled him in safely.

As always, my ability to sense my kin was weakened by the sun. I had to strain to sense them now. When I did, they weren't where I'd expected them to be.

"Sanderson!" I called. Opening the curtain would be a costly mistake for both myself and my friends, as well as Nichols. While I would survive, the rest would quickly burst into flames.

"What's wrong?" the soldier called back.

"They've turned off the road and are somewhere to the east."

Slowing down, the soldiers began searching for another road that our enemies must have taken. Sending out my

239

senses again, I found another group of our kin rapidly approaching from the north. It seemed that the courtiers and their guards had arrived.

"You'd better let your contact know they're about to pass us," I told Gregor. He immediately took out his phone, dialled and spoke into it quietly when it was answered.

General Merwe was the one to spot the point where the enemy had turned off. "I see fresh tyre tracks over there." Naturally, I couldn't see where he was pointing, but the colonel slowed then turned. The convoy of large army vehicles behind us followed. The rumble of a different engine joined us.

The courtiers, I presume. I wasn't particularly looking forward to meeting any of them. My contact with the courtiers hadn't been much fun so far. If the Comtesse had been stupid enough, or arrogant enough to turn up in person, I wasn't positive that I'd be able to stop myself from dismembering her.

"Do you see that?" Sanderson asked. Wherever we were, we'd left the road behind. We'd been bumping over rocks and branches for the past few minutes.

"It looks like a pair of trucks," General Merwe replied.

Sanderson presumably angled towards them. I wished I could see and I wasn't the only one. Gregor stared hard at the black curtain that divided us from the soldiers. Igor checked his weapons, seemingly at ease, but also periodically glancing at the curtain.

Luc twined his fingers through mine, seeking contact. Nicholas glanced at our hands, frowned and looked away. Geordie sagged against his harness with his mouth hanging open, oblivious to everything.

We came to a stop and a long line of vehicles pulled up behind us. "Are they close, Natalie?" Sanderson asked.

Taking comfort from Luc's hand in mine, I sent out my senses. Seconds later, I felt a group of fledglings nearby. "They're somewhere over to the right," I said to the two men.

Their doors opened and they left the truck. Sanderson gave orders for his and the general's men to fan out and search the area. It took the soldiers nearly ten minutes to find an opening to a cave.

I couldn't supress a shudder at the thought of descending into a cave to face my adversaries again. The cavern of doom had been wall to wall with imps. This would be a very different experience, I tried to tell myself. This cave would only hold a small number of fledglings and they would be just as unconscious as Geordie was at the moment.

Sanderson returned and stood near my window. "We've found a tunnel leading downwards. Did you and your people want to go in first, or should my soldiers go in before you?" I wondered how he expected us to leave the vehicle without being fried by the sun. "I've left you all a present beneath your seats," he added. *Can everyone read my mind,* I thought in annoyance.

Pulling open a drawer tucked behind my feet that I hadn't been aware of, I found a long black cloak inside. It came equipped with a hood so we'd be covered from head to toe. We'd have a better chance of survival than any humans if an ambush had been set. I didn't even bother to check with the others about which of us would enter the cave first.

"We'll go in first, Colonel," I called out. "Give us a couple of minutes to suit up, then have people ready to lead us into the cave." We'd need to be guided because we'd be completely blind when hidden beneath the cloaks.

In less than a minute, we had all donned our cloaks. Nicholas barely managed to squeeze into his. He had to clench his fists to make sure they were covered. I didn't like the idea of leaving Geordie behind by himself. He would be very vulnerable all alone in the truck.

Igor gave the teen the best protection he could by bundling him into a cloak and pulling the hood down over his face. If anyone accidentally opened the back door, the kid should be ok. If his cloak was removed, he'd be in serious trouble.

Someone knocked on the back door of the armoured truck. "Are you ready in there?"

"We're ready," Nicholas answered from beneath his cloak. Mine was pulled so far forward that I could only see darkness when I stood. Light flooded inside when the door was thrown open. It was too bright even with the covering of the cloak. I squeezed my eyes closed to shut out the blinding glare.

Nicholas was helped out first, followed by Igor, Gregor, Luc and then myself. The heat took my non-existent breath away. I took a step, stood on the robe and stumbled. Hands steadied me before I could fall. I didn't protest as I was lifted beneath the arms and was rushed across the ground. I caught sight of dirt, rocks and sticks beneath my dangling feet.

Welcome coolness washed over me as we entered the cave. Pushing the hood back, I nodded my thanks at the two African soldiers who had carried me to safety. They nervously nodded back and took small yet powerful flashlights out of their pockets. Sanderson's men had been issued with night vision goggles, but the African soldiers weren't as well equipped.

Steam rose from our robes as we removed them, drawing curious glances from the soldiers. I folded mine neatly and placed it near the rock wall. The others followed suit. The robes would be of no use to us in the cave and would only hinder our movements.

The tunnel was long, narrow and did indeed lead downwards. It reminded me strongly of the First's cavern. None of my companions had been inside the underground lair. Only Sanderson and some of his men shared my misgivings. At the colonel's gesture, one of his men handed his night vision goggles to the general.

"We'll wait for your signal before we follow you down," Sanderson said. This time, I wouldn't be given a head start to buy them time to free hostages. The humans would only join us once we'd ascertained that it wasn't yet another ambush engineered by the Second to decimate our forces.

I drew my swords and took the lead. Luc was right behind me, just beating Nicholas to the dubious honour of having my back. We had all armed ourselves and were as ready as we'd ever be.

Multiple fresh footprints indicated that we were on the correct path. While I could sense a number of vamps ahead, I couldn't hear any movement. Newly made, the fledglings would be out for the day. They had been lucky to find the cave to hide. There hadn't been anywhere else nearby to offer them shelter. *How did they even know the cave was here?* My thought was uneasy.

"I am beginning to wonder if the disciples have been here before," Gregor said after we'd been on the move for a couple of minutes. The tunnel had been angling steadily downwards, twisting in a narrow path.

Turning to see what he meant, I followed his pointing finger to an ancient cave painting. It was down at knee height, as if the artist had been crouching when he'd made it.

The painting was so faded with age that I hadn't even seen it when I'd walked past. It was a stick figure of a hunter holding a spear and stalking a herd of deer. I'd seen similar paintings in the First's private cave. He'd outgrown it and could no longer fit inside after turning into an eight foot tall grey monster.

We were far from where the disciples had been buried, but maybe this was the area that they had originally come from. If that was the case, then the Second and his four remaining brothers would know the cave well. I proceeded with even more caution.

The tunnel eventually levelled out and we were suddenly faced with several openings. "This reminds me of the catacombs beneath the Court mansion," Igor observed warily. Tunnels spread out in front of us as well as to the sides. All were dark and uninviting.

"We should stick together," Gregor cautioned. "To split up would be folly."

No one disagreed with him and we moved down the main tunnel in a tight unit. Some of the side tunnels I glanced down ended after a few short feet. Others stretched on into the distance. It was easy enough to know where to go. We just needed to follow the footprints.

Chapter Twenty-Eight

We continued downward along the gradually widening tunnel until it opened into a circular area. Many paths branched off from it, but the rows of bodies piled in the centre immediately caught our attention. Over a hundred freshly drained humans lay waiting to rise as the undead.

Gregor eyed the small mob suspiciously. "This cannot be all that is left of the disciple's fledglings."

"Speaking of the disciples," Luc murmured, "where are they?"

We all glanced around uneasily, expecting attack from any direction. I'd sensed far more than this paltry number of my kin fleeing from us. *This is a trap,* my subconscious warned me almost unnecessarily. I acknowledged the message with a mental nod.

Thousands of years had passed since anyone had inhabited the cave. There were still faint traces of cooking fires where rocks had been gathered in small circles. More paintings decorated the walls, depicting the history of the people who had once dwelled inside. If I didn't have such pressing matters to attend to, I would have been fascinated by the artwork.

Igor moved to take a step closer to the collection of bodies, but I put a hand on his arm to stop him and unclipped my radio. "Colonel, can you send some of your soldiers down here with their flamethrowers? We found a bunch of fledglings that need to be eradicated."

"They're on their way," Sanderson replied.

Motioning the others to stay where they were, I cautiously walked towards the bodies. Only when I reached the outer edge did I notice one that was far older and more wizened than the others. A disciple lay unconscious directly in the centre of the mob. It probably wasn't very sporting to behead him while he was defenceless, but I was going to do it anyway.

Stepping over the prone forms, I came to a stop beside the disciple. He had fleshed out considerably after consuming a steady diet of fresh blood. His skin tone was still slightly greyish and he looked a bit ravaged around the face, but otherwise he fit right in amongst the throng. The only thing that set him apart was the tattered loincloth around his waist. Most of these humans wore nightclothes, indicating that they had been snatched from their beds from the towns rather than one of the more primitive villages.

I lowered a sword and prepared to skewer the disciple. His eyes popped open just as Luc shouted a warning. I didn't realize the disciple wasn't alone until a spear pierced the top of my head. A second disciple landed lightly in front of me, ramming the weapon deeply into my skull.

My vision went blank only momentarily from the injury to my brain. When it cleared, the disciple who had been pretending to be unconscious was on his feet. He swung his blade at me and I was too slow to react. It cut through both my neck and the spear, severing them both.

As Luc roared in rage and my head spun through the air, I split my consciousness. Possessing my body, I reached out and grabbed the closest disciple by the arms. Before I could unleash the holy marks and melt his arms down to stumps, Luc was there. His sword flashed out and it was the disciple's turn to have a flying head. Unlike me, he didn't survive the blow.

The other disciple turned tail and ran with Nicholas and Igor on his heels. Gregor approached my head and crouched beside me. "Would you like me to remove the haft of the spear?" he asked with a slight grimace.

Rolling my eyes up, I couldn't see the wooden shaft sticking out of my head, but I could feel it running through the bone, brain and other stuff inside my head. "Yes, please."

He yanked it out then picked my head up carefully. My body waited patiently until Gregor was close then reached out. He put my head in my hands and they lifted it up and placed it back on my shoulders. With the usual flash of pain, I was whole again.

Sanderson, Merwe and a team of their men arrived in time to see the performance. Most of the soldiers turned interesting shades of green when they saw the rest of the spear still sticking out of me. The spearhead had exited through my right side and black ooze sluggishly dripped from the tip.

"Do we even want to know how that happened?" the colonel asked.

"Trust me when I say you do not," Luc replied. He circled me, trying to figure out how to extract the spear. "You will need to lie down so that I can pull it out," he decided.

Neither of us was looking forward to the extraction process, but I couldn't leave it in there. We moved into a side tunnel for privacy and Gregor stood guard to keep any curious onlookers away.

Lying down on my back, I kept as still as possible while Luc grasped the haft just above the blade. "Are you ready?" he asked.

"I'm-" before I could finish my answer, he yanked it out in one long, smooth motion. "Ready," I croaked once the pain had faded.

Luc's jaw tightened at the sight of the ooze coating the spear. I was just glad that I had been attacked instead of one of the others. *The Second planned the whole thing. He knew I'd be the one to fall for the trap.* If I hadn't been the marvellous and mysterious Mortis, the ambush would have been fatal.

I took the hand Luc offered and he helped me to my feet. He dropped the spear at the edge of the pile of bodies. A soldier turned his flamethrower on the wood, burning it along with the freshly drained corpses. I didn't blame him for his caution. Not after I'd seen what my blood had done to the fledgling that had accidentally bitten me.

Igor and Nicholas returned a moment later, looking dejected. "The disciple managed to escape," the over muscled one said before Igor could offer an explanation.

Cutting an annoyed glance at Nicholas, Igor elaborated. "It is as we suspected. He knows these caves well and led us on a merry chase."

Nicholas cut in again, keeping his attention squarely on me and ignoring the others. "He jumped into a hole and we heard a splash as he hit water far below. I did not think it would be wise to follow him without backup."

Igor rolled his eyes, looking so much like his apprentice for a moment that I nearly smiled. Then the implications sank in. This whole thing had been yet another diversion. We hadn't seen any sign of the Second, or the older fledglings that he'd amassed.

If I had to guess, I'd bet that he hadn't stopped here at all and had continued on his northward path. He'd sent his two brothers on a mission to distract us, hoping we would kill them both. One was down and now there were only three more rivals standing between him and a clear run at world domination. There would be only two once we dealt with the other disciple in the cave.

Sending out my senses, I located the fleeing vamp somewhere beneath us. I widened my search, but the Second had moved too far out of my weakened range to be able to detect him.

My friends, and Nicholas, gathered around as I strode over to Colonel Sanderson and General Merwe to deliver the bad news. "One of the disciples escaped and is somewhere deeper in the cave below us."

"We can't just leave him down there. He'll start creating new vampires as soon as we leave. What is our best course of action?" Sanderson asked.

"I'll go after him," I offered. Being the only one with the ability to sense where the disciple was hiding, I was the best person for the job.

"I will go with you, my...Natalie." Nicholas offered me a smile and dropped his eyes to the tear in my suit where my white skin peeked out.

Luc bristled at my side, but had too much dignity to argue with the newbie in front of the humans. Frankly, I'd be far less worried about Nicholas dying than I would be if Luc were to accompany me.

"Ok," I said and Luc went still beside me. I'd actually been planning on going in alone, but maybe it would be a good idea to take someone with me. As far as I knew, Nicolas only wanted to sleep with me and didn't have any plans to try to kill me.

Drawing Luc aside until we were out of earshot, I explained my reasons for leaving him behind. "Look, the only reason I'm taking Nicholas along is that I'm sort of hoping the disciple will kill him for me."

Luc's stiffness lessened slightly and one corner of his mouth lifted. "That would be a welcome turn of events," he conceded.

"Make sure none of the soldiers accidentally sets any of you on fire while I'm gone," I told him.

"Do not worry about us, Ladybug." He bent and kissed my light scowl. I still wasn't fond of that particular nickname.

"Take this," Sanderson said and indicated a length of light nylon rope that one of his men held out. "It sounds like you'll need it."

"Thanks." I slung the rope over my shoulder then made sure the radio was clipped to my belt. I doubted I'd have to call for reinforcements, but it was better to be safe than sorry.

Nicholas shot a smug look at my one true love then indicated for me to precede him. With a wave at my friends and a wink at Luc, I took the tunnel that Igor and Nicholas had disappeared down earlier.

Chapter Twenty-Nine

Feeling Nicholas' eyes on me, I stopped to let him lead the way once we'd disappeared from sight. I felt better with my eyes on his back rather than having him skulking behind me, which just proved how little I trusted him.

He unerringly led me to the hole that the disciple had jumped into. Peering down, I could just make out the water below. Nicholas slid the rope from my shoulder, coming very close to brushing his fingertips across my breast as he did. I sent him an annoyed glance, which he blithely ignored.

Securing the rope to a stalagmite, he dropped it through the hole. The tail end hit the water with a tiny splash. Nicholas insisted on going first and squeezed through the opening. He had to work his shoulders from side to side before he managed to make it through. I was tempted to help him by stomping on his head, but he slid through the opening before I could offer my services. I waited for him to reach the bottom before following him.

Sliding down the rope, I stopped just above the water and examined the area. We were in a slender chamber that narrowed even more at both ends. Nicholas stood waist deep in the underground creek, already shivering from the chilly water.

Not thrilled with the idea of getting wet, I aimed for land only a few feet away. Jumping clear of the rope, I landed on the bank. The creek was roughly ten feet wide and we could leap over it easily.

Clambering onto the bank, Nicholas' teeth chattered until he clenched them shut. "Try to find the disciple's tracks," I told him and started casting around for footprints. It would have been quicker to just send out my senses, but it was an excuse to put some distance between myself and my unwanted helper.

This side of the tunnel was clear, so I crossed to the other side. Nicholas joined me and we split up to search in opposite directions. I found scuff marks where someone had recently climbed out of the creek near the end of the tunnel. The body of water narrowed and so did the walls. There was just enough room to walk beside the creek without falling in.

Nicholas came at a run when I beckoned him. The tunnel was short and opened into a confusing labyrinth of caves. My senses pinpointed a lone vampire in the distance and I indicated that we should move slowly. If the Second had been here, he would have felt me closing in on him. This disciple had no idea at all that we were there and was oblivious to our presence.

When we were so close that I could hear a fire crackling, I stopped. Using hand signals, I directed Nicholas to circle around behind the unsuspecting disciple. Waiting for a couple of minutes to allow my unwanted companion to shift into place, I drew my swords and entered a tiny, low tunnel. Bending almost double, I crept forward and beheld my prey.

Still unaware that he was being hunted, the disciple huddled beside a small fire. He fed wood that was so old it was almost petrified into the flames. No vampire in their right mind would fall asleep beside any kind of blaze, no matter how small it was. After his dunking in the creek, he was doing the only thing he could to raise his body temperature again.

I spied Nicholas directly opposite me. He waved to signal that he was ready and the disciple caught sight of the movement. For a moment, he was still as he assessed the danger. Then he was on his feet and was on the move. I'd thought the disciple I'd chased through the jungle had been fast. He had nothing on this guy. Snatching up a knife that lay beside him, the disciple threw it.

Nicholas gave a cry of pain when the blade hit him. My heart gave a tiny lurch of hope that he would no longer be my problem to deal with. Turning, the disciple started when he saw me coming for him and scooped up another blade.

Standing on opposite sides of the fire, we circled it slowly, searching for signs of weakness. "How did you survive my spear strike?" he asked me almost casually in his ancient native language.

"I'm Mortis. Stuff like that has no effect on me."

"I do not understand your words," the disciple said with a frown. "Why do you not speak my language?"

I opened my mouth to reply and only realized he was trying to distract me after he flicked a hand at my face in a pretend attack. Falling for the ruse, I shifted slightly and a blade was suddenly sticking out of my chest.

"The Second warned me that you would be difficult to kill," he told me as I pretended to stagger back a step. "He was foolish to think that a mere woman could possibly best a true warrior in battle."

Reaching me, his hand closed around the hilt of his dagger. He prepared to pull it out, presumably to turn me into a slushy puddle. My hand moved with startling speed and the tip of my sword was suddenly sticking out of his back. "You should have listened to him," I said and slid the blade out.

The disciple's expression of astonishment lasted only for a moment before he was reduced to a watery puddle.

Wiping my blade clean on his tattered loincloth, I crossed my fingers and entered the tunnel where Nicholas had fallen. I was immediately disappointed to see he was still in one piece. Then I saw the blade in his chest. The disciple had been very skilled with throwing knives. He'd managed to stab us both in the heart.

Dropping to my knees beside Nicholas, I put my hand on the blade. I almost groaned out loud in disappointment when his eyes fluttered open. "How bad is it, my...Natalie?" he asked in a weak voice.

As far as I knew, I was the only vampire who had ever been able to survive a wound to the heart. Bending to take a closer look, I widened the tear in his borrowed t-shirt. I hid a frown when I saw that the blade hadn't scored a direct hit after all. "Can vampires survive if their hearts have been nicked, but not punctured?" I still knew surprisingly little about our kind.

Shaking his head, Nicholas grimaced in pain. "I do not know." Moving slowly and carefully, he placed his hand on mine then put it on the blade again. "Would you grant me one wish before you pull the blade free, my Liege?"

Wary, I felt a sense of déjà vu wash over me and suspected what was coming. "What wish?"

"Would you give me the honour of a kiss?" His big black eyes did their best to be pleading, but he was too arrogant to successfully pull it off.

"Geordie already tried that one on me once and I almost fell for it," I told him. "I'm not going to be that dumb twice."

His eyes widened when I pulled the blade free. Doubling over, he clutched the tear in his flesh and came close to swooning from the pain. Disappointment flooded through me again when he straightened up and glared at me. Apparently, other vampires could survive a minor wound to their heart.

"We should head back to the others," I said and stood.

I bent to brush dirt off my knees and then I was suddenly yanked upright and was propelled back against the rock wall. Nicholas' face was tight with rage as he glared down at me.

Finally, we get to see the real Nicholas, my subconscious thought with satisfaction. "You spread your legs for Lucentio yet *I* am not good enough for you! What does he have that I do not?"

"Lord Lucentio has many things you don't," I replied coolly, pretending that the hands biting into my shoulders didn't hurt.

"Name one," he grated.

"I'll name three," I countered. "He has compassion, honour and the capacity to love. You have none of the above."

Staring at me furiously, Nicholas changed his grip so that it became less crushing. A look of cold calculation flittered across his face, altering it from being ridiculously handsome to almost ugly. "*Lord* Lucentio is a monster just like me. He has merely learned how to make your flesh hunger rise whenever he wishes. Any vampire with skill could do the same."

I was a bit slow and only realized that Nicholas intended to kiss me the instant before his lips touched mine. The contact lasted for only a moment before my lust woke. Unfortunately for Nicholas, it wasn't quite the lust he'd intended to arouse.

Orange light burst from my eyes as my battle lust was ignited. Using all the strength that being Mortis gave me, I shoved him backwards. Nicholas hit the wall, bounced off it and went down to one knee. He'd been bigger than everyone else for so long that he'd forgotten what it felt like to be physically afraid of someone.

Moving with speed that a human eye could never hope to follow, I clamped a hand around his throat and lifted him off the ground. His toes barely brushed the dirt at first. They settled on the ground again when I brought him in close enough that our noses were almost touching. "If you every try that again, I will cut your heart out."

Flinching back either from my blazing eyes, or from my rage, Nicholas was unable to speak. His mouth opened, but no words came out. I realized I was crushing his vocal cords and eased up on the pressure. "You have my word that I will never touch you again, my Queen," he forced out.

Dropping him to his knees, I stalked out of the tunnel, uncaring if he followed me or not. *The sheer arrogance of men astounds me,* I thought as I made my way back to the creek. *He actually thought he could force me to lust after him.*

Don't kid yourself, my inner voice said with more seriousness and less sarcasm than I was used to. *You know what his true intentions were. He tried to force you, period. I doubt he cared whether your flesh hunger rose or not.* I knew my alter ego was right and it gave me a sick feeling inside. *I thought I was supposed to be his queen.* Nicholas had a strange way of showing fealty to someone he repeatedly claimed to be his ruler.

Leaping over to the rope, I managed to wet only the toes of my boots, but kept the rest of myself dry. I climbed to the top quickly then watched Nicholas emulate me and leap over to the length of nylon. For a long moment, I debated whether to cut the rope and leave him behind.

You know the old saying, my subconscious whispered, *keep your friends close, but your enemies closer.* Since my inner self was far wiser than me, I listened to its advice.

Chapter Thirty

My friends, and the two leaders of the armies were waiting for us when we returned. "Did you get him?" Colonel Sanderson asked.

I nodded, much to everyone's relief. "He's toast."

Disappointment flickered across Luc's face as Nicholas came into view behind me. He noted the hole in the green t-shirt and raised an eyebrow. "It seems you came very close to death, Nicholas."

Nicholas flicked a quick look at me, then forced a smile. "It is nothing. Barely a scratch."

"What happened?" Luc murmured when I reached his side.

Telling him the whole story would result in an immediate brawl and I wasn't in the mood to deal with the drama. I went with a half-truth instead. "The disciple was very fast and very handy with throwing knives. He nicked Nicholas in the heart."

Gregor flicked his hair back in a gesture that I was beginning to realize masked his true feelings at times. He clapped the muscled vamp on the back. "You were very lucky to have survived, Nicholas. Most vampires die from even the smallest wounds to their hearts."

Looking even more shaken now, Nicholas dropped his eyes to the ground. "I was very fortunate," he agreed.

"I take it that we're done here?" General Merwe declared more than asked. I took in the ashy remains that had once been humans and would have turned into fledglings if we hadn't stopped to roast them. "Do you have any idea where the rest of these creatures are headed?" he asked me.

I shook my head to indicate I had no idea. "They must have split up at some stage without me knowing it. The Second and his last two fellow disciples could be headed anywhere by now."

"Can't you sense them?" Sanderson queried.

"I can only sense our kind at fairly close range during the day. I'll have to wait until nightfall to try to find them." I felt inadequate under the soldier's stares. I was the legendary Mortis and I wasn't measuring up to the hype.

Igor came to my defence. "At least Natalie *can* sense them when night falls. Without her, you would be forever running after the Second without a hope of ever catching up to him."

Grudgingly nodding his agreement, Sanderson began to round up his troops. Privately, I thought Igor had summed up our current situation quite nicely. We had yet to come face to face with our quarry. The only time we'd glimpsed him had been from a distance and only because he had allowed us to. I was beginning to feel like a puppet being led around by the strings.

Back at the entrance to the cave, we donned our cloaks and were led back to the armoured truck. The door was slammed shut once we were safely inside and we stripped the heavy black fabric off. Geordie was still slumped in his harness, covered from head to toe. Igor tugged the teen's hood back, but left the cloak on him.

Without concrete information about where the Second was headed, the colonel took a guess and kept heading north.

Nicholas had been very quiet since our confrontation in the cave. He strapped himself into his seat and succumbed to unconsciousness without a word. Gregor and Igor followed him into oblivion and then it was just Luc and I awake in the back of the truck.

"What happened while you and Nicholas were alone?" Luc asked me.

He wasn't going to be put off with a half-truth this time. "I killed the disciple and found Nicholas with a knife in his chest. He pulled a Geordie and tried to get me to kiss him."

"You didn't fall for it," was his shrewd guess.

"Nope."

Studying me, he took my hand. "Tell me the rest, Natalie."

Hating the fact that he could read me so easily, I checked to make sure everyone really was asleep and that they weren't just faking it and listening in. "He kissed me and tried to make my flesh hunger rise." I debated about telling him the rest then decided I had to tell someone and it might as well be my beloved. "He wasn't going to take no for an answer."

"If you weren't Mortis and lacked your current strength, what would have been the outcome?" Luc's expression was serene, but a muscle in his jaw jumped, indicating rage lurked just below the surface.

I didn't want to say the word and glanced down at our joined hands. "Rape," I finally said quietly.

Luc's grip became crushing and it was my turn to have broken bones for once. Releasing me, Luc's expression was stricken. "I am sorry, Natalie. I did not mean to cause you pain."

My pain had been meagre and the bones had already knitted back together again. Waving away his apology, I took his hand firmly. "Don't worry about it. I owe you more than a few broken bones."

"I would very much like to kill Nicholas." Luc's tone was hushed so the humans couldn't overhear us.

"Yeah, me too." I leaned forward and examined the topic of our conversation. His bulging arms were crossed and his beautiful face was slightly cranky. "Let's hold off on that until after we meet the courtiers the Comtesse sent. I can't wait to see their faces when they realize he's defected to our side."

Mustering a small smile, Luc inclined his head slightly. "He will remain alive for now, but I cannot promise you that he will remain so indefinitely." He leaned over, gave me a brief kiss then clipped up his harness and subsided into an unnatural slumber.

Afraid that if I allowed myself to fall asleep, I might miss the Second or his two remaining cronies, I stayed awake. I periodically sent my senses out whenever we came close to human civilization. Each time we did, my senses came up empty.

Night fell and my companions began to rouse. Gregor waited for Geordie to finally join us in wakefulness before proposing his latest plan. "Natalie, could you send your senses out as far as possible in an attempt to locate the Second and his people?"

"I can, but he'll probably sense me sensing him and will most likely make a run for it." I'd already had that idea and had been unwilling to try it.

"At this point, it really doesn't matter where he runs to as long as we can find him," Gregor decided.

General Merwe drew the curtain back, having overheard our discussion. "What are you planning, vampire?" He was naturally suspicious of any of our kind after his dealings with the fledglings and their masters.

"I think we should stop checking every town the Second has been through and wasting time searching for hidden caches of fledglings. I believe our best course of action would be to continue on until we catch up to their main force," Gregor explained.

Sanderson nodded thoughtfully. "We can delegate some of our troops into clean-up crews, but focus most of our soldiers on pursuit."

"Try to locate them, Natalie," Gregor urged.

Closing my eyes, I sent out my senses. Behind us, I found several small groups of our kind. Ishida and his people had just caught up to our convoy. Sending my senses north, I eventually picked up on a much larger number of vamps.

Widening the search even more, I found no other signs of our kind. "They're still together, somewhere far to the north," I said as I opened my eyes.

Gregor's phone rang and he fished it out of his pocket. Everyone but the humans heard the semi-hysterical female courtier on the other end. "You did not inform the Comtesse that you have joined forces with the Japanese scum!" she accused.

"I informed her of how dire our situation was," Gregor replied blandly. "Our Japanese *allies*," he stressed the word slightly, "have been instrumental in eradicating the threat of fledgling invasion."

"I demand we meet face to face immediately to discuss our terms if you wish for our continued help," the courtier said coldly.

Gregor searched our faces and found weary acceptance. Nicholas looked nervous at the idea. I elbowed Luc in the side and he nodded to indicate he'd caught the ex-courtier's alarm. "We'll ask the Colonel to stop the convoy so that we can discuss your issues," Gregor said then hung up.

"What's going on?" Sanderson asked as he eased the truck to a stop on the side of the road.

"I am afraid that we must have a private meeting with our colleagues for a few minutes," Gregor said.

Sanderson raised his eyebrow at me, knowing he would have a better chance of receiving a straight answer. "The Europeans and Japanese hate each other and the courtiers have just realized that Ishida and his warriors are with us. They've demanded a meeting so they can gripe about it. You might as well make yourselves comfortable because this will probably take a while," I warned both men.

Geordie stood and realized he was wearing a cloak. He plucked at it curiously. "What on earth happened while I was asleep?"

"You do not want to know," Igor said gruffly as he shuffled past. Nicholas was reluctant to leave the armoured truck, but had little choice. He cast an unhappy look in my direction then gracefully leaped to the ground. He was a fool if he thought he'd get any help from me if things went badly between him and the new arrivals.

Luc offered me his hand to help me down, treating me like the royalty Nicholas professed I was. We twined our fingers together as Geordie jumped down beside us. He quickly stripped off the cloak and threw it back inside the truck. "I have a feeling that this meeting is not going to be much fun, *chérie*," the teenager said in a low voice.

Linking my arm through his, I walked between Luc and Geordie towards the growing gathering of vampires. "So do I. But I bet it's going to be interesting."

Chapter Thirty-One

Before we'd even reached the gathering, the arguments had already begun. The vampires had split into three distinct groups; the Comtesse's people, Ishida and his warriors and Aventius and his random European rabble. I could barely see the Japanese ruler behind the guards that had moved to surround him. Weapons had been drawn by almost everyone, but no blows had been exchanged as yet.

"You should have remained on your primitive island," spat a courtier without any actual saliva leaving her lips. Tall, thin, blonde and beautiful, she wore a clingy red dress that was low cut to the point of her nipples almost showing.

The French vampires wore expensive clothing that flattered their figures. Even the men were well dressed. Thirty-five members of the group were courtiers. I could tell by their stiff stances and utilitarian clothing that the remaining fifteen were guards.

"You call us primitive?" one of Ishida's warriors responded. "We have heard of what passes for entertainment in your circles. We are above such childish past times." His tone was insulting and was met with an immediate uproar.

"Please," Aventius stepped forward with his hands held out. "We must try to work together."

"Why should we listen to you, traitor!" the blonde whirled on him to say. "You have relinquished any authority you held over us when you fled from the Court."

"Anna-Eve, this is not about me," the former Councillor said.

"You should try shutting your mouth and listening for five seconds so you can grasp what's going on here," Joshua said to the blonde unhelpfully. Aventius hastily drew his young protégé backwards at the evil glare she sent him.

Glancing at my friends, I saw that none of them were about to step in to quell the fight. Heaving an internal sigh, I cleared my throat pointedly.

Anna-Eve bit back the tirade she was about to unleash and blinked at me. Giving me a head to toe inspection, her pretty mouth lifted in a sneer. Then she noticed Nicholas and switched her attention to him. "So, the Comtesse was correct in her assumption that you had deserted us, Nicholas." Clearly, none of the courtiers liked him. Neither did any of the guards, judging from their expressions of distaste. *That's Nicholas for you, winning friends everywhere he goes with his sterling personality.* Turning back to me, she sneered at my outfit. "What are you supposed to be?"

"I'm supposed to be a manager of a clothing store in Brisbane," I replied evenly. "Unfortunately, in reality I'm Mortis."

Finally recognizing me, the blonde eased back on her aggression. "As I informed Lord Gregor, we were not expecting the Japanese scum to be involved in this affair."

Ishida's people bristled at the insult. I held up a hand to forestall their outbursts. "Every vampire on the planet is involved in this, whether we like it or not. As Aventius said, we have to work together to fix this."

Anna-Eve tossed her head, sending her long golden hair flying over her shoulder. "We refuse to be teamed up with those who are so inferior to us."

Geordie had something to say about that. "You have the nerve to call the Japanese inferior when you treat your food and servants like dogs." His indignant gaze raked across the courtiers. After two centuries of abuse and neglect, he was harbouring a sizable hatred for them. "Emperor Ishida and his people treat their humans and servants with respect and kindness. It is *you* who are inferior to them."

One of the male courtiers lunged forward with his sword, intending to skewer the teen. Igor yanked Geordie out of harm's way as I stepped forward to intercept the blow. My blades were in my hands and were moving almost of their own accord. One deflected the blade and the other came to rest just above his heart.

"You said that we have to listen to your terms before you'll agree to help us," I said to Anna-Eve as her crony stumbled back from my blade.

"I did," she replied coolly.

"I really don't give a crap," I told her bluntly. "You can take your terms and shove them where the sun doesn't shine."

"That would be up your backsides," Geordie said helpfully to those who hadn't heard the term before and were confused.

The blonde opened her mouth for a scathing comeback, but I overrode her. "Your ruler sent you to help us because, as big a bitch as she is, she realizes how much danger the world will be in if we don't act."

"You do not need to be so crude to get your point across," Anna-Eve said almost primly.

Turning in a circle, I met as many eyes as I could before coming to a stop in front of the courtiers again. "Here are *my* terms. You will work together as a team without insults or complaints or I will personally end your lives. Once this threat is over, you can go back to sniping at each other and killing each other for all I care. While you are here, you will do as I say, or you can leave right now and possibly doom us all."

Every single one of them was aware of the prophecies that had been written about me even if they had been written by different authors. All knew that their fate hinged on me and the decisions that I would make.

Proving that she could think clearly when she had to, Anna-Eve bowed her head in submission. "We will follow your lead, Mortis." Her fellow courtiers shifted uneasily, but they didn't protest. The guards were used to following orders without question. They relaxed slightly now that order had been restored.

I turned to Ishida and his entourage shifted enough so that I could see their leader. "Are you with us, Emperor?"

For a moment I thought Ishida was going to pack his bags and leave. At last, he gave me a grudging nod. My relief that we'd managed to come to an agreement relatively easily evaporated when Anna-Eve spoke again. "Three things need to be addressed once this business is taken care of."

I didn't like her smug tone and turned to face her again. "What would they be?"

"He must die." Her finger pointed to Aventius. Joshua took a step forward, but the aged former Councillor stopped him with a hand on his shoulder and murmured something into his ear. "The second traitor will be brought back to face the Comtesse." This time her finger pointed at Nicholas. Her fellow courtiers eyed the muscled one with satisfaction. A few fingered their weapons as if they wanted to put an end to him right now. I knew exactly how they felt.

I hardly even needed to ask my question. "And the third?"

Anna-Eve's gaze moved to Luc and a tiny smile appeared. "One way or another, Lord Lucentio will also face the Comtesse's justice." She switched her attention back to Nicholas and his shoulders hunched.

Luc kept his expression serene, but I read his dread as we headed back to the armoured truck. "That's never going to happen," I told him quietly when we were out of their range.

"We will not let them take you," Geordie said. Igor nodded to offer his support.

Gregor agreed immediately. "Of course we won't."

"What about me?" Nicholas said almost forlornly. "Will I just be left to face my fate alone?"

I looked back over my shoulder at him. "If there's one thing I've learned, Nicholas, it's that you can't fight fate." My smile was wintry and he withered beneath it.

Chapter Thirty-Two

Colonel Sanderson and General Merwe waited for us beside the armoured truck. They both wore almost identical expressions of concern. "Is everything all right with your people?" the colonel asked.

"No," I replied honestly. Things were far from all right, but I didn't want to waste time trying to explain vampire politics. "But they've agreed to work together until we finish this."

"Do we continue north?"

"Yes. I'll let you know if they change direction."

Back into the truck we went with Sanderson behind the wheel. Nicholas sat as far away from the rest of us as possible. Crossing his arms, he subsided into a sulk. Geordie snatched glances at him, plainly dying to make a snide comment. One glare from Igor curbed his childish impulse.

With little to do but engage in conversation, I found myself contemplating the grizzled Russian. As always, my curiosity overwhelmed common courtesy and I voiced a question. "Are you really fifteen thousand years old, Igor?"

Checking the edge of a knife, he flicked his eyes to mine and nodded. "You are going to pester me with questions about my origins, aren't you?"

I gave him my most brilliant smile. "You bet."

Everyone was curious, even if they were trying to hide it. Gregor crossed his legs and tented his fingers, but I caught the gleam in his eye. Luc slid his arm over my shoulder and hugged me to his side, but he kept his attention on his old friend. Geordie turned sideways to stare at his mentor expectantly. Even Nicholas stirred slightly from his sulk.

Giving a silent sigh, Igor put his knife away and crossed his arms. He stared past me at the blacked out window. "The world was a different place when I was a human. It was sparsely populated and months could pass before a stranger could wander near our caves."

I tried to imagine Igor dressed in animal skins and living in a cave and the image came to me with surprising ease. *Come to think of it, he still looks a bit like a caveman sometimes.*

"One freezing winter's night, a stranger did arrive." Deep in his reverie, Igor's hands clenched into fists. "I was walking home from a hunt just after dark when I noticed a man. He was too far away to see his face, yet I could sense that he was watching me."

Remembering my first encounter with Silvius, I shuddered in sympathy. A human's first meeting with a hungry vampire could be a terrifying ordeal, unless they were bamboozled into forgetting about the meeting. Encountering a vampire who intended to make you into the undead was a far more traumatizing experience.

"I felt his eyes on my back as I hurried home. My woman was concerned when I tied the skins tightly across the cave opening. I lied and told her that I had seen a wolf to put her mind at ease." He conjured up a smile so bleak that it nearly broke my undead heart. "I do not think that she believed me."

Geordie's eyes were round. The thin sliver of blue that still showed seemed very bright. Questions wanted to burst from him, but he manfully kept them in and let his mentor tell the tale at his own pace.

"Uneasy at the thought of a stranger lurking around, I checked on my children and was comforted to see them both asleep. I kept my spears close when I lay down to sleep, thinking they would be enough to keep my family safe." Black and full of long-suffering pain, his eyes met mine. "I was wrong."

I could see how hard it was for him to tell his story and I was sorry I'd asked. But now that he'd started, he had to continue or Geordie and I would pester him until he told us the rest.

"The vampire waited until the middle of the night before he burst into the cave. It was too dark to see him properly, but some part of me knew what he was. There had been tales from nearby families of a blood drinker on the loose, but no one had really believed it."

Early vampires had done a pretty good job of remaining inconspicuous. Much better than I had, anyway. As Geordie had not so subtly noted, I'd managed to blow our specie's cover in the first six months of becoming the undead.

Igor continued with his story. "I stabbed the man in the stomach with my spear, but it had no effect on him. He hit me on the head and when I woke, it was to find myself in a cold, dark place." I'd been in a similar situation and could empathize with the fear he must have felt. "The creature was waiting for me to wake before he fed from me and forced me to drink his blood. After my three nights of torment were over, he took me out to feed for the first time."

Shifting his gaze to meet my eyes, he lowered his voice so the humans wouldn't be able to overhear him. "I did not even realize that it was my own woman and children that I had drained to death until days later and my blood hunger had been sated." Dropping his gaze to his lap, his shoulders slumped. "It took centuries before I began to feel remorse for my actions."

Holding back sobs, Geordie reached out and patted his mentor on the shoulder. "It was not your fault, Igor. None of us can control ourselves when we are first made."

Gregor stirred and looked at me slyly. "Until Natalie came along, that has always been the case."

Shrugging off the remark, I urged Igor to continue his story. "What happened to your maker?"

A crafty expression stole across Igor's face. "I remained subservient to him for over ten thousand years before he died in an unfortunate accident."

Luc narrowed his eyes suspiciously. "Did you somehow engineer this 'accident'?"

Grinning widely now, Igor gave a short nod.

Geordie was confused and he wasn't afraid to show it. "None of us can survive killing our masters." Gregor sent another sly look in my direction, but refrained from pointing out again that I'd defied the odds.

"Technically, it was the fall that killed my maker," Igor corrected the teenager. "I simply spooked his horse into falling over the edge of the cliff we'd been riding alongside."

"How did you figure out how to dispose of your master?" Gregor asked, impressed by the Russian's ingenuity.

"I questioned every vampire we encountered and drew my own conclusions from their answers." Igor looked understandably pleased with himself.

"You couldn't possibly know if it would work or not," I pointed out. "You took a massive chance by spooking his horse over the cliff."

Igor's shrug was surprisingly eloquent, but he summed his feelings up with words anyway. "After ten millennia as a servant, oblivion would have been far preferable."

Luc for one could identify with that sentiment. I could see the wheels turning as he speculated how he could do away with the Comtesse in the event that he was ever beneath her control again.

I wanted to reassure him that I would keep him safe, but didn't. I couldn't see the future, except for odd snippets in my dreams. For all I knew, Luc would end up subject to the praying mantis' rule again. Like I'd told Nicholas, no one could fight their fate. But I'd do my very best to make sure he remained free.

Chapter Thirty-Three

As we drove, Sanderson and General Merwe exchanged terse conversation. They were trying to anticipate where the Second and his people might be headed. Gregor shushed the rest of us with an impatient gesture so we could listen in.

"If I was a vampire and wanted to take over the world," the colonel mused, "I'd choose a large city to take over. I'd work my way towards it, increasing my army along the way."

Merwe made a sound of agreement. With the curtain drawn, we couldn't see his expression, but he also sounded thoughtful. "It would be sensible to stop only briefly, snatching a small number of victims per town. We won't know when or where they have struck until the disappearances are reported."

"If they have suitable transportation, they could potentially gather hundreds of fledglings along the way.

Then they could hide in the large city of their choice and wait for their followers to wake before striking."

General Merwe voiced the idea we were all thinking. "They would wreak havoc, killing or converting an entire population in a matter of days."

It was a chilling thought. Whisking the curtain back, I startled the two men who hadn't realized that we were all listening in. "Where is the nearest large city?"

"The closest one would be to the north east," General Merwe replied. The city he named was unpronounceable, at least for me.

"How far away are we from there?"

He barely had to think about it. "It would take us at least forty-eight hours to drive the distance. There are over a million people in residence," he told us gravely and a sick feeling entered my stomach.

Sanderson met my gaze in the rear view mirror. "You don't think he is actually heading there, do you?"

"The Second is smart and infinitely devious," I pointed out. "If both of you think this would be his best option for world domination, then we should head there right now."

Sanderson was quiet for a few moments while he thought it over. Gregor's voice floated forward. "I believe it would be prudent to send as many of your soldiers as you can muster towards this city, Colonel."

"Keep your antennae pointed at them," Sanderson told me. "Let me know if they change course."

My friends chatted quietly as I closed my eyes and sent out my senses to keep a constant vigil on our quarry. They stopped briefly several times, adding weight to Sanderson's guess about the Second's plans to increase their numbers.

General Merwe consulted his map. He was trying to guess where the growing host of vampires might have stopped to add to their numbers during their journey. Sanderson pulled out his satellite phone and contacted his people.

While it was necessary to mop up any caches that were about to awaken behind us, it was far more important to contain the threat ahead. He directed his forces to split and the greater bulk to head for the large city. Merwe also directed his troops to alter their course instead of meeting up with us.

Both Sanderson and Merwe left our truck at sunrise, swapping with two African soldiers. They would try to snatch some sleep as the convoy inexorably closed in on our quarry.

Since it was pointless to attempt to sense the mob we were chasing once daylight came, I slid into a deep sleep instead.

Kokoro floated in utter darkness with her back to me. Sensing my presence, she spoke. "Greetings, Natalie."

Looking around, I saw that we were alone. "Where are we? Is this a dream?" It had to be, but it seemed very real.

"We are inside my vision," the Japanese prophetess explained. "This is what I see every time I close my eyes."

Wanting to avoid being rude, I tried to word my thoughts diplomatically. "Um, isn't darkness what you see whether your eyes are open or shut?"

Turning, her pure white eyes lit on me. "My blindness isn't natural, Natalie," she pointed out gently. "For me, having my eyes open causes darkness. When they are shut, I see very well."

Struggling with that concept, I rubbed my forehead. "What do you usually see when you close your eyes?"

"I would normally see the past, present and future of my people."

"When did your ability to see visions stop?"

"They ceased the night the ten disciples rose. From that moment, I have seen only this." She swept a delicate, pale hand at the blank emptiness around us.

"Maybe your visions have just stopped and you're really blind now." I sounded desperate even to myself.

Kokoro shook her head slowly and her expression was reproachful. "You can sense what I do, *Mortis*."

She emphasized my name and I reluctantly admitted the truth. I could feel what the seer did; I couldn't see anyone else near us, but we were somehow surrounded by death.

A hand shaking my shoulder woke me. "Wake up, *chérie*," Geordie said softly. He had swapped seats with Luc, who was speaking quietly to Gregor and Igor.

"What's wrong?" I said groggily. I'd been so deeply asleep that I hadn't noticed the sun tucking itself into bed for the night.

"You were having a bad dream," the teenager told me uneasily. A vampire that was able to sleep was still a strange concept to him. To me, it was preferable to suddenly blacking out as soon as the sun rose each day.

"Did I say anything while I was dreaming?" As far as I knew, I wasn't a sleep talker, but many things had changed about me since I'd become the living dead.

Nodding unhappily, Geordie lowered his voice even more. "You were saying, 'They're all dead. Everyone is dead.'" He shuddered and huddled against me.

I'd never had, or particularly wanted, a little brother, but Geordie stirred feelings of responsibility in me. I put an arm around his narrow shoulders and gave him a hug. "I'm sure it was nothing, but maybe we should just keep that dream between the two of us."

His smile was partly gratified that I trusted him with a secret and partly disturbed that we needed to have one. "Were you having a vision, Natalie?"

I shook my head and ignored the twinge of guilt at the lie. *Technically, it was Kokoro's vision,* I told myself. "It was just a dream," I reassured him.

"Are you all awake back there?" Sanderson called out. His voice was gravelly and it didn't sound as if he'd gotten much sleep.

Igor pulled the curtain back, revealing the two men up front. "We're awake," I said, slightly embarrassed that I'd been the last to rise.

"It would appear we may be correct about the Second and his two remaining cohorts' intended destination."

General Merwe turned to face us. "We have received reports of dozens of people missing from each town along our current route." Like his American counterpart, he looked ragged.

"Then we are definitely heading in the right direction," Gregor mused.

"Our soldiers have already arrived at the city and are waiting on the outskirts several miles to the north," Sanderson explained. "They won't move in until we are certain that the vampires are settling in to stay."

Merwe wasn't happy about his civilians being sacrificed, but had resigned himself to the inevitable. "We will arrive in another twenty-four hours. By then we should be certain of the creature's plans."

"What is our plan of attack, gentlemen?" Gregor queried.

Sanderson fielded the question. "Your people will be needed on the front lines. I am prepared to loan you the weapons that we've developed in the event of vampire invasion."

We exchanged uneasy glances at that, but Nicholas was the only one brave enough, or foolhardy enough, to speak up. "We will be using the weapons that you have specifically designed to kill us against our own kind?" His disgust was palpable. I would personally make sure he didn't get his hands on one of these weapons. The tiny shred of trust I'd felt for him had been wiped away when he'd tried to force my flesh hunger to rise.

"As Natalie told me when this threat first began," the colonel said, "humans are too slow to keep up with the fledglings. These weapons will be far more effective in your hands." An undertone of unhappiness shone through despite his attempt to hide it. Weapons that powerful in the hands of my kind would be a scary thought for a human.

"What if we aren't exactly skilled with a gun?" Geordie said, assuming that was the type of weapon the soldier was speaking of.

"Can you throw rocks?" Sanderson asked, keeping his eyes on the road.

"Of course." Geordie's tone was affronted that he'd needed to be asked.

"Then I have weapons everyone can use."

"Explosives," Igor elaborated when the teenager still seemed confused. "Just try not to blow your own hands off," he warned his assistant. Geordie gave an uneasy giggle at the possibility.

Chapter Thirty-Four

Twenty-four long hours later, we arrived at the outskirts of the city. Reports had been flooding in that vampires were hiding somewhere in the area. Terrified citizens had begun to evacuate in droves, but the damage had already been done. Thousands were already either missing, or were dead.

As our convoy came to a stop, I sent out my senses and was dismayed at how many pockets of fledglings I discovered. A great many would be insensate for another night or two, but they would eventually wake. When they did, they would immediately begin to search for food.

With so many of the citizens already gone and the rest fleeing, the only meals that would remain would be the thousands of soldiers who were waiting to charge in and cut them down.

"Can you pinpoint exactly where the disciples are hiding?" Sanderson asked me as we disembarked. He looked more ragged than ever and I wondered how much sleep he'd snatched over the past week.

To his disappointment, I shook my head. "There are pockets of vampires everywhere," I explained. "I have no way to distinguish the disciples from the rest of fledglings. They could be hiding anywhere that the sun can't get to."

"Where would you hide if you wanted to avoid the sun?" the general asked me.

I didn't even need to think about it and pointed downwards. "The sewers are usually safe." *Unless they've been taken over by a wannabe mad scientist who enjoys experimenting on hapless intruders,* I reminded myself.

"Does this city have an extensive sewage system?" Sanderson asked the general.

Merwe nodded with a grimace. "It does, but I doubt that it is in very good repair."

A convoy of large army trucks approached and Sanderson moved to intercept it. Thousands of American troops jumped to the ground. They carried huge guns that came equipped with overlarge magazines. The bullets looked far bigger than I was used to seeing on TV.

Hefting the weapon one of his men handed over, Sanderson took aim at a distant tree and pulled the trigger. The bullet hit the target and then the tree was vaporized in a searing flash of light.

Staggering back with spots dancing in front of my eyes, I turned on the colonel. "What the hell was that?"

"This," he said with pride, "is one of the weapons I've been telling you about. Instead of normal bullets, they have explosive rounds that are designed to lodge deep inside the body before detonating."

"What an efficient way to murder our kin," Nicholas muttered and was ignored by all of the nocturnal who heard him. Where he used to bump into me every time I turned around, he now kept his distance. I noticed both Gregor and Igor keeping their eye on him. It was nice to know we all mistrusted the muscle bound one equally.

"What about the other things, the throwy things?" Geordie queried. He was clearly uneasy at the thought of using one of the guns. I had pretty much no experience firing guns either. I couldn't blame him for being squeamish about using something that could cause so much damage.

Another soldier handed the colonel a small device. Gesturing for us to gather around, Sanderson opened his hand to reveal a black explosive much smaller than a grenade. "To arm it, you just need to press the red button." He pointed at the tip. "It will explode in three seconds, so I don't recommend holding onto it for long." He said this without a smile, yet Geordie issued a nervous giggle anyway.

Pressing the button, Sanderson threw the device at another tree. It exploded in mid-air, sending a spray of fire in a five foot wide arc.

Impressed, Gregor clapped the soldier on the back. "They are remarkable weapons, Colonel Sanderson."

"I only hope they never turn them on us," Geordie said to me quietly.

"Gather your people together and I'll have my men start handing out weapons," Sanderson instructed me.

My teams had exited their vehicles and had automatically clumped into their three distinct groups again. Anna-Eve caught my wave and motioned the courtiers and guards in our direction. Aventius saw them on the move and hastened to follow. Kokoro spoke to Ishida and finally talked him into joining us. Arrogance came off the child king in waves as he took up a stiff stance at a short distance from the other two groups.

I was already tired of dealing with the arguments, tantrums and infighting. *This will all be over soon,* I promised myself. In a few hours either we'd all be dead, or the Second and his horde would be. With the weapons Sanderson's men were handing out, we should have a greater chance of survival now.

At my subtle shake of the head to a soldier, he handed Nicholas some of the explosives rather than one of the guns. I didn't like to see them in the muscled one's grip, but figured it would cause too much drama to deny him the use of a weapon at all. It probably wouldn't be wise for our tentative allies to witness dissent within our ranks.

Sanderson had sent one of his men to locate a map of the sewer system. The man was out of breath when he hurried back. Handing over a tattered rolled up piece of paper, he offered his superior an apology. "This is the most recent map of the sewer system that I could find, sir."

Opening the map, Sanderson sighed at the badly drawn copy. It looked like a rabbit warren to me. Some tunnels ended abruptly. Others circled back on themselves and made no sense at all in some cases.

"It's even worse than I thought," the colonel complained. He and General Merwe studied the drawing while my kin practiced with their weapons. Nicholas held the explosives disdainfully. Geordie practiced throwing his, making occasional mock exploding sounds. Igor hefted his gun, sighted down the barrel and then slung it over his shoulder.

Gregor and Luc watched as a soldier showed them how to reload once the magazine was empty. A gun was shoved into my hands and the soldier pivoted and hurried away before I could protest.

"Are you sure you want to use that, *chérie?*" Geordie asked me as he sidled out of my line of fire.

"How hard can it be?" I asked. "You just point it and pull the trigger, don't you?" I held the gun easily, glad for my vampire strength. Without it, my arms would have been trembling in seconds. Sighting on a tree that hadn't been blown up yet, I pulled the trigger. Seconds passed and the tree remained intact.

Leaning over, Luc flicked a tiny switch near the trigger. "It helps if you disengage the safety."

"Oh." Deflated, I pulled the trigger again and the tree disappeared in a burst of fire.

Carefully reengaging the safety, I took the handful of explosives another soldier handed me and looked down at my slick black suit. Without pockets, I had nowhere to stash the tiny bombs. With no other option, I bent and slipped them into the tops of my boots. *I just hope I don't accidentally detonate them and blow my own legs off.* Knowing myself, it was a likely scenario.

When they were satisfied with their plan, the two soldiers asked us to gather around. "Natalie," Sanderson began, "I'd like you to split your people up into twelve teams and have them enter the sewers in these places." He pointed at the spots he and the General had chosen. They were all on the outskirts of the city.

"Our soldiers will back you up and supply you with ammunition," Merwe said. "They will have equipment to help guide you towards the centre of the city."

"Our plan is to drive the creatures into one place, then combine our forces to eradicate them," Sanderson continued. "A large force of our troops will remain on the surface and shoot anything that tries to emerge.

My former team leaders and Anna-Eve had drifted closer to overhear the plan. Eyeing each other suspiciously, none offered any objections. I opened my mouth to split the teams up further, but Luc beat me to it. "Gregor, Igor and I have decided to relinquish our positions as team leaders. We wish to stay with you during the battle ahead, Natalie." Geordie nodded emphatically and I just couldn't shatter his hopes.

"Fine." Turning, I pointed at Nicholas. "Congratulations, you've just been promoted to team leader." With a bunch of soldiers watching his every move, I doubted he'd be dumb enough to do anything stupid.

"You would allow that traitor to lead a team?" Anna-Eve sneered.

"Don't worry, you're now a team leader, too." I smiled at her sunnily. At a quick count, we had one hundred and fifty-four vampires on our side. Working quickly and keeping in mind who would work well together or would be likely to kill each other, I split the teams up.

"We're ready when you are," I said to Sanderson. He'd chosen ten team leaders of his own, with himself and the general as the final two.

"My men have been advised of their entry points and I'm sending soldiers to those locations now. You should make your way to join them and wait for my signal." Now that it was crunch time, the colonel was focussed.

"Good luck, everyone," I said to my troops. As a pep talk, it sucked.

Aventius was the only one to acknowledge me and offered me a bow. Ishida stomped off in icy disdain. Nicholas hesitated, then stalked after the team I'd assigned him to be the leader of. They were already disregarding his authority by leaving him behind.

Anna-Eve looked like she wanted to say something catty, but simply flounced off instead. Her entire team comprised of courtiers. My fingers were crossed that they'd accidentally blow each other up during the coming fight. Somehow, I couldn't see any of them being particularly useful.

I was unsurprised when Colonel Sanderson crooked his finger at me. "Since we work so well together, I thought we should continue the tradition," he said with a tight grin.

General Merwe offered us both a short nod then trotted off. His mixed team of vampires and soldiers hastened to catch up to him.

Our entry point was close by and we were shortly surrounding the rusty manhole. Geordie fidgeted nervously, playing with one of the explosives. Igor sent him a warning glare and the chastened teenager slipped the device back into his pocket.

Booted feet sounded in the distance and rapidly drew closer. A blend of African and American soldiers arrived. Sanderson saluted his men. The two leaders of the armies weren't taking any chances this time. We had hundreds of soldiers at our backs. Sanderson ordered some of his men to shadow each of my people. They carried the ammunition that would assist us in annihilating our common enemy.

My new lackey offered me a nervous nod. I returned the gesture, pretending to be calm. We were about to descend into the unknown and battle beings that were crazed with blood hunger. Our band of vampires was the first line of defence against the fledglings. The meat sacks that had been delegated to be our backup would quickly become dinner if we failed.

Chapter Thirty-Five

We waited in tense silence until the last of the teams radioed in that they were in position. Raising the radio to his mouth, Sanderson spoke. "All teams, move in!"

Igor bent, pulled the manhole cover up with one hand and tossed it aside like it weighed no more than a coin. I was sliding down the ladder before the cover even hit the ground. After a short drop, I landed in water.

The odour of human waste was all pervading. Gagging at the taste in the back of my throat, I shouldered my weapon and turned rapidly in a circle. "It's clear!" I whisper-shouted, then moved aside. Filthy water lapped at my knees, pouring into my boots that only reached halfway up my calves.

Luc was the next one into the sewer. He wrinkled his nose at the smell, but kept his complaints to himself. Geordie voiced his loudly. "Ewww! Why do humans have to excrete so much waste?"

Sliding to a stop beside his apprentice, Igor nudged him out of the way. "We go left," he said and moved off into the dark. The vamps I'd chosen joined us and followed closely behind.

An intersection halted our progress and we waited for Sanderson and his gaggle of soldiers to arrive. They wore night vision goggles, which made Geordie snigger. The colonel checked a gadget he held in one hand and pointed to the right.

Taking point, I sloshed along at a pace that the humans could keep up with, then slowed when I sensed a group of fledglings ahead. Using hand signals, I indicated that we had company.

My chosen team, consisting of mostly European and only a couple of Japanese warriors, gathered close. Sanderson and his men hung back to give us room to fight. Igor pushed Geordie into the middle of the group. The teen immediately wormed his way forward until he was at my back.

Creeping as quietly as we could, we neared the corner. We were careful not to splash the soiled water and possibly alert our enemies. Ducking down low, I peered around the corner. Two dozen filthy, mostly naked fledglings were waiting for us, watching both directions for intruders. One spotted me, pointed and screeched a warning. Whirling around, the group charged.

Staying low, I leaned out, flicked off the safety then aimed at one of the leading vamps. I fired the first round, but Luc was right behind me, backing me up. Stumbling at the twin impacts in his chest, the fledgling continued on for two more steps before exploding. Flesh, blood and guts hit the walls, ceiling and his brethren before he evaporated.

I took down another fledgling, then a glint of flying metal caught my eye. Geordie howled in triumph when his explosive eradicated several of the fledglings in one blast. Then the rest of my team was either lobbing the small black devices, or were firing their guns. In less than a minute, the way was clear.

Far in the distance, more shots rang out as another team ran into resistance. The disciples had to know we were here by now. I hoped the soldiers watching the streets above were vigilant and didn't allow anyone to escape.

Clicking his safety back on, Igor gave his gun a disturbed look. "I am afraid I have to agree with Nicholas," he said grimly. "These weapons are very efficient at killing our kind."

"We shall have to do our very best to remain on Colonel Sanderson's good side," Gregor murmured as he joined us. His latest suit was already ruined and we'd only been in the sewers for a few minutes. My boots were completely full of water. I hoped the explosive devices didn't float away.

"Speak of the devil," Luc said in a low voice as the colonel arrived.

He searched for signs of the battle, but all that remained of the fledglings was their crude weapons and clothing. "Let's press on." He pointed at an opening halfway down the next path. "We go that way."

Despite his very recent acquaintance with the prototype, Luc had no trouble removing the magazine and checking the number of rounds he had left. His lackey was at his side in an instant, offering my beloved a fresh magazine.

My shadow hastened forward when I held out my gun to him. Since he was getting paid for this and I'd just been roped into it through my unfortunate status of being Mortis, he could do the honours.

Freshly loaded again, I took the weapon back and held it ready. Geordie was at my back, grinning excitedly and carrying half a dozen explosives ready to throw. I was much happier having him behind me where he was safe rather than out in front. *He really has become like a little brother to me,* I thought in wonder. While he was still highly annoying at times, I'd hate to see the teen come to any harm.

Sensing more fledglings nearby, I alerted the others. This time when I peeked around the corner, I saw a far larger number of our kin lying in wait. They had gathered at a convergence of intersections. Easing backwards, I turned to indicate how many we were facing. I flashed one hand at them ten times.

"How many is that?" Geordie whispered to Igor in confusion.

He wasn't quite quiet enough and a babble of screeches and howls rang out. Abandoning any attempt at stealth, I rounded the corner and opened fire. Hastening to surround me, my team cut down the first few rows of rabid vampires, but they were gaining too rapidly. Machine gun fire from our shadow soldiers rang out and another two rows went down.

One of the lead vamps leaped into the air just as Geordie lobbed one of his explosives. The device detonated right in front of the fledgling's face and his head evaporated.

Ten blood hungry vampires were left. They closed the distance between us, rendering our guns useless. My swords were in my hands without conscious thought and limbs began to fall as they reached out to claw at us. Focussed on trying to reach the walking meals behind us, the fledglings went down almost too easily beneath my blades.

Igor finished off the last vamp with a knife through his heart. He nonchalantly pulled the weapon free from the astonished fledgling and snatched the vamp's tattered pants up as his body disintegrated. Wiping his blade clean, he offered the scrap of cloth to me.

"My God, but they're fast," Sanderson breathed as he waded over to me. "Even with our new prototypes, we don't stand a chance against them."

I had to agree. Bullets and explosives weren't much use when the targets could dodge out of the way so quickly. Clean again, I slid the blades back into their sheaths. "You're lucky we're on your side, then," I pointed out.

"That we are," Sanderson agreed fervently.

His men replenished our ammo and we pushed on. The night was young and we still had a lot of work ahead of us.

Chapter Thirty-Six

I wasn't sure how much time had passed. I'd lost track of how many groups of fledglings we'd encountered. Several times, we'd stumbled across piles of corpses that hadn't yet risen. Sanderson's soldiers hauled them out of the water and roasted them all with their flamethrowers.

Sensing the largest number of vampires that I'd ever felt before just ahead, I cautioned for everyone to stop. "Where are we now?" I asked the colonel when he strode forward.

"We're pretty close to the centre of the sewer system." His response confirmed my hunch.

"Is there a large area in the centre?"

Sanderson nodded, picturing the map in his head judging by his expression. "I'm expecting most of the surviving vampires to be gathered there by now."

"How close are the others to reaching the centre?" We'd have to time our final attack well. If we didn't, some of the disciples and their servants might escape from our trap.

"They'll be arriving any minute now." The colonel issued orders for his people to check their ammunition.

My lackey gave my weapon the once over and deemed it to be ready. We only had a short wait before Sanderson gave us the signal to close in.

Rushing through dark tunnels with Luc and my side and my friends at my back, I surreptitiously crossed my fingers that we would all make it out of the next battle alive. *You mean* un*alive,* my subconscious reminded me. Even it sounded nervous of the possible outcome of our encounter with the Second.

The sounds of many creatures gathered together in a group echoed around the corner of the next bend. Knowing that the other groups would be closing in as well, I didn't hesitate, but rounded the corner and burst out into the open. Thousands of fledglings were crowded together on higher ground in the centre of a gigantic open space. Water lapped at the edges, leaving noisome tidemarks.

Confronted by over a dozen men wearing familiar camouflage uniforms, I hesitated with my finger on the trigger. I realized who they were just as they brought their weapons out from behind their backs and opened fire.

Being at the forefront of the group, I was instantly cut in half. Gregor gave a cry of pain and went down a few feet away from me. Igor knelt in front of him, shielding his friend with his body. He coolly fired at the former African and American soldiers. They'd belonged to our fallen team and had been converted into the enemy.

Ignoring my lower body for now, I lifted my gun. Propping myself up on my elbows, disgusting water lapped at my chin as I aimed for the soldiers who were still standing. A few shots picked several of them off. Luc moved to my side and gave me a concerned look, but I waved at him to attack. The remaining soldiers exploded and the danger lessened slightly.

Splitting my consciousness, I ordered my bottom half to worm its way forward. I became reconnected with the usual flash of pain. Regaining my feet, I checked on Gregor. He'd been hit several times, but the shots had missed his heart. Unfortunately, a bullet had hit him in the face and had torn half of one cheek away.

Geordie gagged at the sight of Gregor's exposed teeth. Turning away, he armed two explosives and threw them at the mob of fledglings. If he'd been human, they would have fallen far short and have caused no damage at all. Being far stronger than a mere mortal, they landed at the outer edge of the throng and tore a small hole in their ranks.

From twelve different tunnel openings, my kin attacked the force that outnumbered us by at least thirty to one. The fledglings mainly ignored our attack despite the large number of them being cut down. Then one of the soldiers somewhere to our left made the fatal mistake of entering the chamber, most likely thinking he could help. Spying food, the closest blood hungry fledglings went berserk with their need to feed. Whatever control the disciples had over the lesser vamps disappeared as they surged forward.

Sanderson must have crept forward to the mouth of the tunnel to watch because he shouted an order into his radio. "All soldiers, open fire!"

We'd be overwhelmed in seconds and the fledglings would tear the humans apart if we didn't act fast. Hundreds of soldiers spilled out from the safety of the tunnels and unleashed their superior weaponry on the mob of fledglings. Slinging the gun over my shoulder, I bent and reached into my boots. My bombs sailed into the midst of the crowd and fledglings screamed as they burst apart, or caught on fire.

Geordie had lost all traces of excitement and was absolutely terrified now. He staunchly lobbed his bombs, then patted his empty pockets when he ran out. I handed him my last few explosives then grabbed his shoulder to get his attention. "Keep everyone back, I'm going to try something." He had no idea what my plan was, but he nodded then yelled for Igor.

Dashing into the milling, hungry mob, I was completely ignored since my blood wasn't tasty to them. So far, Sanderson's guns were keeping the monsters at bay, but it couldn't last. When I was deep inside the mass of fledglings, I hoped my friends were standing well clear. I also hoped my experiment would work. I'd only tried this particular trick on imps before and that had mostly been by accident.

Reaching out, I grabbed two fledglings by the backs of their heads. They turned curious looks at me, then went back to attempting to claw their way to the food. Concentrating, I let the power of the holy marks grow until I was all but thrumming with it. I had an inkling that my plan was going to work when the ground trembled beneath my feet.

Unleashing the holy marks, I covered my face with my hands an instant before every vampire within a fifty foot radius exploded. Goo splattered me from head to toe. I had the unpleasant sensation of being doused with innards.

"Holy crap, you just unleashed a vampire bomb!" Geordie screeched in awe.

Grinning fiercely, I waded back into the fray and repeated the act. Soon, the fledglings were more worried about being slaughtered than they were with feeding. Soldiers pressed the advantage and moved in closer. Many of the humans were dead and I'd lost half of my own small team. From the glimpses I caught of the other teams, they were faring just as badly.

My human lackey placed a fully loaded gun in my hands when I could no longer get close enough to the fledglings to use my holy marks. I took stock of my team, relieved to see my friends still alive even if they weren't well.

One of Luc's arms dangled uselessly. He patiently allowed a medic to slip it into a sling. Igor had a tear in his shirt and his intestines were trying to slide free as he closed with a fledgling and decapitated her. Despite missing half his face, Gregor kept up a continuous barrage of fire. Still unharmed, Geordie popped up beside me. He smacked a kiss on my goo ridden cheek, then lobbed a couple of explosives at the cringing fledglings.

Somewhere deep in the centre of the enemy, I could hear the remaining disciples screaming orders. The Second's plan for world domination was rapidly falling apart. Sanderson had called for backup and fresh soldiers arrived at regular intervals. We'd already reduced their force to a third of its original size. Now that some of the fledglings were more concerned with survival than with feeding, they were fighting to escape rather than trying to attack.

Shooting a vamp that raced towards him, Sanderson barely waited for his adversary to explode before jogging over to me. "Work your way around to the left," he shouted. I could barely hear him over the clamour of gunfire, explosions and screams of terror and triumph. "We need to push them back into the centre."

Seeing that the fledglings were bulging towards the team to our left, I complied with his order. Word spread amongst the enemy that I was approaching and they instantly surged in the opposite direction. With my remaining team members backing me up, I worked in a gradual circle until the soldiers had managed to whittle the numbers down even more.

In a last ditch effort to overwhelm the soldiers, the disciples ordered their servants to attack. Unable to fight the command given by their makers, the fledglings turned and flowed towards us once more.

I became separated from my team during the initial surge and had to trust that they could look after themselves. My main targets had just become visible. Standing side by side, two disciples stared at me arrogantly. Both wore only loincloths. They'd revived enough from their enforced starvation that their withered flesh had mostly filled out.

Despite their overwhelming arrogance, I instinctively knew that neither of these men were the Second. Somehow, he had escaped from our trap again. He'd once more left his brothers to die in his place. With their servants battling my kin and desperately trying to feed from the soldiers, the disciples were left defenceless. Sanderson, surrounded by a team of men, fought his way through to my side.

Sensing that the colonel was in charge, one of the disciples addressed him. "If you cease to resist us, we will promise you eternal life, riches beyond your comprehension and as many slaves as you could possibly desire."

"What did he say?" Sanderson asked me.

I repeated the offer verbatim.

Pretending to muse over the offer, the colonel flicked off his safety and casually held the gun at his hip. "I already have everything I could possibly desire and eternal life sounds more like eternal suffering to me."

"What did he say?" the disciple said to his brother. The question became moot when Sanderson pulled the trigger and a hole suddenly appeared in the disciple's chest. Gaping down at the wound, the ancient vampire had just enough time to send a despairing gaze to his brother before he exploded.

Screaming in rage, the final disciple went for the colonel with both hands extended. A dozen soldiers opened fire with conventional machine guns. Riddled with bullets, the disciple was driven back and dropped to his knees. I was standing before him with both swords in my hands before Sanderson could order his men to finish the job.

Tilting his head back, he sneered up at me. He was already beginning to heal. Bullets rattled to the ground as they were expelled from his flesh. "You have failed," he told me defiantly. "The Second is far too clever to be caught by a mere female."

That confirmed my supposition that his leader had escaped from my clutches. "Times have changed, you chauvinistic arsehole," I told him. His brow creased from lack of understanding, but I wasn't going to waste time calling for a translator. My swords moved in tandem and sliced cleanly through his neck. "Women aren't considered to be inferior anymore," I said softly as his head toppled and he joined his brothers in death.

"I hate to disagree," Gregor said from somewhere to my right. "But in some cultures, women are still considered to be of less worth than dogs." His cheek had begun to grow back, I was glad to see.

Smiling at his wryness, I turned to see where the rest of my team was and spied Nicholas. The overly muscled former Court guard was acting suspiciously. *It almost looks like he's trying to sneak up on someone.* When the dwindling crowd of fledglings shifted, I understood who his intended target was.

As Nicholas drew his hand back to throw one of the small, but deadly explosives, I was on the move. Calculating the distance, I knew I'd never make it in time to save Luc. Desperate, I detached my left hand and threw it hard.

Nicholas' bomb left his hand as I possessed Lefty. Twisting in mid-air, my hand opened wide and caught the tiny device, deflecting it from its path. Wrapping my fingers tightly around the explosive, I winced in anticipation of pain a split second before it detonated.

Luc whirled around when the bomb went off just feet away from him. Seeing Nicholas guiltily backing away, he tightened his grip on his gun and raised it. The muscle bound ex-courtier turned and fled, dodging away as Luc pulled the trigger. An unfortunate fledgling stepped into the line of fire and took the traitor's punishment.

Without my left hand, I could no longer fire the gun. Handing it over to my human lackey, I drew my sword and fought my way to Luc's side. Still rattled at how close he'd come to dying, he wiped splatters of what had once been my hand from his cheek.

Seeing my empty sleeve, he winced in sympathy. We shared a brief moment of complete accord when we thought of the Comtesse. I'd relieved her of her right hand and now I was missing my left one. *Is this supposed to be some kind of karmic justice?* If it was, then I couldn't help but think that karma had a strange sense of humour.

Chapter Thirty-Seven

Chasing after Nicholas and exacting revenge on him for attempting to kill Luc, and for destroying my hand, would have to wait. Taking down the last of the fledglings was more important.

Left with only one hand, I put it to good use and went to town on the feeding fledglings. A giddy sense of pleasure overtook me again as I cut them to pieces. Most had their mouths buried in necks, wrists and even below the waist.

An African soldier, screaming in terror at being savaged, lifted his gun and blasted the head off the vampire who had her face buried in his thigh. Blood was pumping from his mangled vein. He'd be dead in minutes unless he had a transfusion. Knowing he was doomed, he met my eyes and gave me a tiny nod. My sword slid in and out of his heart quickly. His terror abated as he went slack with death.

Sanderson's voice rose over the din and cut through my battle lust. "Natalie, get your people clear!"

Spinning, I saw that hundreds of fresh troops had just arrived and had the fledglings surrounded. Most of my team members were already clear, but a few still hacked away at the enemy. Kokoro gave a shrill shout for Ishida, but the child king paid no attention. Deep in battle, he speared a fledgling through the heart, then beheaded another.

Shouldering their weapons, the soldiers prepared to fire. Sprinting through puddles of the fallen, I scooped Ishida up under my handless left arm. Ignoring his indignant squawk at being manhandled, I vaulted into the air just as a barrage of bullets and explosives rained down on the remaining vampires.

Landing on the other side of the circle of soldiers, I dropped the emperor, then raced back to check on my friends. Luc saw me and relief crossed his face. We didn't attempt to talk until the hail of gunfire finally petered out.

Waving gun smoke away from his now filthy face, Geordie took a few tentative steps forward. "We did it," he said in wonder. "They're all dead." His smile was huge and very nearly beautiful. "We won, *chérie*!" He launched himself at me and I braced myself for impact.

Sending out my senses as Geordie's skinny arms encircled me, I didn't find any caches of fledglings waiting to rise. Apart from my small army of vampires, the city was free of the undead. We had saved what was left of the population from an infestation of hungry bloodsuckers.

Glancing over the teenager's shoulder, I saw Anna-Eve speaking to Colonel Sanderson. The soldier wore an intent expression that I couldn't read. Whatever she was saying to him, he was giving it serious thought.

Geordie suddenly jerked and took a couple of steps back. "What the?" He looked down at his hands and my gaze dropped. I did a double take when I saw three hands instead of two. A hand that looked decidedly feminine was clutching the teen's wrist. He gave a small scream that I very nearly echoed when it suddenly twitched, turned and launched itself at me.

Lefty landed on my chest, then quickly scuttled down to my left arm and reattached itself. My flesh tried to crawl after the brief flash of pain that reattachment always brought.

Putting his hand over his unbeating heart, Geordie forced out a laugh. "That was a mean trick, Natalie." His expression was reproachful.

I forced a smile of my own. "Sorry. I couldn't help myself." In truth, I hadn't had any control over Lefty at all. It had somehow regenerated and had returned to me of its own accord.

This isn't the first time this has happened, I reminded myself. After I'd been fed imp blood, my body had broken down and my parts had dragged themselves off in different directions. Once the imps had departed, my body parts had returned. It had creeped me out then and I wasn't any less creeped out by it now.

Gregor's face had mostly grown back by now. I could no longer see inside his mouth when he approached. "Where is our heavily muscled friend?" He looked around for Nicholas, but didn't see him.

"If he's smart, he'll be on his way to the Himalayas by now," I said darkly.

"What happened?" Geordie asked without bothering to hide his glee that Nicholas was gone.

Luc appeared at my side and slipped his hand around my waist. "Nicholas attempted to kill me when my back was turned." His face was calm, but his tight grip was a dead giveaway that he was still annoyed by the betrayal.

Igor stomped over to join us. "I saw the whole thing." His expression was even grimmer than usual.

"Tell us!" Geordie begged and danced on the spot like an excited puppy.

The Russian put Geordie out of his misery instead of cruelly drawing the tale out. "From the way Nicholas was sneaking around, I knew he was up to no good. Then I saw him throw one of the explosive devices straight at Lucentio." Geordie's mouth opened and his eyes grew larger. "Something flew through the air to intercept the device and it exploded only feet away from Lucentio's back."

Staring down at Lefty, Geordie pointed at my newly reattached hand. "You tore your own hand off and saved Luc's life by throwing it and catching the bomb?" Hero worship shone from him. "That is the coolest thing I have ever heard of!"

"Thank you, Natalie." Luc planted a kiss on my temple, then grimaced and wiped his mouth with the back of his hand. I was utterly covered in goo, ooze and crud. My suit had been torn right through the middle when I'd been cut in half. Even if I managed to clean it, it still wasn't going to be salvageable.

One by one, the surviving vampires joined us. Aventius had lost nearly half of his group and they were down to twenty. Ishida kept his distance, but deigned to give me a single nod of thanks for saving his life. Out of his original fifty warriors, only thirty-two were still alive. I bowed to my instructor, glad to see he'd come through the fray unscathed. He nodded almost warmly and even smiled a tiny bit.

Anna-Eve gathered her people, of which there were now only twenty-five and stalked over to join us. Her clingy red dress was torn, stained and ruined. Her long blonde hair had clumps of goo in it, but she was still beautiful in a haughty, arrogant way.

Out of a force of one hundred and fifty-four, we had only eighty-two remaining. *The prophecy turned out to be correct after all,* I thought. The First had changed the vast bulk of our kind into imps. Then Sanderson's troops and I had worked together to eradicate them. Our numbers had now dropped significantly.

After the battle we'd just finished, they'd been decimated even more. Worldwide, there was probably only a couple hundred of our kind left. Death had done an excellent job of devouring our species.

Pointing her finger at Aventius, Anna-Eve broke into my mental dialogue. "Now that our business is finished, I demand his life."

"Our business isn't finished yet," I replied then waved at Sanderson, who was standing with General Merwe. The pair had a short conversation then started in our direction. Thousands of their men were either dead, or were seriously wounded. I frowned when I realized the survivors were being treated instead of being killed. They would need to be monitored for the next several days to ensure that none of them turned into the undead. I'd warned Sanderson of the dangers and he'd witnessed it himself after one of his men had turned. *It's his problem, not mine,* I told myself.

"Did we get them all?" the colonel almost demanded when he reached us.

I shook my head in the negative. "Not quite."

Geordie's expression turned glum. "Who did we miss, *chérie?*"

I knew that no one was going to be happy with my next words. "The Second wasn't here. He's probably far away by now, already creating a new batch of fledglings."

"Can you sense him?" General Merwe asked. His gaze strayed to Kokoro. From the knees up, her kimono was still an immaculate white, matching her eyes. It was obvious to me that he had a serious crush on the seer.

I'd already tried to locate the Second, but closed my eyes and sent out my senses again. Straining as hard as I could, I came up blank. "Wherever he is, he's moved out of my range."

Dropping his eyes to the ground, Sanderson's shoulders slumped for a few seconds as he contemplated having to do this all over again. Then he straightened up and reshouldered the responsibility. "Then we'll have to be on the lookout for further reports of disappearances." Examining our faces, he posed a question. "Can I continue to count on your people to assist us in hunting down this monster?"

Now it was my turn to examine my friends and allies. Aventius immediately nodded, which made Joshua scowl. I'd kind of hoped the new vampire had died during the fracas, but he was still around to be a pain. *At least Nicholas is gone.* That was a bright moment in what had been a dark and horrible night.

Kokoro had a quiet word to her emperor and Ishida reluctantly nodded as well. Anna-Eve didn't bother to check with her people. Thinking hard, she also nodded her support. Now that she had seen what the world would face if the Second was allowed to run amok, she saw the value in cooperating.

"It is agreed then," Sanderson said formally. "We will continue to work together until this monster is finally brought down." He smiled, but his eyes remained cold as they swept over us. I wondered uneasily if he was beginning to think that all of our kind should be eradicated. If I were in his shoes, I'd think long and hard about the wisdom of allowing us to live.

Printed in Great Britain
by Amazon